Also by Tajuana "TJ" Butler

Sorority Sisters

Hand-me-down Heartache

The Night Before Thirty

The Desires of a Woman:
  Poems Celebrating Womanhood

Just My Luck

Just My Luck

A Novel

Tajuana "TJ" Butler

One World
Ballantine Books • New York

Copyright © 2005 by Tajuana Butler

Published in the United States by One World Books, an imprint of The Random House Publishing Group, a division of Random House, Inc., New York.

One World is a registered trademark and the One World colophon is a trademark of Random House, Inc.

ISBN 1-4000-6021-4

Printed in the United States of America

First Edition

Text design by Mercedes Everett

Dedicated to Kim, the oldest of Raymond's girls.
Thanks for being a trailblazer for us to follow.

Acknowledgments

I would like to give special thanks to you, the reader. Thank you for choosing to journey into the worlds that I happen to create. Thank you for supporting African American literature. Thank you for sharing my works with your friends and colleagues. Thank you for keeping the written word alive. Thank you for giving me a reason to want to write and create. Thank you for sharing your stories with me. Thank you for your kind words and your prayers.

Thank you! Thank you! Thank you!

Sincerely,
Tajuana "TJ" Butler

Just My Luck

One

As Lanita approached the salon, she could barely contain her excitement. It had been a long time since she'd had the extra time or money to even get her hair done, let alone indulge in the pampering she was about to enjoy, but her husband had insisted she spare no expense during her visit. Today was their special day. Today they would celebrate what had taken years of struggle and sacrifice to complete—their college education.

As Lanita reached for the salon door, she looked down and noticed four quarters scattered on the sidewalk. Smiling, she bent down to pick them up. *Another small gift to remind me of who I am and what I've accomplished,* she thought. She tossed the quarters from one hand to the other and then placed them in her pants pocket before opening the door.

Already feeling more relaxed, Lanita approached the receptionist, a pretty young woman with immaculately groomed hair and a cheerful, welcoming smile. "Hi, my name is Lanita, and I'm scheduled to see a stylist, nail tech, and facialist. I'm not sure in which order," she said with a small laugh, "but I know I'm supposed to begin at ten. I'm a few minutes early, but I believe it's better to be a few minutes early than a few minutes late, if you know what I mean."

"Sure," said the receptionist. "Have a seat over there. Someone will be with you shortly—but are you okay?"

"I'm fine," Lanita said. She touched a hand to her hair. "Why do you ask?"

"I saw you bending down outside. It looked like you'd lost something."

"Oh, that," Lanita said with another laugh. "Thanks for asking, but I haven't lost anything in some time. I was actually reaping my blessing, that's all." Smiling warmly at the receptionist, Lanita glanced around, noting the tasteful, expensive decor. "Wow, this is really a nice salon. It reminds me of the ones on those reality shows where they take people to get makeovers. This setting really makes a person feel like she's privileged to be here."

It was the receptionist's turn to laugh. "Well, we *are* one of the top salons in Los Angeles, the crème de la crème. Our clients include a number of celebrities and their families. I think you'll find our staff is top-notch." The young woman winked at Lanita, giving her a knowing smile.

"Well, it's been a while since I've been pampered—in fact, almost twelve years—but believe you me, there was a time when I would go to places like this weekly." Lanita sat down, easing herself into her chair and unconsciously assuming the air of someone accustomed to the luxurious setting. A heavy sigh followed, and before she knew it, she had fallen into deep thought. As excited as she was about what the day would bring, she couldn't help but remember the events that had led her there. She shook her head, choosing to distract herself by enjoying her surroundings and focusing on the present. After all, that was what today was all about—the present *and* the future. "So what's your name?" Lanita asked the receptionist.

"I'm Natasha," she responded. "By the way, would you like something to drink?"

"Sure. What are my choices?"

"There's bottled water, sparkling or flat, red and white wine, or orange juice."

After a moment of thought, Lanita said, "I'll take the sparkling water. I'm graduating from USC today, and I don't want to begin celebrating too early, if you know what I mean." Lanita snapped her fingers, all but dancing in her chair.

"Congratulations!" Natasha said. "Are you sure you don't want a glass of wine? You should start the day off with a bang."

Lanita instantly felt somber. "To be honest with you, I never touch the stuff—alcohol, I mean. Not after what it did to my mother and me."

Natasha looked down at her phone, seeming unsure of how to respond. Then she said, "I'll get that water for you."

Across the room from Lanita was a large chrome-trimmed mirror. After Natasha left the room, Lanita got up and slowly walked over to it. Gazing at her reflection, she saw an aging woman wearing red Capri pants, a yellow T-shirt, and a silver chain with a silver-dollar pendant. Frowning at what she saw, she ran her fingers through her hair. "Girlfriend," she said, "you're in a bad need of a relaxer, and when was the last time your thirty-eight-year-old self had that dead skin removed from your face?"

She grabbed the pendant and kissed it. Then she placed it so that it lay just so against her chest. "Flat as pancakes," she said of her breasts. Sliding her hands over her body, admiring her trim figure that otherwise had curves in all the right places, she smiled. She then turned her back to the mirror, looked over her shoulder, and placed her hands on her hips, shaking her derriere in the mirror. She might be close to forty, but her backside still looked just fine.

Just then Natasha came back in the room, carrying a glass of water. She cleared her throat unobtrusively and Lanita abruptly stopped dancing. She was caught. She managed a nervous giggle, saying, "You'll have to excuse me. I'm usually more dignified, but I . . ."

Natasha laughed. "No need to apologize. Sometimes you just have to celebrate in your own way." She handed Lanita the water.

"I'm so embarrassed," Lanita said, feeling the flush in her cheeks.

"Don't worry," Natasha said, squeezing Lanita's shoulder. She lowered her voice to a conspiratorial whisper and said, "I won't tell anyone."

"Thank you," Lanita said, her cheeks still hot with embarrassment. She took the glass from Natasha and again turned to view herself in the mirror. "For the past few years, I've been doing my own hair. I use my husband's clippers to keep the ends trimmed. I'm not good at all, but I've gotten better." She smoothed her hand over her short-cropped hair. "Recently I've been going for the Halle Berry look, but I've had so much going on these past few weeks, with finals and all, that I'm definitely missing the mark by a long shot."

Still staring into the mirror, this time Lanita noted the effects of years of living. "Time waits for no one," she said under her breath before looking at Natasha. "I hope the stylist here will hook me up. You know, make me feel beautiful again."

"We have exceptional hairstylists, the best in town. I'm sure they'll do a good job of reminding you just how beautiful you are."

"I sure hope so, because my husband is a good man and he's spending a lot of money on me today, money we really don't have to blow." Lanita turned to look at Natasha. "Don't get me wrong," she continued. "We pay our bills. We've just been putting a lot back saving for another house." She took a sip of water. "He doesn't have much, but he treats me like I'm a princess. When I was a little girl, I used to dream of one day marrying a prince. Let me tell you, the man I married is as chivalrous as any of those men in the royal families over there in Europe—maybe even more so. He's handsome, considerate, loving, and dashing. You know what I mean?"

Natasha rolled her eyes. "I wish I did. They don't make many men like that anymore, especially not in Los Angeles."

"Girl, he's broke compared to the rich men I dated once upon a time. He doesn't have two pennies to rub together to make a dime. He cuts glass for a living, you know, for mirrors and tables and shelves. We've invested a lot of money into our education. We both decided to go for broke and get our degrees."

Lanita walked past Natasha and sat back in her chair. "We're gonna be just fine. After today I'll have my degree and he'll have his. We'll both be able to begin new careers."

The phone rang and Natasha rushed to pick it up, resuming her seat behind the front counter. After listening for a few moments, she said, "Okay, I'll let her know," and then hung up.

She turned to Lanita, saying, "You were supposed to be getting your facial first, but Miss Lina is running a little late, so you'll see Jimmy Choo first. He's going to style your hair. He should be here in a couple of minutes, just as soon as he's finished up in back."

"Jimmy Choo?" Lanita said. "You mean the guy who makes those thousand-dollar shoes does hair too?"

"Well, no," Natasha said. "They do share the same name, but they are two different people."

"Is Jimmy Asian?"

"Yes, he is," Natasha said. "Is that okay?"

Lanita almost jumped out of the chair. "I don't mean to overreact, but is he educated about caring for African-American hair? Everything has to be right today. I've had some real horror stories in the hair department. Once a French lady gave me a relaxer and my mane shed for weeks. I nearly went bald until my mother gave me a protein treatment." Lanita frowned. "I'm sorry, I'm just a little scared. I mean, I can't go across the stage looking all crazy. When I take off my cap, my hair needs to be bouncing and behaving, not embarrassing and shaming."

"Trust me," Natasha said. "Jimmy knows what he's doing. As a matter of fact, he does my hair." She reached up to fluff her smooth, shiny layered bob.

"Well, your hair looks good," Lanita said. "Now that I think about it, the guy who does Halle Berry's hair is Asian too, isn't he?" At Natasha's nod, Lanita said, "Now, that's a good sign. Maybe he'll be able to make me look as good as her.

"So, how late is he going to be? I have to meet my sweetie on campus at one o'clock sharp. Graduation begins at one-thirty."

"He should only be about ten more minutes." Natasha's warm smile put Lanita at ease.

"Oh, that's not bad at all," Lanita said, relaxing back.

Natasha took another call. When she was finished, she looked up and asked, "Do you have any plans after graduation, or are you going straight into job hunting?"

"We're considering a short vacation," Lanita said. "We hope to begin working at the end of the summer."

"Where do you want to go?"

"The French Polynesian islands," Lanita said, sighing.

"But how could you two afford that? I thought your money was tight. I don't mean to be forward . . ."

"That's okay. Yeah, the islands are pricey, but a girl can wish, can't she?" Lanita smiled, crossing her legs. "You'll be surprised at the amazing things that have happened in my life that weren't supposed to."

"But, Tahiti and places like that." Natasha shook her head. "That's a lot to wish for just out of school."

"You're right, but stranger things have happened in my life. My mother always said that just enough of King Midas's blood runs in my veins to turn hard luck into gold, but not enough to keep it."

"Really?"

"Yeah, really. I was born lucky."

"Lucky?" Natasha said, skepticism creeping into her voice.

"Yes. I consider myself an intelligent and levelheaded woman, but honestly, I've had a streak of luck that has followed me since birth. I was born during the Watts riots of 1965, and my birth prevented a man's store from being burned to a crisp."

"You were born in Watts, California, during the actual riots?" The skepticism in Natasha's voice was beginning to turn to awe. "That must have been crazy for your mother."

"Yeah, and because that man's store didn't get burned down, he gave me and my mother a place to live rent-free for years. Isn't that lucky?"

"Yeah, I suppose so," Natasha said. "I remember reading about the Watts riots back when I was in high school. It seems like your real luck was making it out of there alive."

Lanita tilted her glass and took another sip. She made herself comfortable and began easing down memory lane. "Since we have a few minutes before Jimmy Choo will be ready for me, I'll tell you about my birth. It's one of my favorite stories. My mother loved to tell it whenever she and her friends sat around and got drunk on cheap liquor. She told it so many times that I sometimes feel like I saw it with my own eyes."

Two

The night of August 11, 1965, was hot and humid. The day had been depressing, but the night would prove to be even worse.

Earlier that day, my mother, Aretha, had spoken on the phone with her friend Marquette Fry. Both were broken up because of their financial condition. Marquette told my mother that he had been trying to get a job, but nobody wanted to hire him.

"It seems like everybody I know cain't get no work," my mother replied. "I'm so close to being evicted, my baby and me might be homeless soon. Even if the doctor hadn't ordered me to take bed rest, I still wouldn't have a job. I don't know what me and my baby are gonna do after it's born."

"My mother moved us up here from the South because she thought me and Ronald could at least find some work making a dollar twenty-five an hour," Marquette said. "But it ain't no better here than down there. With the delay on that federal antipoverty program, what are we supposed to do? I don't want to spend my day hanging out on the street corner. I want to work, Aretha."

"I know you do, Marquette. Just hang in there. Things can only get better. They have to get better."

"I hope you're right, Aretha, I just hope you're right." Sighing, Marquette changed the subject to a lighter topic. "So what you gonna name your baby?"

"I was thinking Lamont if it's a boy and Lanita if it's a girl."

"Lanita. That's a pretty name."

"I hope it's a girl. In fact, I pray it's a girl because I don't want her to have to deal with what y'all men have to go through with the police."

"But this is the West," Marquette said. "It's supposed to be better, right?"

"Nah, Marquette, North or South, East or West, this world ain't no place of peace for colored people, especially a Black man."

"I guess you right about that. That's why I'm gonna let loose tonight, forget about all the madness," Marquette said. "If you weren't about to drop that baby, you could hang out with Ronald and me. So, Aretha . . . who's your baby by?"

"None of your business!" Aretha snapped. "Stop being so nosy. So what y'all gonna do tonight?" she asked, changing the subject.

"Man, just get a few drinks to chase the blues away," he responded.

．　　　．　　　．

That night, Marquette Fry did just that. He and Ronald partook of that no-good firewater, trying to forget about the woes of life. Then Marquette got behind the wheel of his ten-year-old gray Buick. He and Ronald had just turned down Avalon Boulevard, not far from home, when they heard a police siren behind them.

Ronald, twenty-two at the time, said, "Marquette, what did you do wrong?"

"I didn't do nothing wrong," Marquette, younger by one year, responded, frustrated that they were being pulled over and that his older brother was blaming him.

"I told you, you should have let me drive," Ronald bickered.

"Just sit back and don't say a word, big brother. You've had more to drink than me," Marquette said.

The cop who pulled them over at the corner of Avalon and 116th Street was a patrolman named Officer Lee W. Minikus. He approached the Buick and asked Marquette and Ronald to step out of the car. They cooperated. When the officer asked Marquette to take a sobriety test, the poor man saw his life flash before him. He'd been drinking too much and jail was the last place he wanted to be. It would take a miracle for him to pass that test.

Not only did he fail the test, but he had an audience to witness his humiliation. Because 116th and Avalon is in the heart of Watts, every time something happened, a group of people gathered to watch, mumbling and pointing and discussing what was going on and why.

After Marquette had finished making a spectacle of himself, trying his hardest to pass a sobriety test when he was stone drunk, Officer Minikus announced, "I'm gonna have to take you to jail."

The crowd, which had grown increasingly larger, booed and hissed at the officer.

Egged on by the crowd, Marquette resisted the officer's attempt to arrest him. "You'll have to kill me before you take me to jail," he shouted, struggling against the patrolman as he tried to handcuff the drunken young man.

Shocked by Marquette's reaction and startled by the yelling and screaming around him, Officer Minikus looked at what seemed to be a mob surrounding him and panicked. Fearing things would soon get out of hand, he called for backup.

Within an hour, several patrol cars were on the scene. As more police cars pulled up, more people got involved, the crowd from the neighborhood swelling to several hundred, including Marquette's mother, Rena, and my mother, Aretha, who given her condition shouldn't have been out at all. But there'd been so much commotion outside her apartment window that she had to go down and see what was going on. It seemed like everybody who lived in the neighborhood was out there, expressing their anger and frustration that it was taking so many police officers just to arrest one man.

Aretha pushed her way through the crowd to see Rena pleading with Marquette to go ahead and get in the car with the police. However, the officers were handling him too roughly and Rena couldn't stand to watch them abuse her younger son. Before she knew it, she was trying to pull the officers off him. When Ronald saw his mother fighting with the police—well, that was all he could take. He joined in, helping his mother try to get all those policemen off Marquette.

Unfortunately, there were more police officers than there were Fry family members, and soon all three of them were handcuffed and thrown into a police car. This sight of a woman and her sons in the back of that car was too much for the crowd to take. Somebody shouted, "It's just like Selma!"

With the words "just like Selma" ringing in Aretha's ears, she felt just like she had when she'd first heard the news about Bloody Sunday in Selma, Alabama. How six hundred civil rights marchers had made it to the Edmund Pettus Bridge, only to be pushed back by state and local officers, who attacked them with billy clubs and tear gas, driving them back into Selma. When she heard "just like Selma," she died inside. Her blood pressure skyrocketed. Before she knew what she was doing, she'd spat on one of those redneck policemen. "That's for Dr. King," she whispered.

When she realized what she had done, Aretha backed up quickly and hid in the crowd. But the cop was determined to find the woman who'd spat on him, so he forced his way through the crowd. He didn't find Aretha. Instead he got somebody else, a girl Aretha had seen in the neighborhood before, but didn't know well, Joyce Ann Gaines, who'd rushed out of the salon, where she was getting her hair done, to see what was going on. The officer must have assumed she was the one who'd spat on him because she was laughing when he got to her.

He grabbed her by the arm and pulled her toward the front of the crowd. Resisting, she fell to the ground and refused to move. The cop, stronger than she by far, pulled her off the ground and carried her off. She was kicking and screaming as if he was killing her.

Someone yelled, "You wouldn't treat a White woman like that!"

While the officer forced Joyce Ann into one of the cars, Aretha looked out of the corner of her eye and saw Gabriel Pope, a nineteen-year-old from the neighborhood. He slung an empty soda bottle, glass shattering everywhere. Following his lead, people began to pick up whatever they could find—rocks, bottles, whatever—and started hurling things at the cops. Then the chants began: "Burn, baby, burn! Burn, baby, burn!"

When the cop cars pulled off with Marquette, Ronald, Rena, and Joyce Ann in their cars, the crowd's fury didn't stop. It grew to more than a thousand angry people. The brothers and sisters of Watts united out there on Avalon Boulevard, pounding on the car of every White person who drove by in their fine cars. The policemen tried to contain the mob with their nightsticks, but the crowd was too big to control.

That night things got completely out of hand. Nineteen policemen and sixteen citizens were injured. The uproar drew the attention of the media, some of whom also fell victim to what turned out to be the beginning of a weeklong riot.

Still shaken by what she'd witnessed, Aretha went back to her dismal apartment, only to find another eviction notice posted on the door. She pulled it off and balled it up. Inside, she looked at the tattered old couch and the rickety kitchen table balanced on three legs. A fourth unattached leg was carefully propped in place to keep the table from toppling over.

"How am I gonna do this?" she cried. "I am not ready to have a baby—not in times like these. How can I bring such a beautiful miracle into such a dreadful place?" Consumed with worry, she walked through the small apartment and crawled into bed to sleep off the anguish of being Black, being hated, being broke, being evicted from her run-down apartment.

What hurt the most, although she'd kept it a secret from her friends, was that the man who'd impregnated her was nowhere to be found. My daddy, the fast-talking, good-looking gambling man from Nevada whom she'd met while he was in Watts for two weeks visiting with his cousin, never even knew she was pregnant. He never knew he had a baby on the way. But my daddy—that's another story.

Aretha finally managed to fight through her anxiety and fall into a deep sleep. The next day she stayed in bed and drifted in and out of sleep, having the strangest dream. It began with the events of the previous night, Marquette getting arrested, her spitting at the police. Only this time, when she turned to run from the police officer, my daddy grabbed her by the hand and together they ran into a casino. My handsome daddy had a pair of dice in his hands. "Aretha, blow on the dice and make a wish," he said.

She did. He rolled, and the dice landed on seven.

"We win!" my daddy yelled. "We win!"

Aretha awoke to the sounds of yelling and breaking glass—and the stench of smoke.

She dragged herself out of bed, which wasn't the easiest thing to do because her belly was so big. She wobbled over and peeped out. From her window, Avalon looked like a war zone. The day was over and dusk was drawing near. A hoodlum was smashing a bottle into a liquor-store window, shattering glass everywhere. Five or six people went inside and filled pillowcases with whatever would fit. The building next to it was burning to the ground. "It's still not over," Aretha said to herself.

Suddenly realizing that her building could be the next to burn, she rushed out into the street. She looked around for someone sane, someone who could tell her what had been happening, but she saw no one except good people gone crazy. Walking to the corner, she saw a sign in the middle of the street, reading TURN LEFT OR GET SHOT. Aretha swallowed hard. She looked around her, seeing that everyone seemed to be moving in harmony. What was happening here? Had there been a meeting she didn't know about?

Before she could complete her thoughts, a wave of pain shot through her, cramping so severe that it nearly took her to her knees. She bent over, hands on her knees, and tried to take deep breaths. She looked up, trying to find somebody who could help her—but no one was standing still long enough to take notice of her. Down the street, about a block away, she saw a man standing in front of the corner store, waving his hands. *He's my only chance,* she thought. So she made her way down the block, stopping every few minutes as another wave of pain swept over her.

That night, a distance that usually took only a few minutes seemed to stretch on forever, taking Aretha nearly thirty minutes. As she made her way toward the man, she prayed that he wouldn't go inside or that I would wait and come another time.

She got one of her wishes.

As soon as she reached the store, a pain shot through her that hurled her forward. She wrapped her arms around the neck of Mr. Silverstein, the Jewish man who owned the store, and pleaded, "Help me! I'm getting ready to have this baby."

It took a while for Mr. Silverstein to understand what she wanted because he was hysterical. He was yelling, "I am not the enemy. Please don't rob my store!"

Aretha was yelling, "Please help, I'm having a baby!"

When Mr. Silverstein, who had been guarding his store, realized Aretha was in labor, his hysteria grew. "I want to assist you, young lady, but if I leave my store, they'll rob me blind."

"I understand, but even though I don't want it to, my baby is coming. Please help!" my mother huffed between breaths. She grabbed the elderly man by the hand and squeezed firmly.

The pain ensued. This time Aretha did fall to her knees. "I can't move!" she cried. "This baby is coming right now!"

As she pleaded with me to wait, I was dead set on being born on that day, at that very moment, and nothing was going to stop me from coming, not the looting or the fires, let alone the fact that she was at a corner store, not a hospital.

"Not here. We must at least get you into the store," he insisted.

As he tried to help my mother up, his wife, who had been peeking out through the door, rushed out to help him bring her inside.

As soon as they got Aretha through the door, water started draining down Aretha's legs.

"Her water broke," his wife said. "Plus she's too heavy. I can't go any further. We're going to have to deliver the baby right here."

So they closed the door, and right there in front of the door, Mr. and Mrs. Silverstein began to bring me into this world.

Mrs. Silverstein rushed to the back of the store and came back with sheets and a pail of hot water. They somehow got the sheets underneath my mother and had her propped up and ready to deliver when a bottle flew through the storefront window, shattering the plate glass and scarcely missing my mother's face. An angry young man was getting ready to come inside through the window when he saw Aretha and the Silversteins on the floor in front of the door.

"What's going on in here?" he demanded.

"She's having a baby," Mrs. Silverstein said.

"Ah, man, that's Aretha," he huffed when he noticed her.

Aretha looked up, seeing that the face belonged to one of her neighbors.

He yelled over his shoulder, "Aretha's in there, and she's having her baby. We can't take this place."

"Bobby, is that you?" Aretha asked.

"Yeah, Aretha. It's me."

"Go and get your sister and tell her to come and help," Aretha said before she cried in anguish with the pain of another contraction.

"Okay, Aretha. We'll be right back," Bobby said. He yelled over his shoulder again, "Somebody stay here and make sure nobody tries to rob this place." Then he took off to get his sister.

"Do you think you can push?" Mrs. Silverstein asked timidly.

"I'm scared," my mother replied.

"You're going to have to push," Mrs. Silverstein insisted.

So my mother began to push.

By the time Bobby came back with his sister and a few of the other girls from the neighborhood, I was here, alive and screaming and kicking even more fiercely than Joyce Ann the day before, when that cop hauled her off to jail.

· · ·

A man Lanita assumed to be Jimmy Choo had walked in toward the end of the story and stood by the receptionist's desk, listening.

"Amazing," Natasha said. "I can't believe you and your mother were okay through all that." She shook her head, looking impressed and horrified at the same time.

"Yeah, it was pretty amazing," Lanita said. "Even after my birth, the word was out that no one was to touch Mr. Silverstein's store. The best part was that Mr. Silverstein owned a few multiplexes in the neighborhood. He was so grateful his store had survived because I was born there that he allowed me and my mother to live in one of his apartments, rent-free, until my twelfth birthday."

"Fascinating," the man said, extending his hand. "Hi, I'm Jimmy Choo, and I'll be responsible for styling your hair today."

Lanita shook his hand. "I'm looking forward to it. My name is Lanita, and I'm feeling kinda homely, so let's go to your chair so the magic can begin."

Jimmy smiled, grabbing Lanita's hand and escorting her to the back of the salon, where his chair was located. She sat down, adjusting herself until she was comfortable.

"So what are we doing for you today?" Jimmy said, looking over her shoulder into the mirror, his face above her head.

"The works," Lanita said. "I need a relaxer, a trim, and a style."

"No problem," Jimmy replied. He grabbed a black drape and placed it over Lanita's shoulders, clipping the back together. As he pulled out a large pail of relaxer and began working on her hair, he asked, "Did you and your mother really live rent-free for twelve years? I would do anything to have free rent for even one year. The prices in this city are ridiculous."

"Well, it was close to twelve years. When Mr. Silverstein died of a heart attack, his son blamed it on his father's association with Watts and told my mother that there was no way she should have been allowed to live there for free for so long. He said she was lazy, and he demanded that she begin paying rent or else he would kick her out. When she told him that she didn't have a job, he threw us out without notice or the time to find anything else."

"No!"

"Yep. We'd had it pretty easy until then. After that, life became rough."

Jimmy spun Lanita's chair away from the mirror to begin relaxing the front of her hair.

"If she wasn't working before you got kicked out, how did she pay her bills?" Jimmy asked. "He gave her free rent only, right? What about groceries and utilities and things like that?"

"Oh, well, the word about my birth spread in the Jewish community like ivy. Mr. Silverstein's store was the donations headquarter for about a month afterward. We received diapers, formula, food, clothes, furniture, and money, lots of money. We were even given five thousand dollars in savings bonds. When I turned seven, my mother cashed those in, and we were in the money again. Not to mention that the utilities were waived with the rent. My mother's only bill was the telephone, so sometimes we had a phone and sometime we didn't. I even had money put aside to pay for my college tuition, provided that I graduate from high school. My mother said that back then we were living the life of Riley."

"Riley?" Jimmy asked as he smoothed liquid through her hair.

"Riley. You know, Chester A. Riley? No, you're probably too young. I'm *nearly* too young, but it was a television show in the fifties, *The Life of Riley*. The funny thing about that expression is that things never went right for Riley. No matter what kind of good luck he had, everything got twisted eventually. Just as with him, things wouldn't go right for us either. They might have started out good, but in time they became just as bad as could be."

Three

Before Mr. Silverstein's son kicked us out of the apartment building, I saw my mother fall in and out of love with three men, get the Holy Ghost and backslide into heathenism twice. She swayed back and forth between feeling proud of all we had and being guilty that her friends' struggles were worse than hers. That was soon going to change.

It was 1977, and I had just turned twelve. My mother had been promising me all year that she was going to throw me a birthday party, so I was disappointed when she told me she couldn't. I was angry with her for days afterward. There was a cute guy in my class named Jermaine Powers, whom I was dying to invite. I'd gone over and over in my mind what I would say to him when I asked him to my party. I thought for sure that a personal invitation would get him to notice me. He was so adorable, and he was always nice to me. But it never happened. My birthday came and went, and no party. Days passed and I was still angry. I blamed Lester, my mother's no-good boyfriend at the time, for distracting her from following through.

Lester would come over with a bottle of Ripple, and my mother would send me to my room while she and Lester made out on the living room sofa. He had gotten her addicted to smoking cigarettes and drinking that firewater. They would sit around and drink all night, listening to eight-track tapes, especially Stevie Wonder's *Songs in the Key of Life*. It seemed that when he was around nobody cared about me, so I hated him.

One afternoon when I came home from school, I found my mother sitting on the sofa, bawling her eyes out.

"What's wrong, Momma?" I asked. I hated to see her upset, but if it was because Lester had left her—and I hoped he had—I knew she would be hurt for a while, but she'd get over him soon enough, and I would have my mother back.

Aretha looked up at me, her big eyes framed by a huge afro and giant hoop earrings. Tears were streaming down her face. "Have a sit-down beside me, Lanita," she said, wiping her eyes with the tail of her shirt.

This was more serious than I had thought. Momma seemed more focused than I'd seen her in a while, plus, absent was the smell of alcohol that was normally on her breath.

"Lanita, I need for you to go to your room and pack all your clothes and dolls. We're being evicted. Baby, we have to be out of here by Friday."

"Where are we going to live?" I asked.

"We'll see on Friday," she said.

Her news didn't mean a lot to me at the time because I didn't know what being evicted really meant. I understood that we had to move, but I didn't know why it was so upsetting to my mother. I knew she was attached to the apartment, so I figured that she was going to miss it. I knew I was going to miss it too, but I was already dreaming about how much better our new place would be. After all, when people moved, it was usually to a bigger and better place.

"Why are you crying?" I asked.

"Aren't you gonna miss this place, Lanita? This was our good-luck home. We'll never have another place like this one."

The only thing I thought I would miss was the view from my bedroom. Every night before I went to sleep, I would sit on the windowsill and look at the people walking up and down the street and make up stories about their lives, who they were and what their families were like. I would miss that. Everything else, I had taken for granted. I shrugged and went to my room to pack up my stuff.

But that wasn't the only startling news we received that day. It was a Tuesday, August 16 to be exact. I'll never forget that day because shortly after we were hit with the eviction, Lester walked in with a lot to say.

"Can you believe what happened?" he said, sitting down in the chair beside the sofa. He looked up and noticed that Aretha was crying. "Baby, don't cry about it. He didn't really care a lot about Black people anyway."

My mother stared at Lester. "What are you talking about?"

"You're crying because Elvis Presley died, right?"

"Elvis Presley died?" my mother said, looking bewildered.

"Elvis is dead?" I said. I had come back into the living room when I'd heard Lester come in. I didn't like him, so I made it my business to keep an eye on him when he was around.

"Y'all didn't know?" Lester seemed surprised.

"No," my mother replied.

"Then what are you crying for, Aretha?" Lester asked.

"Lester, we've been evicted from the apartment. I have to be out by Friday."

"Man, that's a bad break," he said. He went over to my mother and put his arms around her. "You gonna be all right, Aretha. You're a strong Black woman. You'll be just fine."

• • •

I took my time walking home from school on Friday. It was my birthday, but we hadn't done any celebrating. We had been packing all week, and facing the empty apartment wasn't going to be easy. As I trudged down the street along my normal path, I saw, laying on the sidewalk in front of me, as amazing as if an angel had neatly placed it there, a fresh, crisp dollar bill. I looked around to see if someone was looking for lost money. I didn't see anyone, so I reached down and picked up the bill.

"Happy birthday to me," I sang, stuffing the money in my pants pocket.

I took that dollar right to the store and spent every penny of it on candy, chips, soda, and an ice-cream cone. Still taking my time, I held my bag of goodies in one hand and my ice cream in the other, trying to lick it down before it dripped all over me. I was in heaven.

When I finally got home, my mother was sitting on one of the moving boxes, smoking a cigarette. "I got everything packed up," she said. "We just have to wait for Lester. He's coming with a truck to move us to the new apartment."

"So, Momma, where is the apartment going to be?"

"Around the corner from here. We're moving back to Avalon."

"Does my new room have a good view, like the one here?"

She motioned for me to come closer. "Baby, a few things are going to change now. I'm sorry to tell you this, but I couldn't afford a two-bedroom apartment. We'll be moving into a one-bedroom." She took my hand and looked up into my face. "You're gonna have to start sleeping on the couch."

I pulled away. "But, Momma, where is my bed gonna go?"

"Oh, Lanita! I'm sorry, baby, but I sold it today. I had to sell your dresser too, and the TV."

I couldn't believe my ears. First I didn't get a birthday party, and then we were moving to a place without a room for me. But no TV! How was I ever going to survive? I looked around the room. Sure enough, the TV was gone.

Trying to smile, my mother said, "I kept your stereo. I know how much you like to fall asleep listening to it at night."

I had heard her words, but was my bed really gone? I had to see for myself, so I rushed past her into what would no longer be my very own room. Just as there wasn't a television in the living room anymore, there wasn't a bed for me. My knees buckled and I fell to the floor in the midst of the dust balls, right where my bed used to be, and howled like a wounded puppy. I was in pain. Something inside me broke. I was realizing that things for my mother and me were getting worse and there was nothing we could do about it.

The move itself was a nightmare. Lester didn't show up to help us. My mother had to go out in the neighborhood and ask around until she got Mr. Jenkins, the old man down the street, to let us use his old truck. He said he would drive, but his back was too bad to do any lifting. So she found two winos on the corner near the liquor store to move us for a bottle each of Mad Dog 20/20.

We finally got to the new place that night. When we opened the door and turned on the lights, a mouse ran across the floor. My mother and I screamed. I threw my arms around her waist and held on tight.

"Momma, let's not live here, okay?"

"Oh, girl, it's just a little mouse," she snapped, peeling me off her. "Come on, y'all. Let's unload this stuff so we can get some rest. I'm tired."

The men moved our furniture in quickly and haphazardly. My mother and I helped carry in the lighter boxes. By midnight, we were finally all done, and Mr. Jenkins was sound asleep on the couch, waiting for us to finish. My mother woke him up and gave the winos a few dollars each to buy some booze. Once they were gone, our world grew quiet. We had been left alone to face the mess that was our tiny new home.

·   ·   ·

The next morning my mother was up early. She had the stereo blasting "Best of My Love" by the Emotions. I was forced to get up even though I wasn't ready. "Rise and shine, Lanita. It's time to turn this dump into a house." She had a cigarette between her fingers and was dancing around the place as if we had just hit the jackpot.

I, on the other hand, felt grumpy. I hadn't slept well the night before. First of all, I'd had to sleep on the couch. Then I was afraid that the mouse would come back, so I tried to stay awake to be on the lookout. All night I could feel him lurking around the corner, just waiting for his moment to attack me. But so much had happened that day, that week, that finally I'd passed out from pure exhaustion. I loathed our new apartment. I felt like I was in a nightmare, one that hadn't gone away when I'd awakened.

My mother walked over to the couch and sat beside me. She put her arms around my neck and smiled. She smelled like cigarettes and Manischewitz wine.

"I don't want to get up, Momma," I complained.

"But you have to, Lanita." She pulled me close to her. "C'mon, this place ain't as bad as it seems. We just have to fix it up. And, baby, it's only temporary. We'll be out of this place before you know it."

I wanted to believe my mother's words. I needed something to hold on to in order to face our new situation.

"And fuck Lester. We don't need him! We don't need nobody, Lanita, because we have each other, and that's all we need." She hugged me tighter, and I rested my head on her shoulder. She seemed to have everything under control.

"Now let's get this place in order," she said and got up off the couch. "Flashlight" by Parliament played over the radio.

"Ah, yeah, that's my song!" she belted and danced her way back into the kitchen. She took a sip out of a big plastic cup and continued to unpack the dishes.

I dragged myself off the sofa, stretched, and followed my mother into the kitchen. That morning we danced around the house until almost everything was put into its place—everything except my clothes, shoes, bedding, and toys. These were still in their boxes.

"We'll just stack these up in the corner of my room, Lanita, until we can figure out what to do with them," my mother said, sounding nonchalant, like nothing was wrong. By this time, she had gone through a pack of cigarettes and the entire jug of wine. "I'm so tired right now that I can't think straight."

Her eyes widened with excitement, "As a matter of fact, let's go to bed early so we can go to church tomorrow. After you get those boxes into my room, why don't you find yourself a dress to wear?"

I couldn't believe my ears. We hadn't been to church since Mother's Day the previous year. I loved going to church. Grant American Methodist Episcopal Church had the best singing, and all my friends talked about being in the choir and going on church trips. Church was this whole world I'd been missing out on. Every time I was there, it seemed like someone would shout and get the Holy Ghost. To me church was fun. I welcomed any opportunity to attend.

By the time I got the boxes moved and picked out a dress, shoes, stockings, and a hair ribbon to match, my mother was stretched out on the couch. I tried to shake her awake, but she shooed me away. "I don't feel like moving," she groaned. "You go on and get into my bed. I'm gonna sleep out here."

I'd had my blankets folded at one end of the couch, so I grabbed one and covered her up and turned out the lights. Once it was dark in the apartment, I remembered the mouse and got a little nervous, so I tiptoed toward my mother's room.

I thought it would be a good idea to try to set the alarm clock on the dresser. As I was turning the dial, a sudden movement caught my attention. I quickly turned in the direction of the motion, but didn't see anything. I thought it must have been a bug crawling across the dresser, but I wasn't sure. I set the clock and crawled into the bed.

This feels so good, I thought, snuggling deeper into the blankets. Just when I had begun to doze off, I heard a noise. "It's the mouse!" I said, jumping up and crawling to the edge of the bed to scope out his whereabouts. I didn't see a mouse, but I saw a roach. It had come out of my mother's closet, and it had an egg sack sticking out of its back.

We had roaches. I was petrified. For the second night in a row, I felt like I had to protect myself. I now had two enemies: the mouse and the roach.

I fought to stay awake, but sleep won out once again.

When the alarm clock went off the next morning, I must admit I was tired, but the thought of going to church gave me all the energy I needed to get out of bed and wake up my mother so that we could get dressed.

I looked around for scary creatures. The coast seemed clear, so I jumped off the bed, landing as close to the door as possible, and then ran to the couch where Aretha was sleeping.

I shook her. "Wake up, Momma," I said.

She didn't budge.

"Momma, you said we were going to church today. It's time to get up so we can get dressed."

She moaned, covering her eyes. "I'm asleep, Lanita."

"I know, but you have to get up. Come on, Momma," I begged.

"Girl, if you don't leave me alone, you better." She pulled the blanket over her head and turned over.

I knew it was a dead issue. I was disappointed, but I knew my mother was tired. I was tired too, so I got back into her bed and went back to sleep.

That evening Momma ran around the corner to get another bottle of Manischewitz, but she came back with Mad Dog 20/20, a pack of cigarettes, and a small bag of potato chips for me. She spent the evening at the kitchen table, drinking and smoking and listening to the radio.

I was bored stiff. I did my homework twice and even did the bonus questions, which I never did. I really missed the TV. That night in particular, I had missed *The Hardy Boys/Nancy Drew Mysteries* and *The Six Million Dollar Man.* I could get used to sleeping on the couch, but life without a television was bleak.

I hoped that Momma would figure something out—and soon.

Four

I hated the sixth grade. It was the beginning of the most isolating and embarrassing time of my life. Our apartment was a roach-and-mice-infested hellhole. Although Aretha had begun drinking and smoking at our old place, which I missed terribly and dreamed about every night, she'd gotten much worse in the new place. She became an outright alcoholic. I tried to convince her to stop a few times, but she didn't listen. Once I even tried to hide her bottle from her. It was early evening, and she'd already had two glasses of the cheap booze she'd taken to drinking. I was doing my homework in the living room when an encyclopedia salesman knocked on the door.

"Hello, I am Mr. Hall, and I would like to introduce you to a new line of encyclopedias," he said. He peered around her and saw me looking on. "My, what a lovely daughter you have. Does she have a set of encyclopedias?"

Aretha was not in the mood to be bothered by a salesman. "Number one, the fact that I have a daughter ain't your business, and second of all . . ."

I knew she was going to be a while letting Mr. Hall know the many reasons why he should take his business elsewhere and need never come back again. I saw that as my chance to hide her bottle of Mad Dog 20/20, but I knew I had to act fast. I listened closely to her words so I would have an idea of when she would be wrapping up.

"Third of all, look at this dump that we live in. Does it look like we can afford to buy your expensive-ass encyclopedias?"

I grabbed her bottle from the kitchen table and hugged it to my chest, moving quickly to the bathroom, where I stashed it behind the toilet. I walked back into the living room to see how Mr. Hall was holding up in the face of Aretha's wrath.

"And last but not least, your breath stinks, you ugly, and I don't want to look at your face no mo', you jive turkey." She slammed the door in his face.

I smirked. Mr. Hall would think twice before knocking on our door again.

"Ain't nothing funny," she said, glaring at me. "I wish I could get some encyclopedias for you, but Momma don't have the money. Maybe one day, Lanita. Maybe one day." She walked past me and back into the kitchen.

It was the moment of truth. Would she notice her bottle was gone?

She sat down at the table, lit a cigarette, and snapped her fingers to "I'm Going Down" by Rolls Royce.

She didn't notice, I thought. I breathed a sigh of relief. I was on the couch, finishing, *Oliver Twist* by Charles Dickens, the book I had been reading, when she figured it out.

"Where is my Manischewitz?" she yelled.

I didn't say anything. I closed my eyes and hoped to disappear.

"Where is my Manischewitz?" she yelled again. Her voice was getting louder as she walked into the living room, her hands on her hips, and stared down at me.

I tried to hide behind the book I was reading.

"Lanita, I might be drunk, but I'm not crazy. I know I had a bottle of Manischewitz on the kitchen table. Do you know what happened to it?"

I didn't budge.

She grabbed the book out of my hands, flinging it across the room. "Lanita, do you hear me?" She was yelling in my ear now.

"Momma, you weren't drinking Manischewitz," I said calmly, pulling at my ear to relieve the tension I was feeling.

"Oh, so you trying to be funny," she said. She grabbed my shirt collar and snatched me off the couch. "Maybe it wasn't Manischewitz, but all I know is that by the time I count to ten that bottle better be back on the kitchen table."

I pulled away from her.

"One, two, three, four, five . . . ten. I don't have time for games," she said. "Where's my belt?" She rushed into her room and was back moments later, me in her grip, whipping me wherever the belt landed.

"Momma, don't," I screamed, trying to cover my body with my hands. "Please don't."

She kept swinging.

I was petrified. My mother had never laid a hand on me. I was in disbelief. I was in pain. It was a lot like the grief from the day we moved, but worse, because the belt stung.

She stopped. "Have you had enough?"

I cried the kind of tears that caused your shoulder, neck, and breath to jerk continuously and unstoppably in unison.

"I was only trying to help," I said, between jerks.

"By hiding stuff from me? Girl, you gonna make me take this belt to you again." She lifted it. I flinched. But for some reason she changed her mind.

"Go get it now," she demanded.

I dragged my wounded body toward the bathroom.

"Move with a purpose," she yelled.

I picked up my pace and came back with the bottle.

She jerked it out of my hand.

The tears came again.

"As long as you live on God's green earth, don't you ever hide anything else from me again," she said, punctuating her words with a finger pointed at me.

She returned to the kitchen, turned the music up even louder, and went back into her own world.

I cried and cried, but I never again asked her to stop drinking. I knew her need to taste that firewater every night was more important to her than my needing her sober. It was a battle that I would not win, so I gave up.

Every day, by the time I got home from school, she had already started her nightly ritual. I used to love listening to music. Now I hated it. My mother controlled the volume, the songs, and the length of time that we listened, which was all night. When she switched from Manischewitz to Mad Dog 20/20, her taste in music changed as well. She wanted to listen to her oldies eight-tracks all the time. She'd get pissy drunk and fall asleep on the couch, so her room basically became mine. I eventually pushed her clothes over in the closet and hung mine in the empty space. I cleaned out one of the drawers in the dresser and used it as my own.

We were on welfare. My mother and I lived off the government. She slept all day, while I was at school, and drank all night. There was never a day set aside for us to go grocery shopping. We just picked up things from the corner store as needed. We never had any proper food, just bologna and government cheese and whatever else she could find for cheap because my mother sold most of our food stamps to get her fire-water and cigarettes. Necessary toiletries, like deodorant and toilet paper, had become luxury items that were hard to come by.

There was no safe haven for me, not even at school. While at one time I'd had lots of friends, the kids in the school now seemed to have turned against me. I guess I couldn't much blame them—after all, I didn't like being around myself much either. Out of necessity, I had become a different person in less than a year after our move.

The more my mother drank, the more irresponsible she became. She used to love to smell good. She used to have a dresser filled with perfumes and lotions. But we very seldom even had soap in the house anymore, and my mother didn't seem to care. I still took a shower every morning. At first I used to use the dishwashing liquid as soap, but when even that became scarce, I was often forced to take soapless showers. Well, what I didn't know is that water alone doesn't erase funk. And wearing clothes for the third and fourth time, clothes that had been washed by hand without soap, didn't make matters any better. I stunk.

The sad part about sixth grade was that it wasn't immediately obvious that the kids stopped liking me; my isolation happened gradually as one at a time they realized that I stunk and that it would not be good for their own social acceptance to befriend me. I wasn't mad at them—I was mad at my mother and myself. Often I would lie in the bed staring at the ceiling and asking God to forgive us for not going to church. That had to be the reason that we were being punished, because we were not attending church and praising the Lord regularly. To make up, I'd pray to God all night and ask for forgiveness until I'd fall asleep.

There was one grueling day in particular that I will never forget. I was running late because I had forgotten to set the alarm clock. I knew something was wrong when I first got up and my mother's room was brighter than usual. I looked at the clock. I had fifteen minutes to get to school, so I didn't even take a soapless shower. I just threw on my brown-and-orange turtleneck and brown corduroy pants and ran out the door. I didn't want to be late because we were taking an important test that morning. My grades and my schoolwork were important to me because they were the only things I had any control over. I could choose to do well, so I did, putting a lot of effort in studying. I had gotten into the habit because there was not much more to do.

I ran all the way to school.

Maybe it was a mixture of the running and my anxiety about being late, but when I got there, I reeked. My usual odor was mild, one you could smell only when you were extremely close to me. But on that day I smelled awful. I was even disturbed by my own odor. I made it to school on time, but once Mrs. Jackson, the teacher, began to pass out the test, the kids in the room started to act out, with loud snickering and sporadic outbursts of laughter. I stared down at my desk, knowing in my heart they were laughing at me.

"Settle down, class," Mrs. Jackson said, irritated. "You are about to take a test. There is no excuse for such behavior."

Someone said under a fake cough, "Lanita Stinkita."

The entire class burst into laughter.

Mrs. Jackson yelled, "What is going on?"

Silence swept over the room and then isolated snickers cropped up.

"Somebody had better speak up or you will all get a failing grade on this test," she said, passing out the last paper.

Silence again.

I was mortified. I didn't want to fail the test, but I was in dire fear that someone would speak up and say why everyone was laughing. I prayed silently to God to make my odor go away.

"I'm waiting!"

Finally Jermaine raised his hand.

"Thank you, Jermaine. Go ahead."

"I don't want to be mean, Mrs. Jackson, but Lanita stinks. How can we concentrate on the test with her stinking so bad?"

The class burst into laughter again and my head dropped further toward my desk.

"That is enough!" she scolded.

I put my head all the way down on the desk, trying to fight the tears, but it was no use. My face turned hot as the tears forced their way down my cheeks.

Mrs. Jackson interrupted their laughter. "I don't want to hear another word out of any of you. Now go ahead and start on the test."

I felt her moving closer to me. The closer she got, the harder it was for me to control my tears. My feelings of humiliation intensified.

Mrs. Jackson bent down close to me. She smelled like sweet perfume, and her voice was soft and comforting. "Lanita, come outside with me for a moment so we can talk," she whispered.

She grabbed my hand and we walked out into the hall.

"I know you're upset," she said, her voice sounding kind. "It's okay to cry."

With her permission, the floodgates opened. For the first time in a long time, I felt everything that had ever hurt me in my life. Never before had I felt it was okay to let go. Although I wanted to throw my arms around her and hug her, I resisted because I didn't want my odor to rub off on her.

When she saw how out of control I was, she said, "Follow me to the bathroom, Lanita."

Once we got inside she asked, "Do you think that what Jermaine said was fair?"

I didn't answer.

"I'll wait until you're ready to answer me."

After a moment I said between sniffles, "Kind of." My finger gravitated to my ear. I slowly pulled at it. Doing so relaxed me.

"I see," she said calmly. "So what do you think we can do about it?"

I was silent.

"Lanita?"

"Nothing," I said softly.

"Nothing?" she said. "Lanita, if you feel that there is nothing that you can do, then nothing can be done. But I believe that for every one of life's dilemmas, there is something that can be done to help make it better."

I hung my head. "I don't know what to do. My mother doesn't buy soap or washing powder or even dishwashing liquid. We barely have groceries in the house. And it's not that we don't get help. My mother has a drinking problem, and she spends all our government money on firewater and cigarettes."

"I see," Mrs. Jackson replied.

"I take a shower without soap every morning, but I forgot to set the clock last night so I was late, and that's why I smell worse than usual." I looked up at her. "I don't want to stink, Mrs. Jackson, I really don't."

"Oh, Lanita," she said, her face concerned. "I'm so sorry. I had no idea."

"I never told you," I replied. "I never told anyone."

"I can help you out, Lanita. This afternoon I'll go home with you and have a talk with your mother. Maybe we can straighten things out. In the meantime, I'll put an out-of-order sign on the door so you can wash up. Use the soap at the sink and the paper towels. When you're finished, just remove the sign and come back in the class so that you can take the test. Whatever you don't finish, I'll give you time to complete while I am visiting with your mother."

Then Mrs. Jackson did the unbelievable. She hugged me and said, "We're going to take care of you."

In my eyes, she was an angel. She had come to my rescue.

While I was washing up, I imagined her talking to my mother. They would walk over to the trash can together, and my mother would throw away her bottle of Mad Dog 20/20 and tear up her cigarettes. We would be happy again.

I don't know what Mrs. Jackson said to the class, but when I returned to the classroom, no one laughed and not even a snicker was heard throughout the room. I was so prepared for the test that I was finished by the time the bell rang.

After class, a girl named Michelle walked up to me. She wasn't my favorite person, but she was so pretty and always neatly dressed and wore two pigtails with the prettiest matching ribbons. She said, "Lanita, I'm sorry that I laughed at you."

"That's okay," I said and put my head down. I couldn't look her in the eye because I wasn't sure if she was being sincere.

Jermaine walked by us. I looked up at him; our eyes locked. I was so disappointed and hurt by his actions earlier. How could he let me down?

Appearing uneasy, he quickly turned and rushed away.

"I mean it, Lanita. I am so sorry. And I'm sorry that I stopped talking to you. It's just that everybody was—"

"It's okay," I replied.

"Can we be friends again?"

My heart skipped. Was she being honest? I hoped so, because I desperately wanted and needed a friend.

"Are you sure you want to be my friend?" I asked.

"Yes, I am. I'll even sit by you in the lunchroom today." She smiled and walked away.

I had two things to look forward to: sitting with Michelle at lunch and Mrs. Jackson's talking to my mother. It was turning out to be an okay day after all.

· · ·

When our class went to lunch, Michelle kept her word and stood in line with me to get our trays. I felt honored. I thought that if Michelle were my friend again, maybe everyone else would like me again too.

As soon as we sat down with our trays, Michelle spoke to me. "Mrs. Jackson told us that we shouldn't laugh at you and that you can't help that you're funky. She asked us how we would feel if we smelled like shit every day." The other girls at our table laughed, except me and a girl named Gloria.

I felt betrayed by Mrs. Jackson. How could my angel tell everyone in class that I smelled like poop? What else had she told them?

"So I want to know," Michelle said, "why do you stink, Lanita, when all you have to do is take a shower every morning?"

A huge lump formed in my throat and heat flushed across my face.

"I'm not trying to be funny. I just want to know."

The girls laughed. Gloria stared at Michelle, stone-faced.

I didn't know if I should answer her. I was beginning to think that this had all been a setup. She was making me the entertainment for the lunch table that day.

"It's just a simple question, Lanita," she said, returning Gloria's stare.

"Leave her alone, Michelle," Gloria said.

I don't know if releasing my sorrow with Mrs. Jackson earlier had made it easier for me to act on my feelings—or maybe it was that after she seemed to care, Mrs. Jackson had betrayed me—but I snapped. I hauled off and slapped Michelle as hard as I could. The sound of the impact was so loud that everyone in the cafeteria turned our way.

Michelle's face jerked hard to the right, and she laid her cheek in her hands, anger sparking in her eyes. "You funky ugmo," she yelled and pushed me hard.

I pushed back and then she grabbed my hair, so I grabbed her hair and yanked it, until Mrs. Jackson rushed over and pulled us apart.

"Ladies, stop this," she said, her face contorted with anger. "I am so disappointed in both of you. We're going to the principal's office right now."

"Lanita started it," whined Carolyn, one of Michelle's cronies.

Gloria looked at Mrs. Jackson and whispered, "She did not."

Carolyn rolled her eyes at Gloria.

"Let's go," Mrs. Jackson said. Michelle and I followed.

As we left the cafeteria, Gloria followed us out. Once we were outside, Gloria said to Mrs. Jackson, "I know Carolyn said that Lanita started it, but honest, Mrs. Jackson, Michelle did. She lied about what you told the class when Lanita was in the hall, and she was being really mean to Lanita. Lanita was just trying to make her stop, is all."

"Gloria, go back inside," Mrs. Jackson said sternly. "I've heard enough of this tattling from you and Carolyn. There should never have been a fight, regardless of who started it."

As a punishment for fighting, Michelle and I had to stay after school every day for an entire week and help Mrs. Jackson clean up the room.

I didn't mind because I liked Mrs. Jackson again once I found out that Michelle had been lying about what my angel had said to the class. I wanted to spend time with her. I wanted to grow up to be just like her.

·   ·   ·

That afternoon Mrs. Jackson walked me home. On the way we stopped by a store, where she bought me a bar of soap, some toothpaste, and a new toothbrush. I was so grateful. You would have thought she had given me gold.

When we walked into my apartment, my mother was in her usual seat at the kitchen table, nursing a half-empty bottle and an ashtray filled with cigarette butts.

"Momma, I brought Mrs. Jackson home with me. She wants to talk to you," I said, and then stepped back to let them talk.

My mother rose and staggered toward the bathroom, away from us. Her afro was lopsided and matted to her head. "Why didn't you tell me we was gonna be having company this evening, Lanita?" she yelled from the bathroom.

"I'm sorry, Momma," I said in a small voice.

She came out of the bathroom, her hair picked out and lipstick on, trying to appear sober. "Hi, I'm Aretha Downs." She shook Mrs. Jackson's hand. "Come and sit down." She rushed over to the sofa, moving the blankets to the side of the couch. I stood on the far side of the couch while they sat down.

"So what kind of trouble is Lanita in? She's a good girl, so whatever it is, I'm sure she's sorry for it."

Mrs. Jackson smiled grimly. "Well, Miss Downs, today Lanita got into a fight with one of the girls at school."

"Why didn't you go to see that girl's mother?" my mother interrupted.

"Both Lanita and Michelle, that's the girl's name, will have to stay after school every day for a week and help me clean up the classroom," Mrs. Jackson said calmly.

"That's fine with me." My mother shrugged.

Mrs. Jackson continued, "But that's not the reason that I'm here."

"So why *are* you here, Mrs. Jackson?" my mother asked, reaching for her pack of cigarettes. She tapped herself out one and then picked up the lighter and lit it while she waited for an explanation from my teacher.

Mrs. Jackson shifted in her seat. "I'm here because, well, I don't know how to put it gently." She took a deep breath and continued. "I'm here because I'm concerned with Lanita and her well-being. I'm concerned because she is so smart, but she's having a tough time connecting with the other children at school."

"Oh, they just jealous 'cause she's so smart," my mother said dismissively. "Every day she comes home and hits her books. I never have to get on her about doing her schoolwork, because Lanita pushes her own self to excel. Who knows, my baby might even end up going to college." She shot me a proud look and tapped her cigarette into the ashtray on the table.

"Of course, Miss Downs, Lanita has a great chance of going to an institution of higher learning." Mrs. Jackson sounded proud of me, too.

"I know," my mother said. "That's my daughter."

"Right. But as I was saying before, Lanita expressed to me that the two of you are having financial problems and that while there is enough money for groceries, there isn't any left over for personal hygiene products. I just want to know if there is any way I can help."

My mother snorted and jumped on the defensive. "Ask the government to increase my AFDC. Can you do that?"

"I wish that I could, Miss Downs."

My mother stared at her blankly. "Then what do you think you can do for us?"

"Do you have a job, Miss Downs?"

My mother glared at her. "Not that it's any of your damn business, but no, I don't."

"I can help you find a job if you would like."

I felt a small ray of hope at that statement. If Momma had a job, then she couldn't spend all day drinking and smoking cigarettes.

"Me and Lanita are doing just fine," my mother snapped. "We don't need no help from nobody. Don't you know that we used to live in a two-bedroom apartment? Nice. We had a color TV and everything we could ask for."

Mrs. Jackson went on. "Have you applied for a two-bedroom apartment?"

"Yes, Miss Nosy! But there's a year's waiting list. We had to take what we could get."

"I know it's not my business—"

"You right about that," Momma interrupted.

Mrs. Jackson looked at her straightforward. "Do you *want* to work?"

My mother stopped talking and looked down, as if in deep thought. After a moment she sighed. "I know I look like a loser to you, like I don't care about my daughter, but this has been a hard year for me and her, and I just gave up. *I* gave up, but not Lanita. She's so strong. The girl is lucky too. My baby never gave up.

"I *want* to get myself together. I do, but I don't know where to start."

Aretha began to sob. I don't know if it was the alcohol she had been drinking or Mrs. Jackson's offer of help that moved her, but she broke down.

"I can recommend some programs," Mrs. Jackson said.

I could tell that she was really concerned about my mother. That made me admire her even more.

"Now, you know we ain't got no money," Aretha came back. "I can't afford no program."

Mrs. Jackson would not be put off. "There are some government-funded programs. I know a doctor you can go to who will help you get started and find you the help that you need." Mrs. Jackson took Aretha's hand. "With time, Miss Downs, you'll have a job, and you'll be feeling good about yourself again."

"It's Aretha," my mother said, sniffling.

Mrs. Jackson smiled, knowing Momma was finally listening to her. "Okay, Aretha. In the meantime, I hope it's okay, but I brought Lanita some soap and toothpaste."

"Thank you so much, Mrs. Jackson."

"It's Ilene."

"Okay, Ilene. My mother always told me I was lazy and wouldn't never do nothing for myself. She's right. I want to do right, but my mind just doesn't help me to know how."

"I understand, Aretha. I'm sure this doctor will help you out." She opened her purse and pulled out a pen and a slip of paper.

"What kind of doctor is he?"

"A psychologist," Mrs. Jackson said, writing something on the piece of paper.

"A psychiatrist!" my mother yelled. "I ain't crazy, and I ain't going to see no psychiatrist!"

"I'm not saying you're crazy, Aretha."

"You don't know me. Call me Miss Downs."

Mrs. Jackson held out the piece of paper. "The doctor is a psychologist, not a psychiatrist. There is a big difference."

"Are you sure?" My mother looked at her, defiant, but still seeming to want her help.

"Yes, I am sure," Mrs. Jackson replied.

" 'Cause ain't nobody gonna say I'm crazy and lock me up and take me away from my baby. She's all I got, you know."

"This doctor will not try to commit you to a mental facility. He will only try to help you improve your and Lanita's lives."

My mother looked skeptical. "You wouldn't lie to me, would you, Ilene?"

Mrs. Jackson took my mother's hand, pressing the slip of paper into her palm. "I'm telling you the truth, Miss Downs."

"Call me Aretha," my mother said and smiled at Mrs. Jackson, who laughed. My mother laughed too, and so did I.

Mrs. Jackson and my mother didn't throw away her firewater or her cigarettes on that evening, as I had hoped, but there was some sort of progress made. My mother was willing to work on herself, and that's all I needed to know. Whatever I could do to help make things better, I was willing to do.

After seeing Mrs. Jackson out, we went back into the kitchen and listened to the radio, instead of my mother's oldies eight-tracks. She talked all night about how she was going to try to be a better mother.

I took it all in and prayed that she would be able to keep her word.

Five

By the beginning of the summer of '78, Gloria Mack and I had become good friends. It turned out that she lived only one block over from me, so we walked home from school together every day. My mother and I were doing better too. Aretha had completed an Alcoholics Anonymous program and had been sober for two months, and she had begun a training program to become a nurse's assistant. She was really beginning to feel good about herself, about taking care of us again. And I loved that.

I continued to do my part by keeping the house clean and making good grades. I remember smiling more and feeling secure again, even though 1978 wasn't a secure time for the world. The Jonestown massacre occurred: More than nine hundred people drank cyanide at the order of their leader, Jim Jones, who later shot himself. Larry Flynt, publisher of *Hustler* magazine, was shot and rendered paralyzed by an unknown assailant.

Gloria and I were unaware of anything except the day camp we attended for two weeks that summer. We walked to the park every day, and we weren't the only ones. Several other kids from the neighborhood went as well. The counselors were fun and friendly, and we got to do arts and crafts and play games, but what I remember most about camp was the songs that we sang at the end of the day: "The Handsome Duke of York," "Bear Hunt," and some song about a boy and a girl in a little canoe. I loved that song because at the end of it, the girls would yell, "Oh, yeah, dumb boys!" and the boys would reply, "Oh, yeah, dumb girls!" This went on until the counselors crowned the louder group. We had that yelling competition every day. We couldn't get enough of it.

I brought home gifts to my mother: a crocheted pot holder, a basket made from woven plastic cords, refrigerator magnets. Every day it was something different.

The best thing about summer was that Gloria and I were becoming just like sisters. The night before our last day at camp, my mother let her stay over.

Aretha let Gloria and me help her fix dinner. Well, sort of. Gloria got the ground beef from the refrigerator, and I got the skillet from the cabinet. We stood around the stove and watched Momma make Manwich Sloppy Joe sandwiches.

"Okay, you two, I need you to get out paper plates and cups. Lanita, you pour the pop."

"Do you want NuGrape pop?" I asked Gloria.

"Yeah," Gloria said enthusiastically, "NuGrape is outta sight."

"Right on," I replied as I took the liter and began to pour it into the cups.

"We need chips too," my mother said.

I went into the cabinet and pulled out the Fritos.

Momma sat down at the table with Gloria and me. Gloria started telling us about all the new clothes that her mother had gotten her for the summer.

"My mother made me a blue-jean purse and bead chokers in all different colors."

"Groovy," I said. "Momma, do you think you can make me a purse like Gloria's?"

"We'll see, Lanita," she said.

"Ooh, and she bought me some clogs and two halter tops," Gloria bragged.

"You know what is really gravy?" I said. "Tie-dyed T-shirts."

Gloria agreed. "They are gravy."

My mother didn't say much during dinner. She seemed preoccupied. But Gloria and I talked on and on about camp and toys and clothes.

After dinner, we straightened up the kitchen while my mother went into her bedroom. A few minutes later she called me in. When I went into her room, she looked like she was about to cry. She was lying in the bed with the Bible beside her.

"Momma, you're reading the Bible?" I said.

"Well, I've been reading it a little lately, mainly Psalms and Proverbs."

"Oh." I didn't know what she was taking about, but if it was in the Bible, I knew it was good that she was reading it.

"Lanita, shut the door behind you for a second."

"But I don't want Gloria to feel like she's out there by herself."

"This will only take a minute," she said.

I closed the door.

"Lanita, I hate that we ain't got a TV, baby. But I'm working on making things better around here. Do you hear me?"

"It's okay." I didn't like her appearing so sad.

"Yeah, but you have company, and I bet you wish that y'all had a TV to watch."

"Gloria? No, we'll make our own fun. We don't need no TV." I meant it. Gloria and I always had a good time just talking about things.

"Lanita, you've always been a good girl," she sighed. "You know that? I just hope that you'll be able to do better for your children than I've been able to do for you. I know you want new clothes too."

"It's okay, Momma." Until our conversation at the table, I hadn't even been thinking about clothes. I was just happy for Gloria. I hated that money was on my mother's mind. We were doing better. I didn't want her to be unhappy. "Maybe when you finish your training, we'll be able to afford a television." I smiled.

"Maybe we will," she said and smiled back.

I turned to leave the room. "Do you want me to close the door behind me?"

"No, keep it open so I can keep an eye on you girls."

"Okay, see ya on the flip side," I said and went back into the living room.

"Are we in trouble for something?" Gloria asked.

"Nah, everything's gravy," I replied.

We listened to the radio and made a pile on the floor of all the sheets and blankets that we could find. We lay on top of our pile and took turns playing tic-tac-toe and made shapes with string. By the time my mother dozed off, we were bored and looking for another way to entertain ourselves.

"Let's do each other's hair," I suggested.

"No. My mother said that if I let my friends play in my hair, it'll all fall out."

"For real?" I said. "Can that really happen?"

"That's what my mother said." Gloria's eyes were big, convinced.

"Okay, then let's think of something else."

We lay there and listened to the radio playing lightly in the background.

I had an idea. "Let's become blood sisters since we don't have real sisters." Gloria had a brother, but he didn't count because he was a boy.

"How do we become blood sisters?" Gloria asked.

"We cut our fingers with a knife, and we touch fingers so that our bloods can mix. Then my blood will be in you and yours in me." I had seen this on television, in the days when we'd had one.

"What if we can't stop bleeding?" Gloria asked, sounding concerned. "Then what?"

"We're not gonna cut our fingers off," I said, rolling my eyes. "We'll make cuts big enough for just a little blood to come out."

"Okay." There was still skepticism in her voice.

"My mother has a razor blade in the bathroom. Come on." I grabbed her and the two of us trotted off to the bathroom, where I found a razor in the corner of the medicine cabinet.

"Give me your right pinkie," I said.

Gloria held out her right hand, squinted her eyes, and turned her head. I pricked her with the blade and squeezed her finger until a drop of blood oozed out.

"Now it's my turn," I said.

"That wasn't so bad." Gloria sounded relieved.

"I told you." I did the same to my finger. Then we hooked our pinkies so that our blood would mix.

"I now pronounce us sisters forever. Power to the sisters!" I said, thinking that an affirmation would be appropriate. Then I threw my fist in the air. Gloria did too.

We both laughed because my "power to the sisters" was a bit loud.

"Is everything all right in there?" my mother said from her room.

"Yes, ma'am," I replied.

We snickered and turned off the bathroom light, tiptoeing back to the living room. That night I told Gloria about how hurt I had been that Jermaine Powers said what he did about me in class. I swore her to secrecy never to tell anyone that I'd had a big crush on him until that day. Gloria shared with me that her mom and dad were not getting along and that they argued sometimes at night. And that she cried sometimes because she didn't understand why they couldn't get along.

It seemed I wasn't the only one who cried at night. Although I didn't want my friend to be sad, I was secretly relieved.

· · ·

The last day of camp was so much fun. When we first got there, we made tie-dyed T-shirts and hung them up so they would be dry by the end of camp. Even though it was still light out, we built a campfire and made s'mores. We ended the day with relay races, like the three-legged race and the sack race. Gloria and I won the water balloon toss and got two free tickets to the cinema.

We walked home with big smiles on our faces, playing with our clackers, toys that had two hard balls on strings, held together by a plastic key. You'd move the key up and down until the balls banged together. Those things were loud, and so were we. It seemed we were trying to outtalk each other about the day and what movie we should go to see with the tickets we'd won.

"Let's go see *Grease,*" Gloria said.

"Right on," I agreed.

"Or we could see *Jaws II,*" she suggested.

"That would be gravy too."

"I think we should see *Grease,*" she reneged.

"Right on." I didn't care what we saw. Momma and I couldn't afford things like movies, so I was happy just to go.

When we got an equal distance from both of our places, I said bye to Gloria and headed in. I unlocked the door to our apartment and found my mother on the couch, making out with some strange man. He was all dressed up in a leisure suit and had gold chains around his neck. There hadn't been a man in our house since Lester, but what could I say? I was just a kid. Nevertheless, I was determined to get Aretha's attention. I slammed the door and stormed past the two of them, stomping my way into the kitchen and slamming my things on the table. Making as much noise as I could, I got a big plastic cup out of the cabinet and went to the sink to fill it with water.

"Lanita, come here," Aretha called.

I pretended to ignore her.

"Now!" she demanded.

I slowly made my way to the couch, where she was sitting with the flashy man. I noticed that one of his chains was silver and had a silver dollar hanging from it. I found myself staring at it.

"Ain't no need in you getting mad at me," she said. "I'm only making up with your daddy."

One thing about my life is that when I least expected them, the winds of change blew strongest. That day the wind blew in my father, Paul Lightfoot.

"My daddy? You're my daddy?" I asked and moved closer to him.

"Yes, I am, in the flesh," he said, flashing a charming smile.

I wasn't impressed, but because he was my daddy, I continued to stare.

"Stand up and give your daughter a hug," my mother said, patting him on the back.

My daddy stood and said, "You're beautiful, just like your mother, Afro puffs and all." He got a good look at me, and then he reached forward to hug me.

It was awkward. Meeting my daddy was overwhelming, like encountering a movie star. Although you know the movie star is standing in front of you, there is a hint of disbelief, like that person seems too huge a personality for you to have the privilege to be in his presence. It was surreal.

He stepped back. "Let me get a good look at you."

"Where have you been?" I blurted.

He did a double take.

"Where have you been!" I demanded. I never thought I would have reacted the way I did, but then again, I never thought I would ever meet my daddy.

He sat back down. "It's complicated, little lady."

"My name is Lanita." I puffed out my chest.

He looked at my mother. "Now, Aretha, you went on and on about her, but you didn't tell me she had such a smart mouth."

"She doesn't. Lanita, mellow out," my mother said, giving me the eye.

I cocked my neck and waited for an answer.

"Well, first of all, Lanita," my daddy began slowly, "for a while I didn't even know about you."

"What about when you did?" I insisted.

"Like I said, it's complicated."

"I'm a straight-A student. I'm twelve years old. I'll be in the seventh grade this year. I think I'll understand."

"Lanita," my mother snapped.

"It's okay, Aretha. I guess she is entitled to know the truth."

My daddy took a deep breath and pulled at his ear, just as I do when I'm upset. "I was married when I found out that you were born, and I thought my wife would get upset if she found out that I had a little girl. So I kept it from her. We lived in Vegas for eleven years, but we divorced last year. So I thought it was high time that I went back to see about my little girl. So here I am."

"Okay," I said nonchalantly. His explanation seemed okay, but I wasn't letting him get off that easy.

He looked surprised. "Is that all you have to say?"

"Yep," I replied. I only wanted to know, and once I knew, I knew.

He laughed. "Aretha, she's just like you."

"She's got you in her too." They giggled like kids.

"Can I go over to Gloria's?" I asked.

"All right," my mother said.

I got out of there as quickly as I could. I didn't understand what I was feeling, but I knew that if I shared my thoughts with Gloria, she'd help me sort through them.

I rushed around the corner, headed to Gloria's, when I ran smack into the waist of an older gentleman dressed in a three-piece suit. Although he didn't stand out like a sore thumb, he still seemed out of place.

I bounced off him. "I'm sorry," I apologized, trying to get out of his way.

"No problem," he said. "Maybe you can help me."

I took a step backward. "I don't think so."

"You live around here, don't you?" He smiled at me, flashing a gold tooth.

"Yes." I was short with him, uncomfortable about talking to a stranger, no matter how nicely he was dressed.

"I think I'm frightening you, so let me start over." He made a little bow. "Hello, my name is Robert Beck, and I just spoke over at the library. My car is parked over there." He pointed to an expensive-looking black car. "I'm an author, and I have a friend in this neighborhood. I'm supposed to be meeting him at the pool hall, and from what I was told, it's nearby. I'm a little turned around, and I'm wondering if you could help me out by pointing me in the right direction."

My curiosity had been piqued. I was meeting an actual author, and I wanted to know more about him. "What books have you written?" I asked.

"You're probably not old enough to have read my works yet, but maybe one day," he said.

"Listen, Mr. Beck, I'm twelve years old. I'm intelligent. I'll be in the seventh grade this year, and my favorite thing to do in this world is to read. I've been reading above my grade level for some time."

"Is that so?" He seemed amused.

"Yes. So what did you write?" I questioned.

"If I tell you, will you direct me to the pool hall?" he bargained.

"It's a deal," I agreed.

We shook on it.

"Little lady, I've written six books and am currently working on another. I'm thinking about calling it *Airtight Willie and Me*," he said. "What do you think about that title?"

"It's okay, I guess," I said. "What are your other books?"

"There's my first book, *PiMP*. Then there's *Trick Baby*, *Mama Black Widow*. Also *The Naked Soul of Iceberg Slim*, *Long White Con*, and *Death Wish*."

I was stunned by the titles. They didn't sound like anything in my school's library.

"What do you write about, mister? There doesn't seem to be anything consistent about your titles."

"I write about what I know," he responded. "In a few years, I want you to research my books, read them, and make sure you experience my world only through my writings."

"Okay," I said, not sure of what he meant. His part of the bargain met, I gave him the information he wanted. "The pool hall is four blocks straight ahead. Make a left at the 7-Eleven, and it's on the right side of the street."

"Are you sure about that?" he asked.

"Yes, I am."

"I believe you. And thank you, little lady. This is for you," he said and placed a dollar bill into my hand.

"Thank you, Mr. Beck," I said and took off running back to my apartment, forgetting all about Gloria's house. I was flooded with excitement. I couldn't believe that man gave me a dollar just because I had told him where the pool hall was. Everybody in the neighborhood knew where the pool hall was.

When I got back into the house, no one was in the living room and my mother's bedroom door was closed. I was so excited that I forgot to be concerned about my daddy's popping up.

I jumped on the couch and opened my hand to unroll my dollar. When I unrolled it, I found a fifty-dollar bill. My head bucked and my mouth dropped open.

I had never seen so much money at one time. I just held the bill out and stared, the way I had been staring at that man's car. Who was he, and how much money did he have to be able to just give me fifty dollars without thinking about it?

I shoved the money in my pocket and fell asleep on the couch with my hand in my pocket, guarding the bill.

I was awakened by an ice-cold feeling on my cheek. I jumped up and saw my daddy staring at me. He had a Slurpee from the 7-Eleven in his hand.

"I hope you're hungry, because I brought us home a bucket of Church's Chicken and coleslaw and corn on the cob."

I smiled when I saw that Slurpee. I guessed he was okay. Before I pulled my hand out to reach for it, I felt to make sure my money was still in my pocket. It was.

The three of us sat down at the kitchen table and ate dinner. I couldn't keep my secret to myself for a minute longer. "Momma, this man gave me some money just because I told him how to get to the pool hall."

Momma looked concerned. "Lanita, don't get in the habit of taking money from strangers," she said. "He could have kidnapped you."

"Can I keep the money?" I asked and began to pull at my ear, as I always did when I was nervous. I remembered that my daddy had done the same thing when he was talking to me earlier. *He is my daddy*, I thought. It was confirmed.

"Well, I guess you can't give it back," Momma said, smiling. "So you can keep it."

"Thank you, Momma!" I cheered.

Paul opened the newspaper he had gotten from the store. "Listen to this, Aretha. There's a story in here on that pimp turned writer, Iceberg Slim. Word has it that he's over at the pool hall right now. The fellas in front of the store said his friend was over there bragging about how he used to be king of the streets while he was trying to downplay his past, talking about how he wasn't pimping anymore. Says he's a writer now, that he had just spoke over at the library tonight."

Paul kept reading.

"Yeah, right," my mother said and rolled her eyes.

"That's him, Momma," I said. "That's the man who gave me the money."

"I heard about that Iceberg Slim," Momma said. "That he got his name because he never showed any emotions toward his whores. People like him don't change," she said to Paul. Then she turned to me. "I'm gonna let you keep the money this time, because it's too late to give it back. But if that jive turkey ever says another word to you, you turn and run the other way. You hear me?"

"Yes, ma'am," I said and put my head down. I wondered why my mother didn't like him. He seemed nice to me.

"Listen to what the article says," Paul insisted.

"I don't want to hear no pack of lies," Aretha said, and that was that.

That night my parents went back to her bedroom and closed the door. This time I tiptoed up to listen to what they were saying.

"Can you believe that lowlife Iceberg Slim had the nerve to say something to Lanita?" Momma was saying. "I should go up to that pool hall and give him a piece of my mind."

"Mellow out, Aretha. First of all, he doesn't go by Iceberg anymore—he's Robert Beck."

"Well, I heard he moved here from Chicago when his mother took ill."

"He moved to LA, but when he did, he had gotten out of the pimping game. Now he writes books and lectures at colleges."

"He might be writing books," Momma said, "but that don't mean he stopped putting prostitutes on the street. Now he's after my daughter."

Prostitute. I wondered what that word meant, so I went and got my dictionary off the shelf and looked up the word. My mouth dropped and I covered it with my hand. I couldn't believe what I was reading. *Yuck,* I thought, and went back to eavesdrop.

Now Daddy was talking. "Aretha, sometimes life has a way of changing people."

"He just better stay away from Lanita," she insisted.

"I'm gonna let it go," Paul said.

I didn't want to spend that money because maybe it meant I would become a prostitute. So I went to the kitchen and rummaged through the cabinets until I found a cleaned-out jelly jar. I unscrewed the top, put the fifty dollars inside, and sealed the jar. Then I found some black electrical tape, which we never used, and I carefully wrapped it around the jar so that the contents inside couldn't be seen. Then I took a butcher knife and slit a hole down the middle of the lid that was big enough for quarters and maybe even fifty-cent pieces. I knew I had to find a hiding place for the jar, so I pulled up a chair and put it in the very back of the cabinet over the refrigerator, the cabinet no one ever went into. For some reason I felt accomplished. I promised to keep that money in the jar forever and forget about it.

Years later, I took the time to read each of Robert Beck's books in chronological order. He was a talented writer who sold six million copies. In reading his works, I saw how much he had grown from his pimping days in Chicago until the time I met him. He died in 1992 of liver failure. I felt blessed and lucky to have met Robert Beck instead of meeting Iceberg Slim.

After I completed my mission that night, I crept back over to the door to see if I could catch more of their conversation.

"She's so much like you, Aretha," Daddy was saying.

"I know, but she has your tendencies. You know, that whole ear-tugging thing, and she never even saw you before now."

"I know." Daddy sounded proud.

"And she's so smart. She's always checking books out of the library to read. She's read more books at the age of twelve then I have in my whole life," she said.

"Is that so? That's my daughter."

"Yep, she is."

"I was thinking, Aretha. Lanita needs a TV. I don't understand how y'all have gone so long without one. I know she likes to read, but I'm gonna go down to the pawnshop and pick one up tomorrow," Paul promised.

"Right on!" I said under my breath and squeezed my fingers into fists with excitement.

"Paul, I'm so glad you're here," Aretha whispered.

Nothing else was said, and if they were kissing again, I didn't want to hear it, so I held on to my daddy's words and daydreamed until I fell asleep, fantasizing about how wonderful it would be to have a television again.

I hadn't seen Paul Lightfoot in twelve years, but if he kept up his generosity, he would quickly make up for lost time.

Six

Pamela, one of the hairdressers who had dark skin, but wore her hair in platinum blond curls, was stationed next to Jimmy. She interrupted Lanita. "I met my dad for the first time when I was eighteen. He welcomed me into his life with open arms." She continued curling her client's hair, focusing on each strand as she continued. "It was his children who didn't want to have anything to do with me. I have two brothers and a sister and they never acknowledge me as their sibling. Talk about feelings being hurt."

"I'm sorry to hear that," Lanita said sympathetically.

"Don't worry about it, girl. I have my own family now. I'm married and I have two bad-ass kids."

"Tell me about it," Jimmy Choo said, combing through Lanita's hair. "The relaxer took well. Your hair is going to be fabulously fierce."

Lanita smiled.

"It's nothing like having a good relationship with your dad. Once my father and I connected again and I began to understand him better, I released the anger that I had toward him and men in general," Pam said.

"Well, I'm still angry," Pamela's client said, looking straight ahead and frowning. "I never met my father. Don't want to meet him. Don't have a man and will be fine if I never have one."

"That's harsh," Pamela said.

"Life is harsh," her client shot back. "I'll never give my heart to a man. From my daddy to every man I've dated, they are all the same—selfish, inconsiderate children. And I don't have time for childish games."

"Excluding your daddy, maybe it's your fault that you've run away every man who's been in your life," Jimmy joked.

Everyone laughed.

"I'm just kidding," Jimmy chuckled. "But you shouldn't be so hard on us poor men. There are still some good fish swimming around in this vast ocean of life."

"I agree with Jimmy," Lanita said. "My husband is the best. And when my daddy was in my life I considered him a good man."

Seven

Paul Lightfoot was a knight in shining armor. When he showed up at our doorstep that summer, it was like he had been there all along. Life was better. My mother was better. We even got a telephone. We were a family.

I don't know if he ever got around to asking my mother if he could move in with us. After that first night, he just stayed. With a third person in that small apartment, things got tight, but neither my mother nor I minded one bit. The three of us shared the closet space in my mother's room, and Paul set his footlocker at the foot of the bed and kept the rest of his belongings in there.

I did more things during my summer break that year than ever before. My daddy borrowed a car from an old friend, and the three of us went to Disneyland. One day he took Momma and me riding around Beverly Hills to show us where the movie stars lived. We went to Hollywood and strolled down the Walk of Fame, pointing out our favorite celebrities' stars. We even went to the park sometimes, just because we could.

On a lazy Sunday afternoon, my daddy would say, "Let's get out of here."

Momma would respond, "Where do you want to go?"

"Let's go to the park," I'd say.

"Okay, let's go to the park," he would agree.

Momma would make us some sandwiches or we'd stop and get fried chicken, and we'd take a walk to the park with all our stuff in bags. We went to the park so often that one day Daddy went out and bought us our very own picnic basket. We went to the park that day too.

Sometimes we'd even barbecue at the park. I loved when we'd lay back on a blanket and stare up at the clouds in the sky. Daddy would be in the middle, and Momma and me would be on either side.

Once I said, "Daddy, that cloud looks like an angel. Do you see it?"

"It looks kind of like that foxy momma Freda Payne to me," he joked.

"I think it looks more like Billy Dee Williams, you jive turkey," Momma said and punched him in the shoulder.

When my mother got her first real job as a licensed practical nurse he took us all out to eat at a sit-down restaurant. It was more like a diner. It reminded me of Mel's Diner on that television show *Alice*.

The waitress came over to us and handed each of us a menu.

"Order anything you want," Daddy said. "This is a celebration, and I'm sparing no expense."

After looking over the menu, my mother said, "I think I want the smothered pork chops."

"That sounds good, Aretha. I think I'll have that too."

"Can I get a steak burger with everything on it and a strawberry milkshake?" I asked, tugging away at my ear.

"I said anything you want," Daddy reminded me.

"Gravy!"

The waitress came back and took our orders.

After being around Paul Lightfoot a little while, I had come to realize that he was a man of few words. Usually Momma or I did most of the talking. He was a great listener, which made him charming. He had this quiet strength that was a welcome presence in our family. He knew a lot of people and was friendly to everyone, especially the ladies. But neither Momma nor Daddy had a lot of close friends. It was always just the three of us.

In the mornings, I'd wake up to him and my mother in the kitchen. Momma would be making breakfast and Daddy would be sitting at the kitchen table, reading the newspaper. When I went to the bathroom, I was hit with the smell of my daddy's aftershave mixed with my mother's perfume. I smiled every morning I woke up to that wonderful combination.

I'd get dressed for the day, eat breakfast, and go out and play all day with Gloria. By the time I came in from a long day of running around the neighborhood, my mother would be getting ready for work and Daddy would be sitting in front of the television, mellowing out. He had chosen the perfect time to come live with us: By midsummer Aretha had completed her nursing-assistant program and was placed in a nursing home. Because she was new, they put her on the night shift, working Sunday through Thursday nights from 5:00 P.M. until 1:30 A.M. She wouldn't have felt comfortable leaving me by myself that late; by the time she got home I was fast asleep. Paul assured her that I was his daughter too, and that he would be there to take care of me every night.

And he did. Every evening he'd either cook or walk to a fast-food restaurant and bring us chicken or burgers, or he'd pick up a plate from the market around the corner. I liked when he cooked because I would be his helper. We had fried catfish almost every Friday night because he knew catfish was Aretha's favorite. He'd go to Church's to get coleslaw and French fries, but during the week, he'd make cold-cut sandwiches with chips and canned green beans. His favorite was HLTs—hot dog, lettuce, and tomato sandwiches. We'd have that with Tater Tots and canned corn. My favorite was his fried Spam and mustard sandwiches with chips.

When we wanted to rush to see a good program on the tube, he'd open one can of Vienna sausages for me and two for him. We would pull out the crackers and open a cold can of baked beans and sit in front of the TV, smacking on our quick, delicious meal, drinking beer—mine would be root beer, his the real thing—while thoroughly enjoying the television program.

Paul took pleasure in spoiling Momma and me. He didn't work, but he was never short on money for little gifts and the things we needed around the apartment. I was puzzled about how he always kept money. Before he came into our lives, Momma and I had been in bad shape financially since there wasn't any income coming into our home. Mrs. Jackson always said that in order to be able to have a comfortable life, we had to finish school, pick up a trade, or maybe even go to college so that we could get a good-paying job. I wondered why you needed a job to have money. My daddy had what seemed like plenty of money, but he never worked.

One day I got the courage to ask him. It was a Saturday afternoon and

Momma was in her room, taking a nap because she had just gotten home from working a double shift, and Daddy and I were in the living room, watching television. We were sharing a quiet moment over a couple of beers, as we often did.

"Daddy, can I ask you a question?"

"Go ahead."

I tugged at my ear. "How can you spend money every day?"

"What kind of question is that?" he asked.

"Well, you don't have a job, Daddy, and I'm just wondering how you can spend money when you don't have a job?"

He laughed. "Well, it's complicated."

I gave him a look.

"I know. You're old enough to understand. How do I explain this to you?" He stopped and thought about his answer. He tugged at his ear and finally smiled. "Your daddy is lucky."

"You are?" I said in amazement.

"You see, in Las Vegas, they have these casinos, and you can go in and give them money to play their games. If you win, they give you money. If you keep winning, they keep giving you money. And sometimes I keep winning."

"Outta sight," I said. I had heard of casinos before, but I didn't know you could make money by going to them.

"Before I came here, I won a lot of money, enough to hold me over for a while. So I don't have to work."

"That's solid, Daddy!" I said. "Momma always tells me I'm lucky. Do you think I can go to one of those casinos with you one day?"

He laughed. "Well, when you get of age, you can."

"Do you think I'll win like you?"

"There's a good chance. My blood does run through your veins. You'll probably win real big."

I smiled at the thought of making money in a casino. I wondered what kind of games they had there and if I'd be any good at them. Gloria and I had won the balloon toss at camp. I was sure that whatever games they had, I could beat anybody in there because my daddy was lucky, which meant I was lucky.

I wondered if my luck had rubbed off on Gloria when we became blood sisters. I hoped so, because I wanted us to be friends forever. I figured if both of us went to the casino with my daddy, we'd make a whole stack of bread.

.   .   .

Since Momma had begun to work so much, I got to spend a lot of one-on-one time with my daddy, experiencing firsthand just what he meant about being lucky. He always seemed to be in the right place at the right time.

One time, when my parents and I were in the park, a nicely dressed man walked up to my daddy and said, "I got four tickets to the Dodgers game tonight. My old lady and I got into an argument, and she said if I go to another baseball game she was leaving me."

We all just looked at the man.

"Do you want the tickets?" He held them out in his hand. "I can't use them."

"Okay," my daddy said.

We borrowed Mr. Jenkins's truck, and since Momma had to work that night, Mr. Jenkins invited one of his friends to go with us. The four of us piled into the truck and went to see the Dodgers play. My daddy didn't have to spend any money that night; Mr. Jenkins's friend was so excited to be going that he bought us peanuts and hot dogs and cold drinks. We had the time of our lives.

When we went grocery shopping, my daddy would smile at the cashier and tell her how nice her hair or her clothes were or how foxy she looked and the next thing I'd know, we'd be paying for only half the groceries.

When we picked up fast food, there was always an extra burger or drink thrown into our order just because my daddy told the cashier that she reminded him of Diana Ross or something simple like that.

Sometimes when we walked down the street, it was as if God threw change from the sky for my daddy to find. We'd be walking to the apartment and all of a sudden my daddy would stop in his tracks. "What do you know, a quarter. Why don't you pick that up and put that in your pocket, Lanita."

I was amazed every time. Once we even found a dirty five-dollar bill in the gutter. My daddy pulled out his handkerchief and picked up the bill with it. When we got back to the apartment, he washed it in the sink with soap and hung it to dry.

"We'll use this to get you a treat from the ice-cream truck every day until it runs out."

"Outta sight!" I said.

Paul was a magician. He was special, and I felt special because he was my daddy and he was there for me. And he sure had a way with the ladies. Every time he walked by them and said hello, they'd swoon all over him. There was a certain way they looked at him. Women gave him so much attention, always putting folded-up pieces of paper into his hand. Sometimes I felt like I was walking with a movie star.

I didn't know what was on those pieces of paper, but when he got one, he always reacted the same way. He'd smile and play along.

I'd ask him, "Daddy, what do those women write on those pieces of paper?"

"Nothing," he'd say. "It's just paper that they're through with, and they want me to throw it away for them."

When we finished walking the neighborhood and got outside our apartment building, he'd throw the papers into the trash can.

I knew his story couldn't be true; after all, I was going into the seventh grade. So one day after he threw one away, I went back outside and rummaged through the trash to see what was on it. I found out that those women were coming on to my daddy and slipping him their telephone numbers and apartment addresses, wanting him to come and spend time with them.

I smiled. I was proud of my daddy because he didn't fall for their tactics. He was in love with my mother, and nobody was going to take her place. I went back inside and pretended I didn't know anything. But I secretly admired him and decided I wanted to grow up to be just like him—charismatic, attractive, and committed to one true love.

. . .

A few weeks before school started, I awoke to the sound of loud voices. When I realized my parents were arguing, I jumped up and ran to the bedroom door to get in better listening range. I put my ear to the door, but I couldn't get over the fact that it was still dark out, so I rushed to the kitchen to find out the time. Trying not to miss too much information, I took a quick glance at the clock. It was three-ten. I ran back to the bedroom door.

I had never heard the two of them arguing. I don't know if it's because they never did or if I usually slept through it. But that night they were definitely getting some things off their chests.

"Why can't you find another job working during the day?" Daddy was saying.

"Paul, these are the hours they gave me. I have to deal with it until an earlier shift becomes available."

"Why do you need to work? I told you that I want to take care of you."

"You said it yourself—you're running out of money. How are you gonna take care of me? You don't have a job. And I know you, Paul, you're not gonna get one."

"But I told you I just need to go back to Vegas for a few weeks and I'll make some more money."

"Paul, Vegas is a long shot. What if you lose, then what? I want us to move into a two-bedroom apartment and maybe even a house one day."

"I know you do, Aretha, but don't forget I'm Lucky Paul Lightfoot. I can't lose."

"You have always been such a dreamer." Momma sighed. "Come into reality, Paul."

"So what do you want me to do?" Daddy was starting to sound angry.

"I can't handle you asking me to quit my job all the time," Momma said. "I haven't had a job since Lanita was born. Now I do. I have to follow this through because I want to make her proud of me. I can't quit now just because you want me to."

"I'm not asking you to quit, Aretha. I'm just saying I want to hold you at night. This bed gets so lonely. By the time you get home, it's almost three o'clock in the morning and you're too exhausted to move."

There was silence.

"Aretha, when was the last time we made love? You're always tired and now I'm tired too."

Silence.

"Aretha, I'm a man and I have needs, baby."

"Grow up, Paul."

"Are you saying I'm not a man because I want to make love to the woman I love?"

"If the shoe fits," Aretha yelled.

"Don't go there!"

"Stop pressuring me and I won't."

"No pressure," he said calmly. "No pressure at all."

Nothing else was said.

.　　.　　.

School would be starting in one week, and I was so excited. Gloria and I were going to take seventh grade by storm. We'd spend hours on the phone, talking about what we thought the boys would be like, which classes we thought would be the most difficult, and what we planned to wear on the first day. For me, it was like having a clean slate. Maybe no one would remember Lanita Stinkita. We were not in elementary school anymore. We were going to be in middle school, and kids who'd gone to several different elementary schools would be thrown together. There would be lots of kids who'd never seen me before, who'd never known me as anything but just plain Lanita.

I even had a more mature look. My momma wouldn't let me straighten my hair yet, but I no longer parted my hair down the middle with two Afro puffs on either side. Instead I wore one puff at the top of my head, just like Thelma Evans from *Good Times*.

I was bouncing off the walls in anticipation. Momma was gonna take me shopping for some new clothes that weekend, and I couldn't wait to pick out my school supplies.

"Not including today, I only have five days until school starts," I said to Daddy as we made our way through the neighborhood. It was early in the evening and the streets were buzzing with activity.

As usual, the women were on the prowl, checking out my handsome daddy as he strutted down the street, looking confident and handsome.

"So what do you want to be when you grow up?" he asked me.

"Lucky, just like you."

He laughed. "Well, you'll probably be lucky. You already are. But what kind of job do you want to have? Where do you want to live, Lanita? You know, there's a huge world outside of Watts."

"Yeah, I know. But I never really thought about it. I like it just fine here, with you and Momma." I slipped my hand into his.

"You say that now," Daddy said. "But as you get older, you're going to find that you can't move out of here quickly enough. Plus, you're so smart. Don't you want to go to college?"

"Yeah, I do. Maybe UCLA." One of Gloria's uncles had gone to UCLA, and she'd told me all about it.

"I don't know about that . . . What about Spelman in Atlanta or Howard in D.C.?"

"That's so far away!"

"Me and your momma didn't even graduate from high school, you know. We want you to have a better life than we did. You should start getting your mind to lean toward going to college, any college." He put his arm around my shoulder. "I know it would sure make me proud."

"Well, then I'm going to college," I said.

"Hey there, handsome." We turned around and saw a lady dressed in a tight red dress. She had long, thick wavy hair and wore bright red lipstick. "Hi, how are you?" she asked, smiling.

"I'm feeling real good, thanks. Just spending the day with my daughter," he replied.

"I see you walking around here with her all the time," she said. "You sure are a good daddy. It's a shame that you don't have no wife to help you take care of her." She held out her hand. "My name is Lola, and I live a few blocks in the other direction."

"Paul," my daddy said and extended his hand to shake hers.

"Well, Paul, I sure would like to get to know you better," she said. She slid a piece of paper into his hand and then blew a kiss at him.

I just stared at her. *You don't have a chance,* I thought.

When we got to our apartment, I lifted the lid to the trash can, but my daddy walked right by me.

"Don't you want to throw the paper away?"

"Nah, Lanita, and it will do you some good to stay out of grown folks' business," he said, opening the door and going inside.

I knew that lady's address or phone number was on the piece of paper, so I watched Daddy like a hawk to see if he would call her, but he never did.

The following night, even though I was sleepy, I tried to stay up as late as I could because when school started, I knew I would have to start turning in earlier.

My daddy was sitting beside me on the couch. We were watching the end of *Dallas*.

"I see you trying to fight that sleep," he said. "Go on and lay your blankets out on the couch. When this lie goes off, I'm gonna go into the room and listen to some music." My daddy called every television show a lie, including sporting events and the news.

"Okay," I replied.

When the program was over, he stood and stretched.

I got the blankets from his footlocker. Then I began to lay them down on the couch.

"We're gonna have to get a let-out couch for you so that you can be more comfortable, at least until we move into a two-bedroom," he said from the bedroom entrance.

"A two-bedroom!" I said. "Right on!"

"Right on," he replied.

"Good night, Daddy."

"Good night."

"Daddy, do you mind if I fall asleep with the TV on tonight? You can turn it off later."

"Okay, Lanita. As long as you don't make a habit of it."

"I won't. I promise."

I lay on the couch dozing, trying to stay up later. I was fading fast when I heard my daddy's voice.

"Hey, Lola, how you doing? This is Paul," he said.

Instantly I was wide awake.

"Man, you were wearing the hell out of that dress yesterday. You are one foxy lady," he said.

I was fuming.

"I live with my girlfriend. She usually doesn't get home until three o'clock." There was a pause. "Yep, every night."

I wanted to run into that room and snatch the phone from my daddy and tell the woman, "Leave my daddy alone!"

"Naw, you cain't come over here. My daughter sleeps on the couch in the front room, and she'll hear you walking in."

"That's right!" I said quietly.

He chuckled. "Oh, so you'll be quiet."

"You can't come over," I said, talking into the pillow.

"I don't know about that," he flirted.

My daddy was all chuckles.

"It's hard to resist a woman as foxy as you. But you have to be out of here by two-thirty."

That woman was not about to come up into my mother's house. I didn't know what I was gonna do, but I knew that I had to do something. I yawned real loud and walked into the bedroom.

"Daddy, I can't sleep. Do you mind if I lay in here with you for a while?" I crawled into bed beside him.

"Listen, my little girl is up, so I'll have to talk to you later," he said. Then underneath his breath, "Shit."

"Are you okay?" I asked him.

"Don't worry about me. You just try to get some sleep."

Before I knew it I was fast asleep on the bed, happy that woman was not going to see my daddy.

The next morning I awoke to my mother sleeping next to me. I got out of bed to look for Daddy. He was stretched out on the couch. So I crawled back into bed and snuggled up close to Momma.

"Lanita," she said groggily.

"Hey, Momma."

"I'm tired," she said.

"I hate that you have to work so late," I complained. "Is there any way that you can change your schedule?"

"No, there's not," she said, sighing. "And let's not have this discussion right now. Momma's trying to get some sleep."

"I don't want you to work at night," I said softly. *It's messing up everything!* I screamed silently.

"I know, but if you want to talk, go wake up your daddy," she fussed. She snatched the pillow from under her head and covered her face with it.

"Never mind," I huffed and rolled back over, trying to come up with a plan to prevent my daddy from bringing that woman over. I fell asleep before I could come up with anything.

Eight

The first day of school came with a big bang. I was so over-whelmed by the events of that day that I began to write in a journal for the first time. It turned out that Gloria and I were in the same home-room, and our teacher was one of the grooviest in the school, one of the few male teachers. His name was Mr. Gary Stephens. I had a big crush on him; so did Gloria and every other girl in our class. The other good thing about having Mr. Stephens for homeroom was that he allowed us to choose where we wanted to sit.

As we walked into the classroom and looked around to figure out where we would be assigned to sit, he stood in front of his wide wooden desk and then leaned against it, as cool as you please, and announced, "Because you are all young adults, I'm going to attempt to treat you as such and allow you to choose where you want to sit. If we find that it doesn't work out and that you are not mature enough to handle this arrangement, we'll have to govern ourselves as other typical seventh grade classes would, and I'll issue assigned seats.

"There are prime seats in the front middle," he said as Gloria and I stood in front of the room, trying to decide where we were going to sit.

Our decision had been made. We sat in the two front-row seats in front of the grooviest teacher in the entire school. Our day was made.

Then in walked Jermaine Powers.

He looked at Mr. Stephens for direction as to where to sit. "There are no assigned seats," our teacher said. "The choice is yours."

Jermaine nodded and looked around. There were few options left.

"The seat behind Miss Lightfoot is available," Mr. Stephens suggested.

Jermaine shrugged and walked toward the empty chair. "Hi, Lanita. Hi, Gloria," he said before taking a seat.

Gloria and I waved. I swallowed hard and hoped we'd never run out of soap again.

At school that day, I had no major confrontations. No one seemed to stare at me and frown. Most of the people in my homeroom were from other schools. Other than Jermaine, the kids I saw from school the previous year were not the troublemakers. I went through the rest of the day, nervous every time I had to switch classes, but I found nothing but satisfaction in each of them. It was a stress-free experience. I even spotted a few potential new friends.

Gloria and I met after school, outside by the tree that would become our meeting place for the rest of the year.

"Was your day as groovy as mine?" she said with excitement as I got close.

We grabbed hands and laughed and hopped up and down. "The grooviest!"

We calmed down just enough to head toward our apartments.

"What about Jermaine?" I asked. "Do you think he'll start any trouble?"

"Oh, I think he's harmless. Besides, he spoke to us nicely."

"He did, didn't he?"

"I can't wait to go to sleep, wake up, and do this all over again," Gloria said.

"I can't either," I agreed. "Especially for homeroom, to see . . ."

"Mr. Stephens," we said in unison. And giggled.

"He is so dreamy," I said, sighing.

"I think he's my favorite teacher," Gloria said.

"Mine too," I agreed.

We continued down the street in this manner. As usual, there were students and parents coming to pick up their kids headed in our direction. When Gloria saw this boy she liked walking with two of his friends, she grabbed my hand and gushed, "Don't look now, but there's Bobby. I have the biggest crush on him. Oh, he is so groovy."

We walked straight ahead, and she slyly pointed to the right of her, where he and his friends were walking. I tried my best not to look until I couldn't take it anymore. I looked over my shoulder and to the right and saw three boys walking and talking about boy stuff.

"Which one is Bobby?" I asked.

"He's the one wearing the ball cap."

I peeped over my right shoulder again to get a closer look.

"Oh, he is cute," I said.

"I told you. But don't look anymore because they'll know we're talking about them."

"Okay," I said.

But I had to take just one more glance at Bobby and the other boys walking with him. Apparently Gloria couldn't help herself either because we both looked at the same time.

When we realized what we had done, we fell out laughing and took off running. Instead of splitting at the corner the way we usually did, we kept walking together toward my apartment.

"I might as well walk you to your door, and then I'll rush home," Gloria said. "It'll give Bobby and his friends a chance to go by."

"That's a good idea," I said.

We giggled some more at how silly we were, trying not to be so obvious in our admiration.

"Who are his friends?" I asked as we approached the steps to my apartment.

"I don't know their names, only Bobby's," she said with a huge grin.

"You don't know their names?" I said.

"No, but I can find out. Which one do you like?" she asked me.

"Neither," I replied.

"Do you like anybody yet?" she asked.

"Mr. Stephens."

"Me too."

We both sighed and reluctantly agreed that he didn't count.

"Do you think they've walked by yet?" I asked.

"Probably."

The door to my apartment flew open, startling us. When we looked up to see what all the commotion was about, we saw my dad with Lola, bright red lipstick and all, in his arms. He was pulling her close to him and whispering in her ear.

"But, Paul, I'm not ready to go yet," she whined.

"You have to. My daughter'll be home any minute."

He kissed her, smack-dab on the lips, right in front of us. Only he didn't know we were there until I yelled, "*Daddy!* How dare you!"

He pushed that woman to the side and faced me. "Let me explain," he said.

But I didn't want an explanation. I couldn't even bear to look him in the face. I couldn't handle standing there in front of him, that woman draped all over him, so I took off running—to where, I didn't know, but I knew I had to get away from that scene, as far away and as quickly as my legs could take me.

"Lanita, wait," Gloria called, taking off after me.

But I didn't want to talk to her, either. She'd been a witness, someone who would always know my daddy was a cheater. The more I ran, the sadder I became. The tears came, so I was running and crying and trying to figure out where I was going.

Gloria caught up with me.

"Are you okay?" she asked, running alongside of me.

"What do you think?" I snapped.

"You're probably not okay," she said.

I didn't reply.

"You want to come over to my house for a while?" she asked. "I have some Tang. We can get two cups and go into my bedroom, and I won't say anything to you if you don't want me to."

At least that solved one of my dilemmas—where I was going.

"Okay," I said and slowed down. I used my shirtsleeve to wipe my tears, but they kept falling.

We walked in silence to her apartment. Both her parents were still at work, but her big brother was there. He was a junior in high school and watched her until her parents got home from work. We rushed past him as quickly as we could, hoping that he wouldn't tease us the way he always did.

"The little baby is home, and she brought her little baby friend with her," he mocked.

"Shut up, you jive turkey!" Gloria yelled as we rushed by him.

Safe in her room, I fell face-first on her bed and burst into tears again.

"I'll get us some Tang," Gloria said and rushed out of the room, closing the door behind her.

I heard her brother yelling at her in the kitchen, "I bet you're getting bottles of milk for you and your little baby friend."

"You're so pathetic," Gloria shot back.

"Spell it, you little baby," he yelled.

Gloria didn't respond.

"Didn't think so," he said.

The door opened and Gloria came back in.

"Do you want some Tang?" she asked.

"No."

She set my cup on the dresser.

"I brought you some Kleenex."

Keeping my head buried in her bed, I held my hand out to receive the tissue.

Gloria kept her word and didn't say anything else to me. She pulled out a library book and sat at the foot of her bed, reading silently until I calmed down.

After a while, I sat up and faced Gloria. "My daddy is cheating on my mother. What should I do about it?"

We were both only in the seventh grade—the first day of the seventh grade, at that. What did she know?

"I wouldn't say anything," she answered solemnly.

"I don't think I have the guts to say anything," I agreed.

"If you tell, maybe your daddy will have to leave. Do you want him to leave?"

"No, I don't. But he shouldn't be cheating on my momma. She worked a double shift, didn't even come in last night. I'm just gonna have to figure out a way to convince her to stop working so hard—or at least not to work more than one shift in a day. I have to persuade her that she needs to work during the day, no more than eight hours, like regular people."

"That's a good idea," Gloria said.

We sat in her room and talked for a while over our cups of Tang until I found the courage to go back home.

When I got home, my daddy was in the bedroom with the door

closed. I was glad because I didn't want to face him. I sat down on the couch and turned on the television. I realized I was hungry, so I went in the kitchen to see what I could find. I got some sandwich meat, bread, and chips and began to put together a meal for myself.

After I finished eating, I went to the bathroom and took a bath and found some folded-up pajamas in the laundry basket outside the bathroom. I needed to go into the bedroom to find school clothes for the next day, but I dared not knock on that door. Instead, I rummaged through the laundry basket and found an outfit. If my daddy and I were going to meet face-to-face, he was going to have to be the first to open that door.

I went back to the couch and lay down without my blankets because they were in the bedroom too. I watched television until I fell asleep.

I awoke to loud noises from the bedroom. They were arguing. My first thought was, *Did she find out?*

I heard my mother say, "If you're gonna leave, go ahead and leave, then."

I sat straight up and noticed that someone had put covers over me. I pulled them off me, and just as I was about to move off the couch and get in better listening range, the door swung open.

"I think it's the best thing for everybody," my daddy said.

"No, not everybody, only you," my mother yelled, following him.

I fell back on the couch and pretended to be asleep.

My daddy was lugging his footlocker out of the bedroom when my mother jumped on top of it. Towering over him, she yelled, "You're not going nowhere, Paul. I need you here. Your daughter needs you here."

"Don't do this, Aretha," he said, his voice low and calm. "Believe me, I've had plenty of time to think about this, and my time here is over."

She didn't budge.

"Get off my trunk, woman," he insisted.

My mother sat down on the footlocker and folded her arms. "Make me," she yelled.

I was dying to see, so I eased off the couch and crawled to the corner and peeked around to see what was happening.

"Let's not end it like this," Daddy said. "This is childish!"

"I'm not trying to end it, Paul, you are."

"Here we go again. Haven't we already been through this?"

"What if I don't want you to leave?" she said.

"Why should I stay, Aretha? You haven't been giving me what I want.

I've begged you. Hell, I've even pleaded with you to either find another job or not work nights. I thought you would try to meet me halfway and at least try to move to a day shift, but instead you start working doubles. I don't see how that's supposed to make things better."

Momma just sat there, staring past my father.

"Tell me, Aretha, is your working doubles all the time supposed to make things better for us?"

"In the long run it will," she said calmly. "But you never hear me when I tell you that working doubles will allow me to eventually move to mornings."

"Yeah, that's what you say, but when is that supposed to happen? I have tried, but I am losing patience with you, woman. When was the last time we had sex? When was the last time you screamed my name? When was the last time you had the energy to make me feel like a man?"

"Look at the big picture, Paul. I'm working for our future. If you would just grow up, you would see that."

Paul began tugging at the footlocker again.

Aretha stood on it again. "You are so impatient!" she said. "Why can't you wait this out?"

He let go of the handle and stood in front of Aretha, squeezing her arms, pulling her close to him. "It's over," he said, gripping her shoulders tighter and lifting her off his trunk. He placed her down beside it and then reached for his footlocker.

In what seemed like one last desperate attempt to get his attention, she said, "What about your daughter? So you're just gonna walk out on Lanita? Who's gonna be here when she comes home from school?"

I was wondering the same thing.

Paul let go of the footlocker, dropped his head, and plopped down on the trunk. "You know how I am, Aretha. I need to be stimulated. I need excitement. As much as I want to be, I'm just not happy here. If we go on like this, you will hate me, and I love you too much to have you hate me."

He grabbed her hand and stared into her eyes. "Lanita will be just fine. She'll be better off without me being here. You know that."

She pulled away from him, drew her hand back, and slapped him with all her might. "Fuck you, you jive turkey." Aretha strode to the front door and opened it wide. "Now, get the hell outta my house!" she yelled.

Instead of waiting for him to leave, she took her time, eyeballing him the whole time, and walked back into her room, slamming the door behind her.

My daddy sat there for what seemed like forever. So did I. I couldn't move. I was frozen behind the couch. All I could do was stare at him. I was so in love with that man. Having him in my life had given me security. Everything in the world was all right with him around, and now he was leaving. How was I supposed to continue? I couldn't reverse time, and as much as I wanted, I couldn't fix my parents. It all seemed so absurd. My parents were not going to be together because my mother had a job. Adults didn't always make a lot of sense to me back then, especially Paul. When he finally moved off that footlocker, he would be walking out of our lives forever. And that's exactly why I sat there staring. I just wanted to absorb him, take in his presence.

Paul Lightfoot was truly a knight in shining armor. He sat there in his powder-blue slacks, powder-blue and brown shirt, and brown dress shoes. His lean body was bent over as if he were in physical pain, while his head rested in his hands. I wanted so badly to inch closer and wrap my arms around him, but I was too frightened to move. There was something about the way his long legs were bent, his knees higher than his waist, that seemed so masculine.

He stood and rubbed his eyes. I think he had shed tears, but I wasn't sure. Then he did something I would have never expected. I followed him with my head as he walked over toward the couch and leaned over it to check on me. I squeezed my eyes shut, hoping to disappear so that when he noticed I wasn't where I was supposed to be, he wouldn't be able to find me. He wouldn't be able to say good-bye. Seconds later, I felt his hand patting my shoulder.

I slowly opened my eyes. He was squatting down, right in front of me.

"How much of that did you hear?" he asked.

"All of it," I whispered.

"I'm sorry about that, Lanita, but that's just the way it has to be."

"But I don't want you to go, Daddy."

He reached his long arms around my small body and embraced me warmly, tightly. He had never hugged me like that before, and I'll never forget the way it felt. I was so overwhelmed with what was going on that I fell limp. He picked me up and laid me down on the couch. Tears were streaming from my eyes and his too.

"It's not that I don't love you or your mother, Lanita." He knelt down next to the couch. "You might not understand this now, but listen to me when I tell you, when you meet a nice young man—and you will—and you fall in love, make sure that his heart belongs to you, because if he ever expects you to share him with other women, he's not worthy to be in your life." He squeezed my hand. "Do you understand me?"

I nodded in agreement.

"Your momma is a good woman. The best! I'm just no good for her. She deserves better than me."

My daddy kissed me on the cheek. Then he took off his silver chain that had the silver-dollar pendant hanging from it and fastened it around my neck. He walked around the couch, picked up his footlocker, and was gone out of our lives forever.

I cried all night until my mind became feeble and I could only sleep.

I had to stay at home for a few weeks by myself because Momma still had to work. Then Gloria told her mother about my situation and asked if I could start coming home with her after school. Her mother talked to Aretha, and I was set to finish the rest of the school year going over to Gloria's every day after school.

Even though I missed my dad tremendously, I enjoyed going over to Gloria's every day. We drank Tang. And even though her brother was usually a pain, he sometimes popped us popcorn over the stove, and we would sit down in front of the television every day and watch the *ABC Afterschool Special* or *The Wonderful World of Disney*. From the first day I began to go over to Gloria's, I ate dinner there five times a week and slept at the foot of her bed every night until my mother would pick me up at 1:00 A.M. and we would walk over to our apartment. I would immediately fall back asleep the moment I hit the sofa.

I didn't mind my mother's working so hard. For a while I didn't even see her as my mother. Back then, I didn't understand what kind of sacrifices she was making to take care of me. She didn't depend on the government for a check anymore. As heartbroken as she was when my daddy left, she kept trudging forward. Unfortunately, I blamed her for my daddy's leaving. Now I wish I had been more supportive of her. Instead, I began addressing her by her first name.

Daddy was no longer a part of our lives, so I no longer looked on us as a family. I viewed Aretha as only my caretaker, someone who worked hard so that we would have a better life, but somehow things never seemed to get better. And then there was me, left alone.

But when I was with Gloria and her family, I saw them as my very own. When her parents returned home from work in the evenings, we would all sit down at the table for dinner, and they would always ask us how our day went. I enjoyed sharing that dialogue with them. As far as I was concerned, my mother could continue to work ten-hour shifts, so long as I would be able to experience being part of a family, spending time with people I pretended belonged to me. I pretended that Gloria was my sister and her brother was mine as well. I pretended that my parents didn't exist, and that Mr. and Mrs. Mack were mine. When it was time for bed, I pretended that the bed that Gloria shared with me was ours.

In the whole time that I spent over at their house, Gloria and I never argued, not even once. Sometimes I could tell that she felt she had to protect me. Whenever I was down, she did whatever it took to help to lift my spirits.

It was as if God knew I loved Gloria and her family more than I loved my own. Evidently, He wasn't pleased with that because just as I had settled into my life with Gloria's family, he took them away from me.

It was two days before Thanksgiving. I sat down in homeroom, a little anxious because I had to give an oral presentation in first period that day on what Thanksgiving meant to me. I had worked on my presentation in private because most of what I was presenting was a lie. I couldn't say I was thankful about my home life, because I wasn't. I couldn't admit that I cared more about Gloria's family than my own. There was essentially nothing to be thankful about, so I fabricated a presentation. My words would be nice and pleasant, wrapped up in a bright bow of lies.

As I read over what I had prepared, Gloria walked in and sat down in the desk beside me. Her face was long, and we didn't do our usual "I can't wait until Mr. Stephens walks in. I wonder if he'll be wearing the dark blue, light blue, black, red, or multicolored tie." He switched up every day, but wore the same five ties every week. Gloria and I had made a game of guessing which it would be.

I had a lot on my mind with the presentation, so I didn't push the issue at first, but I knew something wasn't right. I could feel it in my stomach. I felt like throwing up, and the longer the silence between Gloria and me, the stronger the urge became. But never in my thirteen years did I think she was holding in the words that would seem to be a death sentence to me.

"I am so nervous about my presentation this morning," I said as I looked over at my best friend, who stared intensely at the empty chalkboard as if the most important assignment of the year had been listed there.

She didn't respond.

"Are you okay?" I asked.

"No," she replied and continued looking forward. "I'm not."

I had never seen her so solemn. My only thought was to change the subject to get her mind off whatever was bothering her—and mine off my presentation.

"So which tie do you think he's going to wear?" I halfheartedly asked her.

"I'm telling Mr. Stephens that both of you have a crush on him," said Jermaine, who sat behind me.

"We do not," I replied. Jermaine often threatened to tell Mr. Stephens about our interest in him.

"Do so," he shot back.

"I'm not paying you any attention," I said. Then I turned my direction back to Gloria. "Which tie?"

She didn't respond. Jermaine lost interest in us.

"I think he's probably going to wear the multicolored one," I added. "What do you think, Gloria?"

Gloria took a deep breath and bit her bottom lip. "Lanita, you're not gonna be able to come over to my house anymore," she said.

"Why not?" I asked, panicking. "Did I do something wrong?"

"No. You didn't do anything wrong."

"So why can't I come over anymore?"

"My daddy got a good job in Oakland, and we're moving up there. We'll be moving into a house and everything, but I don't care about no house because after Thanksgiving, we'll be gone from Watts for good. And I won't ever see you again."

She put her head down as a tear fell from her eyes.

I wanted to believe she was joking, but tears don't lie.

"Today is my last day of school. My brother didn't even go to school today. He's staying home to help them pack. They asked me if I wanted to skip school to help out, but I just had to come here to let you know."

I gasped for air. I felt like I was suffocating.

"My mother assured me that she had told your mother last night when she came to pick you up, but I wanted to make sure you were all right."

"She told Aretha!" I said in disbelief.

"Don't you mean Momma?"

"No, I mean Aretha."

"That's not nice, Lanita," Gloria fussed. "Anyway, that's what she said."

"Aretha didn't tell me anything. I wonder why she didn't say anything to me about it?" I was furious with my mother for keeping this from me.

Just then, Mr. Stephens walked into the classroom, looking as handsome as ever. He had on black slacks and a crisp white long-sleeved shirt. Just as I had predicted, he was wearing his multicolored tie. However, I couldn't celebrate. I just didn't see much reason in gloating to Gloria. What was the use? My family was leaving me, and there was nothing I could do except mourn.

Nine

Jimmy rinsed Lanita's hair. A brownish-yellow color flowed over his gloved hands as he sprayed her hair with one hand and smoothed it with the other. He shook his head. "Now, that's a sad story if I've ever heard one."

Natasha rushed around the corner to the washbowl station. "What did I miss?" she asked.

"Too much to go back and catch you up now," Jimmy said. "But let me tell you this, her dad left."

"No!" she said. "I really liked him."

Jimmy began filling her in as if Lanita were not even there, as if he were updating Natasha on a movie that she had missed parts of.

Pamela laid her client back, draping her hair into the bowl.

Although Lanita was amused by their interest in her story, she could still feel the sting she'd felt when her daddy and her surrogate family had left. Just talking about those incidents caused a rush of memories to flood her mind, things that were yet to happen to her younger self. If Jimmy Choo thought that the first part of her childhood was sad, he would be appalled by what else she could tell him.

Lanita wondered if she had already shared too much, but then decided it didn't really matter as long as her audience was interested. Talking about the peaks and valleys of life with strangers had always been therapeutic for her. Her philosophy was that if you shared your intimate thoughts with people close to you, they might hold those thoughts against you someday, but if you shared those same thoughts with strangers, they will certainly forget all about you as soon as you walk out of their lives. Meanwhile, speaking of these memories gave her a chance to examine the life she'd lived and think about the choices she'd made.

Natasha was so involved in listening to Jimmy's update that she ignored the phone ringing on her hip.

Jimmy stopped and motioned to the phone. "Um, Natasha, you might want to answer that. After all, this is a business we're trying to run here."

"I know," she replied and pushed the button on her hip to answer the phone. "Thanks for calling Opulence Beauty Salon and Spa. May I help you?" She walked toward the front of the salon.

Pamela stopped spraying her client's hair and slowly primped her own blond locks, pushing them behind her ear.

Jimmy shook his head. "You've catapulted into super diva status since you dyed your hair."

She smirked. "They say that blondes have more fun. I wanted to find out for myself."

"So do they?" Jimmy asked.

"Blondes turn heads, but black women with blond hair mesmerize. Isn't that right?" She tapped her client on the shoulder. They slapped a high five.

"Pamela, you are too much," Jimmy said.

"Don't hate on my blond ambition," she said confidently. "Lanita, you should try going blond."

"I don't know about that," Lanita replied.

"Go easy on her, it's her first time here. We wouldn't want to scare her away," Jimmy joked. "I understand the blond way works for you, but please don't keep pushing all our clients in that direction."

"Jimmy, I'm not studying you," she said rolling her eyes. Then she went back to shampooing her client's hair.

As Jimmy worked on Lanita's hair, the salon had gradually become extremely busy and buzzing with customers. Several hairdressers were servicing their clients with cuts, relaxers, color treatments, locks, braids, or shampoos. All the hairdressers expressed their own style, but were clean-cut and wore black slacks and black smocks that read OPULENCE across the front. To Lanita, the customers all seemed very cosmopolitan and worldly, a far cry from the people in the neighborhood in which she had grown up. She felt accomplished, somehow further along socially, just by being in Jimmy's chair. The light-hearted social interaction among the stylists was an added bonus.

Natasha walked back around the corner. "So who took care of you after school once your father and the Macks left?" she asked.

"My mother."

"I know that. I mean, when she was at work."

"She quit her job to take care of me."

"That seems a bit drastic," Jimmy said, taken aback.

"You're right. It was drastic," said Lanita. "There was more to it, though. She had been working doubles as often as she could, right through Christmas and the New Year. After she put her all into that job for seven or eight months, she finally got the courage to ask her boss for daytime hours only, and her boss flat-out said no! So she quit right then and there."

"Follow me to my chair." Jimmy patted Lanita and motioned for her to follow.

Lanita got comfortable in the chair at Jimmy's station.

"I'm gonna trim you up nicely and make you gorgeous," he promised.

She smiled, but her mind raced back to how defeated Aretha had felt when she was unemployed, especially because she had chosen employment over Paul.

"At first, Aretha thought that with a little effort, she would have no problem getting another job. But it wasn't that easy. She applied everywhere, and her search became long and drawn out."

Jimmy spun the chair around, turning Lanita away from the mirror.

Lanita continued.

.   .   .

While she was looking for a job, we got back on government assistance, but Aretha was catching the blues. Nothing was materializing. Her drive slowly diminished. The longer she went without a job, the more doubtful she became of her own abilities, and the less she tried, the more she accepted that maybe she wasn't meant to work. She hunted for a job as a licensed practical nurse straight through my seventh grade year, but it seemed that every other mother trying to work her way out of the system had those jobs locked down, and none of them were quitting or getting fired. Although Aretha never shared her feelings with me, she was obviously experiencing bouts of depression and regret.

The summer came and went, and nothing memorable happened. She eventually got used to me calling her Aretha because I wouldn't stop, even when she threatened a spanking. I realized that Aretha had become too tired to use harsh discipline. I think she and I slept through most of that summer. We watched a lot of television, spending most of the day together. The only activity of mine Aretha didn't participate in was when I wrote letters to Gloria. But when Gloria's letters came, I'd read them to Aretha, and she'd sit back and listen while puffing on a cigarette. I wasn't looking forward to eighth grade without Gloria.

Although we were back on welfare, Aretha and I had become friends again. However, our relationship wasn't quite healthy. I didn't encourage Aretha to stick with the job hunt, because if she had been hired to work nights again, it would have destroyed me. On her part, she didn't encourage me to go out and make friends, probably because she was afraid of being in that apartment by herself, alone with her thoughts. So we sat around and gained about ten pounds each that summer.

We were happy in our own closed-off, dysfunctional existence until her ex-boyfriend Lester came back into the picture. He dropped by the apartment every few days or so, bearing gifts, probably because he knew he was wrong for the way he'd left her before. He would stop by with a pack of cigarettes and a bottle of Manischewitz. I don't believe Aretha was interested at first because she would meet him at the door, snatch the cigarettes out of his hand, and slam the door on him and his bottle of wine. She'd yell, "I don't drink no more, you jive turkey!"

She'd come back and sit down with me in front of the television and throw the cigarettes on the coffee table and say, "Now, that's one less pack of cigarettes that I have to buy."

We'd go back to watching TV.

Then one day when Lester came knocking on the door, Aretha let him in. I don't know what was going through her mind on that day, but I should have guessed that it would eventually have happened, because each time he appeared, she lingered at the door a little longer than before. He made her laugh. During all the times they stood at that door, she had never laughed before. Once she felt the emotion that went with the laughter, he had her.

Maybe Aretha was fed up with spending so much time with me. Maybe it was because she knew that summer was coming to a close and I would be going back to school, so she needed someone to fill the void. Or maybe she was just horny or vulnerable and needed the touch of a man. I don't know exactly, but she and Lester took the radio, which had always remained in the kitchen, into the bedroom and closed the door behind them.

Nobody said anything to me. He didn't say hi. And she didn't say, "Excuse us." I no longer existed. I no longer mattered.

After that night, Lester became a regular fixture in our house once more, and Aretha began to indulge in firewater again.

I didn't know what to do with myself, but I couldn't stand to be in the same room as Lester. Aretha would wake up and make breakfast for the three of us, like we were some big happy family—a family I wanted no part of. For the rest of that summer, I woke up as early as I could, quickly fixing myself a meal and rushing out of the house. I'd spend my days at the library, writing to Gloria and soaking up the fascinating worlds I found in literature.

With the assistance of my favorite librarian, Miss Rita Page, who was always so nice and helpful, I learned about and fell in love with literature by Black writers. I read the works of Zora Neale Hurston and Langston Hughes, absorbed the poetry of Nikki Giovanni and Sonia Sanchez. I even read works by W. E. B. DuBois and Frederick Douglass, finding solace in their struggles. I found comfort in knowing that I wasn't the only one who had seen hard times.

If only I could've moved into that library, everything would have been all right. Coming home at night was the pits. I'd have to turn up the television my daddy had brought us to drown out the sound of my mother giving herself to Lester. I'd try to get all absorbed in the evening's programming, but sometimes the thought of my mother being in that room with that man doing God knows what would be louder than the volume on the television could go.

I thought about running away to Oakland and just showing up at the Macks' front door. Gloria wrote to me in her letters that she and her family had moved into a beautiful and spacious home, unlike their apartment in Watts. Before I went to sleep at night, I would imagine Gloria's surprise when she saw me standing there when she opened the door. Then her parents would show me to my very own room and say something like, "We kept this room available for you, just in case. Welcome home." They'd embrace me, and we'd all sit down to a lovely dinner. When it was time to sleep, they would tuck me in, and I'd have the most comfortable sleep that I'd ever had in my whole life.

I plotted for days about how to run away. I would use the money that Robert Beck had given me, which I'd stashed over the refrigerator, along with money that I had added to it over the year, and get a one-way bus ticket to Oakland. I even went as far as calling the bus station to price a ticket.

I couldn't stand to see my mother return to her former self, and I couldn't live another week in that little apartment with Lester. It wasn't that he was mean and cruel—he wasn't. However, he wasn't Paul Lightfoot. What got underneath my skin about Lester was his sleazy niceness, the way he walked through the door with a bottle of liquor, bringing my mother back down to his level. I hated that he tried to bribe me into liking him by giving me fifty cents here and a quarter there. I simply pocketed the money and added it to my getaway stash.

I had it all planned: a bus seat reserved for 6:00 P.M. on the Friday before school would begin. I wanted to give the Macks the opportunity to digest the shock of my being there. I stashed a big trash bag in the corner of the closet in the bedroom, filled with my good clothes and shoes, a toothbrush, and other necessities I thought I would need for the trip. I took out the taped-up jar and retrieved the money I had stashed—eighty dollars and some change.

Aretha had not talked about school shopping because she didn't have any money to take me. I didn't push the issue because I didn't need to—I wouldn't be there. The Macks would take care of me once I got to Oakland. Plus, I would still have plenty of money, even after I bought my ticket, so I could help buy the things I needed once I got to Oakland. I had even written a letter to Gloria, in which I'd told her, "Be on the lookout. I have a big surprise for you!"

When the big day arrived, I was sweating bullets. My heart raced all morning and I was a bit scatterbrained. I went about my day as usual, trying not to call any attention to myself. The previous night, I had put

my packed garbage bag under the stairs to the apartment. That morning
I raced to the library, but I didn't read a single page of *The Bluest Eye* by
Toni Morrison, the newest book Miss Page had given me. She had it at
the counter waiting for me when I walked in.

"You're gonna love this book," she said. "I'm adding it to my personal favorites list." She proudly placed the book in my hand. "Your favorite corner is waiting for you. Go and enjoy."

"Thank you, Miss Page," I said and trotted off, hoping that it wasn't
obvious that I was planning to run away that evening.

I was restless. I looked forward to devouring that book, but I couldn't
concentrate. I thought about how exciting yet scary my evening would
be. I got out an atlas and attempted to chart the route we would take up
the coast. I assumed we would take the Pacific Coast Highway all the way
up. I imagined the beautiful ocean views that I'd get along the way. Even
though I lived in California, it would be a treat to see the ocean. I sometimes forgot just how close it is.

I found a book about the Bay Area and read up on the culture, about
Jack London Square and the Oakland Bay Bridge. Before I knew it,
the library was closing for the day, so I walked to the counter to return
The Bluest Eye.

"Thanks for suggesting this. I finished it already," I said. I placed the
book on the counter and headed for the door.

"So what do you think about Pecola?" Miss Page asked me.

"Pecola?" I asked.

"The main character in the book. Don't you just love her?"

"Ah, well . . ." I hadn't read a word. So I lied. "Yeah, she's great. I'm
just surprised that Miss Morrison would write about a White girl as her
main character."

"Huh?" Miss Page seemed stunned. "Pecola's not White. You haven't
read the book yet, have you?"

"Uh, no, ma'am, I haven't. I . . ."

"You seemed a little flustered when you walked in this morning. Is
everything okay?" she asked.

"Yeah, everything's fine," I said.

"You don't want to check it out and read it? I promise you'll be glad
you did." She eyed me as if I had committed a crime. "Wait a minute. It's
a Friday and you usually get two to three books for the weekends."

"I've got a busy weekend ahead of me, plus school starts on Monday, and I won't have much time for reading," I replied, tugging away at my ear.

The real reason I didn't want to check out any books is because I wouldn't be returning whatever I walked out with that evening, and I didn't want to steal any books from the library.

"Nonsense. You're gonna wish you had this book. Go ahead and take it," Miss Page insisted. She stuck my return card in the sleeve that was glued to the back page of the book and walked around the counter to where I was standing, holding the book out for me to take.

I knew that when I received that book, I became an instant criminal, so I said a small prayer and asked the good Lord to forgive me. I knew then that it would be my last time seeing Miss Page. Instead of taking the book, I threw my arms around her waist and gave her a big hug.

"Thank you," I said.

"It's just a book," she replied and shoved it in my hand. "You be good."

I rushed out the door without responding. My plan for that evening couldn't be considered "being good," and I felt nothing but guilt.

On the way home, I debated whether to just grab the bag underneath the steps and head for the bus station or to go inside and get one last look at my mother before I left. I was unsure about what would be best until I got to our doorstep. I knew I had to see her. She was my mother, and as flawed as she was, I loved her and would miss her. So I had to say good-bye. I owed her that much.

I checked to see that my bag was still there. It was. I walked into the apartment and saw Aretha had a huge smile on her face. She rushed from the kitchen table and met me near the couch.

"Lanita, I understand that you love to read, but you've been spending too much time at that library. It ain't natural. I started to go over there and get you because we need to talk."

I gulped. She had found out about my plans and would be stopping me. I should have left when I had the chance.

"Okay, Aretha, but I need to rush back to help Miss Page shelve some books. The library is extra messy, and she wants to work overtime to get it back together."

"You're not going back out to the library this late."

"She's gonna pay me, Aretha."

"We'll have to discuss that later, but right now I got some news that I want to share with you. Let's go sit down at the kitchen table."

I followed her and took a seat.

"Lanita, you're not gonna believe this. Sit down. What I'm about to tell you is gonna blow your mind."

"I am sitting down," I replied unenthusiastically.

"Lanita, me and you, we're moving."

"Where are we going?" I perked up. My first thought was that Aretha had found out I was moving to Oakland and decided that she was going to run away with me.

"We're going to be moving into a two-bedroom apartment. We finally made it to the top of the waiting list, and now you're finally gonna have your own bedroom. Can you believe it?"

Aretha was so happy.

"We got to figure out how to get you a bed, but I guess you can sleep on the floor until we can afford one. I'll finally have my own closet and so will you. You'll be able to get to your things quicker and without the hassle of rummaging through boxes."

I sat there, dumbfounded. I had wanted my own room again since we had moved from our old apartment. Part of the reason I was planning to run away to Oakland was to get one. And Aretha looked so happy. How was I gonna let her down, especially when she was trying so hard? Even though I couldn't stand to have Lester around, I would have my own space in our apartment, a haven where I could retreat when things got bad. I could decorate my own room the way I wanted. I would be able to close the door to my room and escape, the way I did when I went to the library. I made up my mind right then and there that I was staying. I was gonna give Aretha another chance. Oakland would have to wait.

"So when do we move?" I asked.

"We move in the first day of September, before your fourteenth birthday. I know I've never given you a party, Lanita, and unfortunately I can't give you one this year, but maybe us getting a new place and you getting your own room will be gift enough."

"It is, Momma. This is the best news ever," I said.

I hadn't realized what I had done until Aretha raised her eyebrows and flashed me a wide smile. She didn't comment on me calling her Momma, but I could tell that she liked it. I had become fond of calling her Aretha, but when I saw how much it meant to her that I called her Momma, I began going back and forth between the two names.

She put my hand in hers and rubbed it against her cheek. "We gonna be just fine, Lanita. I promise."

I wrapped my heart around her words and squeezed her hand. I wanted so badly to believe what she had said to me. Her optimism and the idea of a new bedroom were what I needed to sustain me during a time when there wasn't much in my life that made sense.

Ten

The eighties came in with a bang, bringing the good with the bad. Richard Pryor was badly burned trying to freebase cocaine, John Lennon was assassinated by Mark David Chapman, Ronald Reagan defeated Jimmy Carter to become the president of the United States, and in the midst of all that, everybody was asking, "Who shot J.R.?"

The year 1979 and the eighth grade had been a blur, flying by before I knew they had passed. Then it was 1980, and I was about to turn fifteen, in my own corner of the world, trying to figure out how I was going to make it through the ninth grade without a best friend by my side. Although she had been gone for almost two years, Gloria and I had continued to stay in touch through letters, but she wasn't physically there. Eighth grade had been bearable, but I really needed her now that I was going to be in high school, where I would have to incorporate into a school with already established upperclassmen. I needed her for my own confidence. I wrote her, telling her about my anxieties, saying that I was excited about finally being in high school, and I wanted to make my mark and stand out somehow, but I wasn't sure how to go about doing so.

Gloria gave me some advice that I was sure would help shape my high school life. She suggested that I go out for a sport or join an organization immediately. That way I would be able to meet potential friends with interests similar to mine, and I wouldn't be stuck in the library every day, reading. I loved to read, but she was right. I was more than ready to expand my extracurricular activities beyond the stacks.

During the first two weeks at Jordan High School, I began speaking to my teachers, talking to students I had known from the eighth grade, and looking at flyers hanging around the school, trying to find out what extracurricular activities I might like. Jordan was a predominantly Black high school with a few Hispanics. As with most schools, the students were either extremely active or totally uninterested in sports, extracurriculars, or school in general. Those who cared about being well-rounded were fierce and serious about their participation, and Jordan was known for producing elite athletes and garnering support from the teachers, students, and parents for all their afterschool programs.

After some serious consideration, I narrowed my options down to the fun stuff. I would try out for cheerleading, the dance team, and choir. I was confident that with effort and luck, of which I believed I had plenty, I was bound to be chosen for a spot in at least one—if not all—of my endeavors.

Cheerleading tryouts were at the end of the first week of school. A workshop was held on Friday, in which the older cheerleaders demonstrated cheers, jumps, stunts, and gymnastics. The actual tryout was the next day, Saturday.

That Friday after school, I walked into the gym and was faced with a room filled with girls just as excited and anxious about what the next two days would bring as I was. The captain of the cheerleading team, a senior, stood in front of us, seeming confident and upbeat. I admired her instantly. She wore a huge smile and perfectly fitted athletic shorts and a matching T-shirt with the word CAPTAIN printed on the front.

"Hello, ladies, my name is Heather McKnight, and I was chosen captain of the cheerleading team at the end of the last school year. There were nine other members of the cheerleading team last year, and five graduated, so there are five spots available in the varsity squad. The top five girls will make varsity, and the eight below will become our junior varsity squad."

There were at least fifty girls in the gym. I hadn't realized just how tight the competition was going to be until that moment. I figured I would be as good as anybody else, but I knew then that I had to get my act together and really pay attention if I wanted to have a fighting chance.

Heather continued, "There will be five judges tomorrow, and you will have the opportunity to display for them everything you will be taught here today. You will be judged on skill, grace, poise, projection, appearance, and overall talent. So remain focused today and pay close attention to what you learn. Go home and practice, and come back tomorrow morning ready to audition."

The other four cheerleaders stood beside Heather and helped lead us through the initial stretches, which I enjoyed because I knew I was good at it. I was pretty flexible. Next, the cheerleaders told us to remain seated on the floor while they demonstrated the things we'd need to know.

Heather moved to the side of them. "Tomorrow you will have five options for jumps you can do for your audition: the toe-touch, hurkie, spread-eagle, pike, and double-nine." As she said each jump by name, the four other cheerleaders demonstrated them. "You are obligated to perform the toe-touch, the hurkie, and the spread-eagle. The pike and double-nine are advanced jumps and are optional, but if properly executed, they will help to increase your score."

I had never before paid attention to the talent it took to do jumps. Come to think about it, I had never really paid attention to cheerleading at all. I wasn't sure how fast I would be able to catch on.

"Okay, now we're going to show you two cheers," Heather announced. "You can choose either one for your audition."

The five cheerleaders got into a formation and began. Heather yelled, "Ready, okay."

Then, in unison, they cheered: "Two bits, four bits, six bits, a dollar, all for Jordan, stand up and holler! 'Cause our team is hot and we can't be stopped!" They did uniform arm motions and perfect toe-touches coordinated to the words. Their movements seemed complex but doable. I was sure I would be able to catch on with ease.

They changed their formation and began the next cheer, incorporating the spread-eagle jump. "Beat those Bears! We will beat those Bears! B-E-A-T, beat those Bears! Beat those Bears!" That cheer seemed easier to perform than the first, so I knew it was the one I would learn.

"If you have any gymnastics ability," Heather said, "you can increase your score. We require that you do the splits, a cartwheel, and a round-off." A cheerleader performed each move. "But you can earn more points by performing anything more advanced, like the back handspring, the tuck, or any gymnastics series." She moved to the middle of the floor. "I'll demonstrate," she said with confidence. She whipped her body backward, her hands hitting the ground, and before I knew it, her body flipped over and her feet were back on the ground again.

"That is a back handspring," she announced.

Then she jumped backward in the air, tucked her knees to her chest, flipped over, and landed on her feet. Her hands never touched the ground.

"That is a back tuck."

Heather walked to one end of the gym, all of us glued to her every move. She took off running, did a round-off, moved into several back handsprings, and ended with a tuck. All the girls stood and applauded. I had never seen anything like it, except on TV, during gymnastics competitions. I couldn't believe that someone in my school was so dynamic. I knew I would never be as great as Heather, but I was confident that none of the other girls sitting around me would be either.

Following the demonstration, we were split up into four groups of twelve to thirteen girls. Each group rotated between each of the four cheerleaders, spending hours learning the cheers, jumps, and a bit of gymnastics. I had no experience in gymnastics, ballet, or any other kind of dance. I had a natural athletic build and could move, but I lacked grace. I gave it my all, nevertheless.

In my group, one girl, a sophomore, stood out as exceptional. Another girl was also good, but the rest of us were mediocre to horrible. I fell somewhere in the middle. I did have a good sense of humor about the whole thing, and the other girls in my group, most of whom were freshmen, were apparently as nervous as I was and seemed to appreciate my attitude because several of them asked my name. A few commented that they had a class with me. I was proud to be noticed, so I pushed myself as hard as I could to do the best that I could.

That evening I practiced with some of the girls in my group. We all decided to do the "Beat Those Bears" cheer. We chanted and chanted and practiced our moves. I was confident that I was as good as the girls I had been practicing with; however, I wanted to somehow stand out from the rest of them, do something flashy that would impress the judges.

"I think I can get my back handspring by tomorrow," I said.

"You must be crazy," Lisa, one of the girls, said. "It sometimes takes years of lessons before a gymnast gets a back handspring—and they usually start learning when they are five years old or something like that!"

"Yeah, but I think that I can do it," I protested. "I got a good feeling about it."

Apparently I was convincing because Stacia, another of the girls, said, "I've had some lessons and know how to spot. I can spot your back handspring if you want me to."

"I don't need a spot," I announced. "I watched Heather flaunting her back handspring all during practice today. I watched her closely every time. I think I've got it."

"You're gonna just do it on the ground like this?" Stacia said, gesturing at the hard-packed dirt and grass on which we were practicing.

"No, I'm gonna put a blanket down," I said, running around the corner to our apartment, grabbing the blanket I slept under every night, and then rushing back outside. I spread the blanket on the ground. Stacia shook her head in disbelief. Lisa watched intently.

I stood at the edge of the blanket, took a deep breath, took another deep breath, closed my eyes, and just went for it. I prepped my body and then jumped backward with all my might, praying all the while that my hands would hit the ground. They did; however, when my hands made contact with the blanket, the pressure and momentum caused the blanket to slide and my hands and arms went with it. There was no foundation to hold my body up, so I came tumbling down flat against the earth—face, chest, thigh, knee, feet!

I just lay there, my face covered with grass. I couldn't move because my whole body was in agony, but Lisa and Stacia were standing over me, staring.

"Are you okay?" Lisa asked.

"I'm fine," I said in the most upbeat voice I could muster. "I'm not hurt." I pushed my body off the ground and began brushing the grass stains off me.

"It looked like you would have made it over if the blanket hadn't slid," Stacia said. "Do you want to try it again with me spotting you? I think maybe you can do it!"

My body was in so much pain that I wasn't even sure how I was going to walk back to the apartment. "Nah, that's okay," I said. "I don't need no back handspring to make the team. I know that if I really wanted to, I could do it."

"Okay!" Stacia said.

"Wow, I can't believe you did that. Are you sure you're okay?" Lisa asked.

"Yeah, I'm all right, but I think I'd better turn in and get some rest for tomorrow." I kept a good game face on so these girls wouldn't know how awful I really felt.

"Me too," Lisa said.

"Me too," Stacia agreed. "I'll see y'all in the morning."

She must have known that I was really hurting, maybe by how carefully and slowly I moved my legs and arms and neck, because Stacia reached down and grabbed the blanket and shook it. Then she folded it back up and handed it to me. "You get some rest—we have a long day ahead of us," she said.

"Good night." I waved. I didn't move. I watched Stacia and the other girls walk away. Lisa stayed behind for another minute.

"You sure you're okay?" she asked.

"Girl, I'm okay," I said, sighing. "Go on. I'm just gonna stretch a little before I go in."

Lisa walked away. When she was out of sight, I slowly dragged my aching body inside, moaning and groaning all the while. When I got inside the apartment, Aretha took one look at me and shook her head. "They done wore you out today, huh?"

"You don't know the half of it." I sat on the couch with no plans of moving, period.

Aretha smiled and walked past me, into my bedroom. I didn't know what she was doing, and I was too tired to care. Then I heard water flowing into the tub. She came back to the couch, helped me off the sofa, and led me to the bathroom, where she had prepared me a hot bath and had soft music playing on the radio.

"Thank you, Momma," I said.

"You're welcome, Lanita. The only thing I seen you put more time and effort into is reading. Cheerleading must be important to you. I just want you to be as rested as you can be for tomorrow."

She walked past me to the door. "Soak until your muscles are good and relaxed, and then lotion up good—it will help you to release the tension."

Aretha walked out, closing the door behind her. She seemed more calm in our new apartment, more confident, more at peace. I had felt peaceful too, at least during the week. Lester came creeping in first thing Friday afternoon. He and Aretha drank all weekend, but Momma usually kicked him out by the end of the day Sunday so she could rest up for work. She had gotten a new job as an LPN at the county hospital just before I'd finished the eighth grade and was back to being focused on her work. Now she had a good schedule, working from 6:00 A.M. until 4:00 P.M. I often wondered if things would have worked out better for us if she'd had that job when Daddy was here.

That night I went to bed without eating. I was too anxious and too tired. After what felt like hours, I got out of the bathtub, dried myself off, and went to my bedroom. I had been in that bedroom for over a year, and I still adored it. I had taken the money I was going to use to run away to Oakland and, with Aretha's help, purchased a used full-size bed and dresser set, as well as a bed-in-a-bag outfit that stayed on layaway at Kmart for over a month. I put up posters from my *Right On* magazines and filled my walls with pictures of Michael Jackson, DeBarge, Kool and the Gang, Prince, Lionel Richie, Marvin Gaye, and Diana Ross.

I plugged in my radio and got into bed, going over the cheer lyrics and routines in my head. As I was falling asleep, I got a glimpse of myself doing a back handspring as good as Heather's. I kept imagining my body flipping over and landing perfectly. Then I thought about my fall earlier that day and what had gone wrong. I convinced myself that I could have made it over if the blanket hadn't slid. Even Stacia said so. I imagined how it would feel when first my hands and then my feet hit the ground. There would be no way I wouldn't make the team if I landed that back handspring. I fell asleep with the image of my perfect back handspring drifting through my mind.

Aretha woke me up at nine-thirty with a breakfast of eggs, bacon, and toast waiting for me in the kitchen. My body was extremely sore, but I felt revved up by adrenaline and anticipation. I gobbled down the food because I was starving. Then I took my time getting dressed, putting on red shorts and a red-and-white-striped T-shirt, tube socks with a red stripe that circled my calf, and my new white Keds tennis shoes. I put my hair in a ponytail at the top of my head and brushed my baby hair out. I looked pretty good—at least *I* thought I did.

Aretha wanted to come with me, but I wouldn't let her. I was going to be nervous enough without my momma watching me. Besides, none of the other girls would have their mothers there with them. I wanted to stand out, but not like that!

When I got to the gym, the adrenaline was pumping hard. I really wanted to make the team and knew what I had to do to make it. I was given the number seventeen, my favorite number, my lucky number. That was a good sign.

Heather and the rest of the cheerleaders led us in stretches. She had on the same socks as I did, which I took as another good sign. Then we went over all the jumps as a group. I was especially fond of the hurkie, which I felt I did well. My toe-touch was decent, but I knew it would get better with time.

Then those who were going to audition with the "Two Bits" cheer stood and went through the routine with one of the cheerleaders. Next, those who were doing the "Beat Those Bears" cheer went over their routine with another cheerleader. I was confident that even though I was not necessarily better than the rest of the girls, I was as good as anybody else trying out.

Finally the cheerleaders had all of us take a seat on the gym floor and brought in the judges: Miss Carla Slaughter, the cheerleading adviser; Coach Janet Victor, the head coach for the girls' basketball team; Coach Lyle Dunbar, the head coach for boy's basketball; Miss Monique Butler, the adviser to the dance team; and Heather, the cheer captain. After the introductions, we were all ushered outside the gymnasium to be called in one by one to audition.

All the candidates were up and buzzing, working on their weak areas. I, on the other hand, found a corner and sat down, continuing to visualize myself completing my back handspring. Stacia and Lisa must have seen me sitting by myself because they came over to see what I was up to.

"Are you still hurting from yesterday?" Lisa asked.

"I was a little worried about you," Stacia said, seemingly concerned. "Are you sitting over here because you're not feeling well?"

"I never felt better," I responded, smiling.

"Well, come and go over the cheer with us," Stacia said.

"Okay," I replied, getting up. We went over the "Beat Those Bears" cheer a few times, each of us doing it with no problem.

"I'm gonna take a break and conserve my energy," I said. I sat in the corner until finally they called my number.

"Number seventeen, you're next," someone yelled from inside the gym.

I jumped up and went inside.

"Let's see your cheer," Heather said. She was sitting in a chair next to the other judges.

I was nervous, but I knew what I was there to do, so I did my cheer. Time rushed by so quickly, my body was just flowing with the words until I came to an end, yelling, "Beat those Bears! Beat those Bears!"

The judges watched in silence. Then Heather said, "Now we need to see your jumps."

I did the required jumps, making sure my legs were straight and my toes pointed. I tried to get as much height as possible.

"Would you like to do either of the optional jumps?" Heather asked.

"Yes," I replied. "The pike."

I positioned myself to do the pike. My legs flew in the air, perfectly together, and my toes were pointed. I touched my toes, thinking I had done a good job, but wishing I'd been able to jump higher.

"Okay, now we need to see your gymnastics ability," Heather said.

I moved over to the mat and performed the splits, a cartwheel, and a round-off.

"Would you like to perform any additional gymnastics?"

"Yeah," I said. "I'd like to do a back handspring."

"Are you sure?" Heather asked. "I didn't see you do one in practice yesterday."

"I'm sure," I replied. I walked to the edge of the mat and prepared to do my back handspring. This time I was determined not to fail. I told myself, *Don't close your eyes. Keep your arms straight, and just throw your legs over as quickly as you can. You can do this.* I pulled out my silver-dollar pendant and rubbed it, and then I tucked it back into my shirt. I took a deep breath and jumped back with all my might. My legs were wild and bent as they went into the air. My hands hit the ground and I was upside down. I threw my legs over to the ground as fast as I could. They were spread apart because I was trying to get them down as quickly as possible, and jumped up.

I had made it over.

I had completed my back handspring. As ugly, atrocious, and un-structured as it was, I had succeeded. I was so proud of myself that even if I didn't make the team, I would still be pleased with my courage and my ability to do what Stacia said took most people a long time to learn.

"Thank you, number seventeen," Heather said. "Ask for number eighteen, and you are dismissed to go home. The winners will be posted inside the principal's office first thing Monday morning."

I rushed out, floating on a cloud. I yelled for the next person and said good luck to both Stacia and Lisa. Then I rushed home.

Monday morning couldn't come fast enough. I woke up early, all but ran to school, and made it to the office as quickly as I could. A girl walked out, looking sad.

"Did you make it?" I asked her.

"No," she answered, sounding like she was going to cry.

I went inside the office and over to where the list was posted. A group of girls was huddled around it, looking it over. One of them shrilled at the top of her lungs, "I made varsity! I made varsity!" She was hopping all around, so I pushed past her.

The varsity list was on top. It didn't have names, just numbers. I looked for mine, but it wasn't there. Then I lifted the top sheet to look at the JV list. I took a deep breath and was beginning to go down the list when Stacia and Lisa rushed through the door.

"Lanita, did you make it? Did you make it?"

"I don't know yet," I huffed.

I really wanted to find out by myself because if I didn't make it I wanted to be disappointed alone.

They crowded next to me.

"Who made varsity?" Stacia asked.

We looked at the list. "We didn't," Lisa replied.

We lifted the sheet again, and I finally got to go through the list, scanning from the top to the bottom. I couldn't believe it, but the very last number was seventeen. I had actually made the junior varsity cheerleading squad.

I yelled and jumped around just like the girl who had just made varsity. "I made it! I made it!"

I noticed Stacia was doing the same dance. We held hands and jumped together until we noticed that Lisa wasn't participating.

"Congratulations," she managed.

"You said you would try out for the dance team if you didn't make it.

I know you'll make the dance team," Stacia assured her. "You're really good at dance."

"Yeah, I'm sure I'll make the dance team," she said and rushed out past us. I think she might have been crying, but I couldn't really tell.

"I'll see you at practice on Tuesday," Stacia said.

"We made it," I said, this time not as loud.

"We did, didn't we?" Stacia smiled. Then she went after Lisa.

I went out the door behind her, heading toward my locker, and ran into Heather.

"Congratulations, Lanita," she said.

I couldn't believe she had singled me out, that she even knew my name.

"Thank you," I said.

"You did a good job," she said, smiling. "If you get that back handspring together, you just might make varsity next year."

"You think so?" I could not believe what I was hearing.

"Yeah, there are six seniors this year, so we'll have six spots opening up next year. I think that if you work hard, you'll have a good chance. I saw a lot of potential in you. Just don't get lazy."

"Thank you, Heather! I'm gonna be the hardest worker on the JV squad."

"I know you will," she said. "You didn't do your back handspring in practice. Had you ever done one before the tryout?"

I thought back to biting the dust on my blanket. "Yeah, I'd done it before."

"Okay. Well, we take time out of every practice to focus on gymnastics. By the end of the year, I expect that your back handspring will look as good as mine." She gave me a stern look.

"Thank you, Heather."

"I'll see you around," she said.

"Okay, see you around." I smiled. I wanted to jump and scream again, but instead I let out soft short squeals all the way to my locker.

Eleven

In the nearly sixteen years that I had lived on this earth, I had never had a birthday celebration. Every year since I had known such events took place, I had asked for a dinner or dancing or slumber party for my birthday. Aretha always said no.

I longed for a special party to celebrate my birth, but there was always a reason I couldn't have one. Either we were broke and didn't have any money, or Aretha was so drunk that she forgot it was my birthday. Whatever the case, we never made a big deal about my birthday—hers either, for that matter. I guess we just weren't birthday people.

It was 1981. Prince Charles and Diana Spencer were married on July 29. Not long after, Luke and Laura wed on *General Hospital*, garnering just as much attention. Love was in the air as I was embarking on my sweet sixteenth birthday, yet there was no sign of me having a sweetheart of my own.

I was going into my sophomore year and determined not to be disappointed if Aretha either forgot or didn't have the resources to give me a sweet sixteen party. I didn't even begin asking at the end of my freshman year in school, as I usually did, because I wouldn't have been able to handle being let down once again if it didn't happen. Plus, I had found cheerleading during my freshman year; it had become my second love, next to reading. I was good at cheers. By the time the basketball season came to an end, my jumps were exceptionally good, and I had mastered the back handspring. I had helped create some new cheers for the JV squad and was looking forward to trying out for varsity at the beginning of the new school year.

This year my birthday fell on the weekend before school started, but I was not going to spend my summer torturing myself, worrying if I would get a party or a boyfriend. Instead, I chose to focus on preparing for cheerleading tryouts, which would take place at the beginning of the new school year, and completing my summer reading list. There were fifteen books on my list, and I had already checked out *A Raisin in the Sun* by Lorraine Hansberry and *Uncle Tom's Cabin* by Harriet Beecher Stowe, and I'd begun reading *Roots* by Alex Haley, which had been made into a miniseries that aired in 1977. Although I was really young then, I remembered how captivated the world had been over the course of six days, as they watched the life of Kunta Kinte play out: growing up in Africa; being imported into the United States through the Middle Passage to become a slave; heading a household and raising a daughter, Kizzy Kinte, whose son, Chicken George, became a free man. I was so fascinated by the saga that once I felt I was old enough, I just had to read the book. As I absorbed the pages, I imagined how much of a labor of love it must have been for Mr. Haley to write this book. It inspired me to trace my own ancestry.

Eager to learn as much as I could about the people in my family who had come before me, I asked Aretha about my ancestors.

"Momma, what can you tell me about our family and our lineage?" I asked one Saturday afternoon as she stood beside the stove, blowing on a hot comb she was preparing to straighten my hair. I was finally old enough to have my hair straightened.

"Lineage? What are you talking about, girl?" She pulled the comb through a section of my hair.

I flinched at the thought of that hot comb getting too close to my scalp or missing my hair altogether and coming in contact with some part of my body, scarring me for life. As the comb moved further away from my scalp, I was able to relinquish my tight grip on the chair's arms and speak again. "I'm talking about our ancestors. Tell me about your parents and their parents," I begged.

"Ain't much to tell." Aretha replaced the comb on the eye of the stove to reheat it.

"What do you know?"

She blew on the comb and then rubbed it against a rag, proceeding to the next section of my hair. "My daddy was an alcoholic. Got hit by a train walking home one night, pissy drunk. Served him right. He was a poor excuse for a father. My mother, God rest her soul, died from anemia when I was twelve. My aunt Bertha raised me. I despised her, and she resented the fact that she had been forced to take care of me when she had four kids of her own to raise. So we didn't get along. I hated the way she treated me, so when I got old enough, I moved as far away from Nebraska as I could."

"Nebraska! We're from Nebraska, Momma?" I asked.

"Yeah, that's where your family is from. I thought you knew that!"

How would I have known? Momma never talked about the past. "I didn't think Black people lived in Nebraska," I said.

"Black folks are everywhere."

"When did you leave?"

"Well, I fell for Luscious Johnson when I was sixteen. He was nineteen. We both dreamed of moving to California, with the ocean, the palm trees, and the wonderful weather. His cousin had been here for about a year and promised Luscious that if he ever made his way to Los Angeles, he would help him get a job constructing the Southern Pacific Railroad."

"So you came with him?"

"Yep. I worked washing and folding clothes for White people, and Luscious did odd jobs until we had what we hoped would be enough to make it cross-country in his old beat-up car." Aretha sighed. "We got out here, and it turned out that his cousin couldn't get him a job. We were broke, and then he got homesick and wanted to move back. There was no way I was gonna take that long drive back to Nebraska. I felt like my future was here in California, and I didn't want to leave, so he left me stranded and heartbroken. I made do and tried to build a life for myself. Believe me, it wasn't easy. Things got better, though, when I met your daddy."

"Did you love Luscious?" I asked.

Momma got too close to my scalp with the hot comb. I flinched, ducking low in the seat. "Ouch!" I yelped.

"I'm sorry, Lanita. Be still and you won't get burned," she fussed. I reluctantly straightened up. She went back to pressing my hair.

"I did love Luscious, and I'm not even mad at him for leaving me. I would have never gotten out of Nebraska and away from Aunt Bertha if it weren't for him."

"What about your parents' parents?"

"My grandmother, God rest her soul, worked as a maid all her life, until she died of old age. My grandfather, a shoe shiner, died shortly after her."

"What about your grandfather's parents?" I said, marveling at all this new information.

"I don't know, Lanita, they were probably slaves." Aretha was beginning to sound exasperated.

"Momma, slavery ended in the late 1800s. My great-great-grandparents were not slaves!"

"Your guess is as good as mine." She shrugged. "I don't know anything about my great-grandparents."

Frustrated with Aretha's limited knowledge about our family, I shifted the questions to the other side of my genealogy. "What about Daddy's family?"

"He's a California boy, grew up in Fresno. That's where his family is, but I never met them."

I took a deep breath, feeling overcome with excitement. My daddy's family was in the same state as I was, and I had never met them. Fresno wasn't so far away. I turned and faced Aretha. "Can we go there?" I begged.

"Where?"

"To Fresno, to meet my grandparents. I bet I have aunts and uncles and cousins there. We could visit and find out more about my heritage."

Momma was at the end of her patience with me. "Stop all that nonsense, Lanita. Even if we went, which we are not going to do, we wouldn't know where to begin to find Paul's folks. Now turn around and let me finish up. I ain't trying to be on your hair all day."

As Aretha continued pressing another section of my hair, I sat there in silence, praying she wouldn't accidentally burn me again. I also wondered who my people were, what they looked like, and what it would be like to meet them. I made a promise to myself that if Paul Lightfoot ever made his way back into my life, I would make him take me to meet my family.

There was a knock at the door.

"Who's that knocking at my door?" Aretha yelled, rushing to find out.

I could hear the person on the other side. "It's me, Miss Aretha."

"Oh," she said and unlocked the door. "Lanita, it's Stacia," she yelled back to me. "Stacia, we're back here in the kitchen. I'm pressing her hair."

She followed Aretha back to where I was sitting.

"Hey, girl," she said.

Removing the hot comb from the fire, Aretha set it on the rag to cool.

"What's going on?" I asked.

Stacia took a seat at the kitchen table. "I saw Heather and her boyfriend over at the record store, and we were talking about the cheerleading team for next year. She started going over the expenses for being on the varsity squad."

"I already knew it was going to cost a little more than JV," I said.

"JV was practically free. I don't know how I'm gonna be able to afford varsity." Stacia appeared flustered as she huffed her way down the list of expenses. "First of all, the letterman's jacket is not free, and because varsity uses two uniforms instead of one, there is a small uniform rental fee. Then, unlike the JV team, the tennis shoes have to match. We can't just wear the tennis shoes in our closet. We have to buy a special pair."

"I thought that was what the fund-raisers were for," I said.

"No, the fund-raisers take care of the cost for our yearly physicals and the bus we use to travel to away games."

"That sounds like a lot of money coming out of our pockets," I complained.

"It is. That's why I'm gonna try to find a summer job. I went ahead and asked for an application from the record store, since I was there, but they're not hiring."

"That's too bad. I guess I should be looking for a job myself," I said.

"That's a good idea, Lanita," Aretha said. "I'm gonna have a tough enough time trying to get school clothes for you this year. I'll be able to get you a few things, but if you had a job, you could get more."

I was stumped. I didn't have a clue about where I would want to work, but I knew that I had better get on the ball if I wanted to find something.

Aretha finished straightening my shoulder-length hair and then pulled it all back into a ponytail. When she was finished, she shooed us away. "Go on and talk about all that cheerleading mess in your room, Lanita. I'm getting ready to listen to the radio and start on dinner."

Stacia and I went to my room to try and figure out how much money we needed to make to cover the expenses we'd have if we made the varsity squad. Things seemed pretty dismal.

.   .   .

Once I completed my first three books for the summer, I rushed them back to the library. Miss Page was wearing a broad smile when she saw me walk through the door.

"Guess what, Lanita?" she said.

"Please don't tell me about any new books that just came in," I groaned. "I have my list for the summer, and I'm sticking to it."

"No, I have something else to share with you." She rushed around the counter and walked me over to my usual table in the corner. "There is a part-time summer-job opportunity for someone, I hope you. The job just came available, and it only requires shelving books. We got additional funding and the position is extremely flexible, just fifteen to twenty hours a week. I don't know what you have planned for the summer, but I'm sure you can find some time to make some extra money. Plus, you'll be around the books you love so much."

"Okay!" I said. "Sign me up." I kissed my lucky silver-dollar pendant.

"I thought you'd say that, so I have an application right here. I need you to fill it out now. Do you think your mother would mind?"

"No, not at all. Just the other day, we were talking about the possibility of me getting a summer job. This is right on time. How much will it pay?"

"Minimum wage," she replied.

It really didn't matter to me how much it paid—I was just happy to have a job.

.   .   .

Even though Miss Page had always been nice to me, we built a special bond over the months while I worked with her shelving books. Early on in the summer, she had decided to do an extensive book sweep to fix the cataloguing problems that tended to crop up, so that was my main project. We began with the first shelf and worked our way around the entire library, making sure that each book was in its proper place. We also made sure that each book had a card catalogue number on its spine and a sleeve in which the return cards could be placed. Also, if there were broken spines, Miss Page would repair them to increase the longevity of the books.

Mornings were my favorite part of the day because the library was usually peaceful until noon, when parents and children and people of all kinds began rotating in and out, populating the aisles and needing attention. In the afternoons, Miss Page and the other librarians would scatter, dealing with the problems that arose, but in the mornings, Miss Page would sit at a table in the middle of the library, sorting through books and munching on M&Ms. Sometimes she'd go through three bags before lunchtime, complaining all the while that she should have eaten a healthier breakfast.

There was something about the way she would lay the bag on the desk and, in between slathering glue on the spines of books, would pull out one chocolate-covered peanut at a time and place it in her mouth. Her way of eating the candy made it look like the most delicious treat I could imagine. I found myself craving peanut M&Ms at the oddest times, even when I was away from the library.

Sometimes when I would bring from the shelves books that needed to be repaired, she would stop me and initiate mini-conversations. It was through those talks that I really got to know Miss Page. It turned out that she was a single woman with no children and no intention of getting married—ever. She had been born and raised in Watts and unfortunately was involved in a taboo love affair. She enjoyed tasting fine cheeses and taking long train rides up and down the coast whenever she got the opportunity. As the summer progressed, she became more and more comfortable sharing information about her personal life with me. She even felt comfortable telling me about a secret that was the cause of great distress in her life.

The first time she disclosed her secret to me was during a casual conversation. "Hey, Lanita, come sit down for a minute and take a break," she said, throwing an M&M into her mouth. As I sat down, she continued. "So how are you enjoying working here so far?"

"Oh, it's been like a dream," I said. "It doesn't really feel like work."

"Remember this feeling when you choose your career, Lanita. Make sure you'll be doing something that doesn't feel like work."

We sorted through a few books in silence. Then I asked, "Do you like it here?"

"I love working here," Miss Page said. "The only thing better would be to work at the main branch, but with the discrimination I would have to deal with there, it wouldn't be worth my while. Plus, working in Watts keeps me close to my home. When there are only a handful of workers, such as we have here, there are fewer politics to deal with."

"Oh," I said, a little confused. The idea of politics was new to me, and I didn't really understand what she was saying.

"In larger companies," she continued, "you're more likely to be fitted into a certain mold. Just because of your skin color or your sex, they feel there are limits to your capabilities."

"I've heard my mother say something similar," I said.

"Yeah, I guess that's the way the world is as a whole, but here at this library and in my own home, I feel safe."

"I feel safe here too," I agreed. "But I want to move away and go to college in Atlanta or D.C. I don't want to stay here forever."

She sighed, sounding dreamy. "You're so young and optimistic, Lanita. I remember when I felt the same way, and it's a good thing. Just remember that although there are limits the world will try to put on you because you're a Black female, you don't have to conform to them."

"What kind of limits?" I asked.

"Well, for one, you will forever be expected to date only Black men."

"I haven't found anybody in particular that I like, but as far as I know, dating only Black men would be fine with me," I replied.

"Yeah, for now, but what if you met a nice White or Asian or Latino guy and decided that you wanted to get married to him, then what? Do you think our society would accept your choice?"

"Well, it wouldn't be their business whatever I decided to do with my life," I said.

"I wish it were that simple," she said and shook her head.

"But isn't it?" I was confused again. Why would anyone care who I married?

"Oh, Lanita, you don't understand just how cruel this world can be," she said bitterly. Her eyes slanted and her mouth tightened. The Miss Page I had always known was upbeat, optimistic, positive. I had never before seen such resentment and anger spew from her.

"My daddy used to tell me that when I went to compete in this world, in order even to be considered for anything that I attempted, I would always need to be better than my White counterparts. I accepted that it was the way things were. But as far as my personal life goes," I said, "I never felt like it could ever be dictated by anyone."

She took a deep breath and looked at me closely. "I'm gonna share something with you, Lanita. The only reason I'm telling you is because I want you to be aware of the kind of injustice waiting for you after you leave the sheltered life you have here, in good ol' Watts."

"What do you mean, sheltered?" I exclaimed. "There's nothing here in Watts but poverty and crime."

"Yeah, but at least you know where you live and understand the people around you. You're welcome here in your neighborhood. Other places, people are not so welcoming."

"I guess you're right," I said, unsure of where this conversation was going. Was Miss Page trying to convince me to stay in Watts all my life?

"I know I'm right, Lanita. See, I've been forced to live a lie because of the evils I would have to face if I ever exposed my relationship with my one true love."

"A lie?" I was more confused than ever.

"Yeah, a lie. That's why I will never marry or have children."

"I don't get it," I admitted.

She took a deep breath, as if she were about to confess some dire sin. "Lanita, I have been dating and am madly in love with a man who is forbidden to a woman like me. My boyfriend is Jewish, and if we ever came out with our relationship, he would more than likely lose his job and have a difficult time finding work anywhere. Donald has a very good job as an accountant downtown. If he's fired, his reputation will be forever tarnished."

My mouth dropped. "So why do you continue to see him?" I asked. I didn't want to hear what Miss Page was telling me, but I was trying to be there for her, as she had been there for me so many other times.

"Well, Lanita, we're in love. I couldn't imagine my life without him in it, and he feels the same as I do."

I wanted to ask her how, if they knew they weren't supposed to be together, they had managed to get so involved with each other, but instead I asked, "So how long have you and Donald been a couple, Miss Page?"

She sighed and looked me directly in the eyes. "For the past three years. Lanita, we don't date like normal people. My family knows about him, but his doesn't know about me. We're limited in our public interaction. We go out of town a lot, so we won't be spotted by any of his colleagues. He usually comes to my house. I never go to his place. We cook dinner together, and we have so much in common that if people saw us interacting, they would know we belonged together."

I wanted to be as far removed from this situation as I could. I was too young to give her any advice she could use—and why else had she come to me, if not for advice? There was nothing I could say.

I looked at Miss Page through new eyes. She was the same person, but somehow everything about her had changed. She had become a vulnerable human being in dire need of guidance, and it seemed she didn't know where to go to get it. If I was her choice for counsel, then she really was in bad shape.

We sat in silence while she seemed to reflect on her predicament. I felt sorry for her and wanted to help, but I didn't know how.

"What are you gonna do?" I asked.

"Continue in the same way I have been," she replied.

"With all due respect, Miss Page, that's insane." I was suddenly finding my voice.

"What?" She sounded taken aback.

"Doing the same thing over and over and expecting things to get better," I said. "That's just crazy, if you ask me."

"I don't expect things to get better," she said, sounding resigned. "I know they won't, which is why I don't push for change."

I was overcome with disappointment in Miss Page. She had always recommended books to me, saying things like "Lanita, this book will help you develop a sense of willpower," or "This book will inspire you." She'd say, "I love fiction because it offers the possibility of changing the course of your life." I had devoured her advice, hoping the books I read would help me to improve myself. And she wasn't practicing what she preached. She wasn't encouraged or motivated from the literature she was reading, but was continuing to accept the cards that had been laid out for her.

"From what I've learned, pushing for change is the only way to achieve it," I said, challenging her.

A well-dressed man walked over to where we were sitting. "Excuse me, but could you tell me where to find information about getting grants for nonprofit organizations?"

"I sure can," Miss Page said. She got up from the table and directed the gentleman to the reference section.

It occurred to me then that Miss Page and Donald were wimps. After all, even Tom and Helen Willis on *The Jeffersons* were open about their interracial marriage. Tom was a publisher, and he hadn't been fired because of his marriage to a Black woman. Donald needed to bite the bullet, come clean with his colleagues, and take the chance on losing his job. Who knows? Maybe he wouldn't get fired and they'd be able to live in peace without any hassles.

When Miss Page returned, I said, "What about Tom Willis? He didn't hide his relationship with Helen."

After a moment of confused silence, Miss Page asked, "Are you talking about *The Jeffersons*?"

"Yes. They live in that high-rise apartment together, and she goes to his office functions, but nobody says anything—with the exception of George."

Miss Page smiled a sad little smile. "That's TV, Lanita—a fantasy world. Maybe I would be convinced if that show wasn't so afraid of properly portraying the family. I mean, how does a group of writers decide to make one daughter completely Black and the son completely White? Not one of them thought of how ridiculous it would be to have a completely White son born to a mixed couple. No one had the guts to discuss the reality of mixed children, that when a White man and a Black woman produce a child, the odds of him or her not taking on a good mixture of the characteristics of both races is slim."

I had to admit, "I was always confused about that."

"You're not the only one, Lanita. But that aspect of that show is just another example of America's fear of truly accepting interracial couples, let alone the results of their unions."

Miss Page was adamant about her convictions, and there was nothing

I could do to convince her to see the bright side of her dilemma. In her mind, there wasn't a bright side.

Maybe she understood more about the world and the way it worked than I did. My high school was predominately Black. My friends were all Black. I saw few White or Jewish people on any consistent basis, and most of the ones I saw were teachers or store owners. The issue of racism was never prevalent, except that Aretha always joked that "White people have, and Black folks have a hard time."

That night I prayed for her and Donald. I asked God to somehow find a way for them to be able to freely and openly display their love for each other. I hoped that I would never be faced with loving a White man and prayed that if it ever happened, people would not have the ability to force their will on me.

Miss Page never again mentioned the consequences of her relationship with Donald, but she did start dropping his name in conversations. She would refer to a meal they had cooked together or something they'd watched on the television or a comment he'd made about a particular subject. It seemed she was happy to have someone with whom she could talk about her life, even if it wasn't as happy as she'd like it to be.

For my part, I never looked at *The Jeffersons* quite the same again.

Twelve

The summer came quickly to a close. I was proud of myself because I had read all fifteen of the books on my list. Because of my success that summer, I continued to incorporate a reading list into my summer schedule every year that followed.

Miss Page and I had cleaned up the entire card catalogue of books. It was a Friday, my last day of working at the library and the week before school would be starting, and she thought we should celebrate, so she invited me over to her place. She said she wanted to give me a gift, something she couldn't give me at the library because she didn't want any of the other employees to become jealous. So we decided that I would ride home with her and she would take me back over to my apartment afterward. I had cleared it with Aretha earlier.

All day at the library, I was excited, looking forward to seeing her house. When she talked about her life with Donald, I often imagined them in her place, in the kitchen, preparing a gourmet meal or sitting snuggled together on the sofa, watching television, his taboo White arm wrapped around her dark brown shoulder. I wondered if they noticed their complexion differences, or if he really smelled like a dog when he got wet. At least that's what Aretha once said she'd heard; I had never spent time with any White people, so I wasn't sure if it was true.

From what Miss Page shared with me about him, Donald seemed to be nice, considerate, and charming. However, because he wouldn't take a stand regarding their relationship before his family, friends, and colleagues, I also felt he was a wimp. But Miss Page loved him and for him had forfeited the opportunity for a normal life, so I figured he had to be incredible. I hoped I'd get the chance to meet him.

We rode over to her house, a beautiful three-bedroom home with a fence around the yard. When we went inside, I saw the house was decorated even better than I had envisioned. We walked over her hardwood floors onto the dusty rose carpet in her living room, which had a dusty rose and gray floral-printed overstuffed couch.

Miss Page had never told me she was an art collector, but huge original paintings and numbered prints hung on the walls of her house.

I stopped and stared at one.

"It's abstract expressionism. All of it is," she said, beaming with pride.

"What's that?" I asked.

"It's a movement in art that combines emotional intensity and self-expression. It has an image of rebellion, wouldn't you agree?"

I looked at each of the paintings. I had to agree. Each of the paintings included lots of bold colors. It seemed as if each artist was trying to say something, only I didn't get the message. But I nodded in agreement anyway.

Her home was meticulously kept, cozy, and welcoming. She had an eclectic style of decoration. From the moment I walked through the front door, I wanted to move in and stay forever.

I followed Miss Page into the living room, where she motioned for me to take a seat. "So, Lanita, would you like something to drink?" she offered.

"Yeah, you wouldn't happen to have any freshly squeezed lemonade, would you?" I winked, assuming she would laugh and say no. But sitting in her house felt like being in a dream, so I might as well ask for lemonade.

She smiled. "You're in luck, Lanita. I made some fresh just last night."

I laughed inside, tickled pink. In my dream world, the next thing that would happen would be for Miss Page to tell me my mother had asked her to take care of me for a while and then usher me down the hall and show me to my room. Yeah, right.

As Miss Page walked into the kitchen, I looked around. On the fireplace mantel were photographs of her and a man. I got up and walked over to get a closer look at what must be Donald. In one picture, Miss Page and a red-haired White man, their arms wrapped around each other, were saying *cheese*. I couldn't believe she had fallen in love with a redheaded Jewish man. There was nothing about them that matched. I was beginning to think she was fooling herself, that she should move on and find a nice Black man who would be able to marry her and give her some children and a happier life.

Miss Page walked back in with two glasses of lemonade.

"Thank you," I said, taking a glass.

"You're welcome," she replied and took a sip.

I did the same. I couldn't remember ever tasting anything so sweet and sour and delicious all at once. "This is so good," I said.

"I love homemade lemonade," she sighed. "I make it often because Donald loves it so much." She gestured toward the couch. "Have a seat on the sofa."

Her sofa was so comfortable, and it didn't sink in when I sat down, but kept firm, holding my body weight with no problem. Our couch had stopped supporting me years before, giving in anytime a bottom came in contact with it.

"I love lemonade too," I said. "But I never get it homemade. When I'm grown and have my own place, I'm gonna make homemade lemonade every day."

"I doubt you'll make it every day, Lanita," she said, moving over to her stereo. "If you did, you'd get tired of it too soon. At some point, the quality that makes it so special would be gone." She put on a cassette tape and hit Play.

"What are we going to listen to?" I asked.

"This is my current favorite music," she said. "The sound track from the Broadway musical *Les Misérables*." She closed her eyes as loud, dramatic music filled the room.

I didn't know what to say. I'd never heard of that play before. "So when do I get my surprise?" I asked.

"What do you think it is?" she asked, as if she was attempting to be suspenseful.

"I have no idea," I replied.

"You don't even want one guess?"

"Okay, I'll try." I closed my eyes and tried to imagine what kind of gift someone like Miss Page would give me for my last day working at the library. I drew a blank. "A book, maybe?"

"You'll never guess," she said. "Sit back and enjoy the music and your lemonade, and I'll go and get your gift." She walked out of the room.

At the time, Broadway musicals weren't my thing, but there was something about hearing that sound track play in her home that made the music enjoyable. I imagined what the live performance might have been like and wondered if I would ever get the opportunity to see it. I also wondered if Miss Page had ever seen it and, if so, whether she and Donald had gone together—or was seeing plays and musicals something else their forbidden relationship prevented them from doing?

Miss Page was taking a long time returning, so I found myself looking over my shoulder impatiently, anticipating seeing her shadow or hearing her footsteps, but the only thing that I heard were the upbeat words of "Master of the House" from *Les Misérables*. I figured that maybe she needed to wrap the gift or something, so I continued to drink my lemonade and wait. There was an oversize book sitting on her coffee table, *From Harlem to Hollywood*, so I picked it up and began to thumb through the pages. I found myself caught up with the vivid photos depicting Black actors from the sets of movies and television shows, chronicling the changes over the years in the portrayal of African Americans in Hollywood.

I had finished my lemonade and looked at every picture and read most of the text in the book, but Miss Page still hadn't returned. I had stayed up late the previous night and was feeling a little tired.

When Miss Page takes me home, I'm gonna take a nap, I promised myself. Yawning, I looked behind me to see if she was coming. Nothing.

I wanted to walk around the house to see what was going on, but I didn't want to ruin the surprise, so I sat. My exhaustion clearly got the better of me because when I picked up another book to help ease my impatience, I dozed off right there on her comfortable sofa.

•   •   •

I was awakened by a voice.

"Lanita, wake up!"

Then my shoulder was being lightly shaken.

"You fell asleep on the couch, Lanita. It's time to wake up."

I opened my eyes and jumped, my eyes widening. I squeezed them closed before opening them again to make sure I was awake and seeing what I thought I was seeing. Either my mother was in Miss Page's house or I was dreaming. I pinched my arm. I wasn't dreaming.

I was spooked. Nothing made sense. "Momma, what are you doing in Miss Page's house?" I asked.

"Follow me," she instructed.

"Where are we going?" I asked. "Where is Miss Page?"

"Stop asking questions, girl, and follow me."

I followed my mother reluctantly. She led me though the house and into the kitchen, where there was a sliding door leading to the patio and backyard. I rushed past my mother and slid open the door, only to see people popping out of nowhere, yelling, *"Surprise!"*

I was drowning in excitement, trying to take in everything about Miss Page's cemented-in backyard, which was beautiful and spacious. Mature orange, lemon, and avocado trees were scattered about, with lanterns strung between the trees. "Celebration" by Kool and the Gang was playing, and Stacia, holding a cake covered with candles burning brightly, was surrounded by a group of people, some of whom I knew and others I had never seen before. Miss Page was snapping pictures with an instant camera.

Aretha, close behind me, stepped closer and put her hands on my arms. "Make a wish, Lanita, and blow out the candles."

There wasn't much I could wish for. At that moment I had everything a girl could want. The only thing missing was my daddy. I stepped toward the cake, squeezed my eyes shut, and blew with all my might. Sixteen candles are a lot to extinguish, but I enjoyed making it happen. My wish was that my daddy could be there with me.

Everybody cheered. I felt like I was going to cry from sheer excitement. I was actually in the middle of my very own surprise party. Ten long years I had begged for a party, and the moment I decided that I would be fine the rest of my life without one, I received it.

I stared at the smoke coming off the candles, unsure what I was supposed to do next.

"I'm just gonna take this over to the table," Stacia said, and I was left standing in the middle of everyone.

"Speech! Speech!" my audience insisted.

After a moment I said, "This is the best night of my entire life. I can't believe that this is really happening to me."

Applause.

"Thank you so much, Miss Page," I said. "Thank you so much, Momma."

I turned around to give Aretha a hug and noticed she was crying. She had a huge smile on her face, but the tears were streaming down.

I rushed over to her and hugged her as tight as I could. "I love you, Momma," I said, feeling my own tears begin.

"I know you do, Lanita." Momma held me tight, resting her head atop mine. "I love you too."

"Ain't this supposed to be a party?" Stacia said. "Cut out all that crying."

Aretha and I shared a laugh, and I wiped the tears from my eyes.

"Come on, Lanita. Come see your presents," Stacia insisted, pulling my arm.

Along the way to my gifts, everyone greeted me. Two ladies Miss Page introduced as her sisters were the first to approach me. Neither of them had a dry eye.

"We've heard so much about you," the older sister, Betty, said. "Your momma and Rita have been working on this party for the past few weeks. We are so happy for you." She and Linda, Miss Page's—Rita's—younger sister hugged me.

"Thank you," I replied. I was so used to calling Rita "Miss Page" that it sounded funny to hear her first name.

Just then, Miss Page—Rita—walked up with Donald on her arm. "Lanita, I want you to meet Donald." He looked the same as he had in that picture I'd seen, except his hair was a little different.

"So I finally get to meet the child wonder," he said, smiling. "I've heard a lot about you."

"What do you mean?" I asked. I had never thought of myself as a child wonder before, but I kind of liked it. The name made me feel special.

"Rita goes on and on about how intelligent you are and how bright a future you have ahead of you." He shook my hand.

"Really." This was news to me.

"Yeah, really. I hear that you are one of the most well-read young ladies in Watts."

"Make that California," Miss Page added.

"I can't argue with that," I agreed, tooting my own horn.

"Happy birthday to you, Lanita, and if Rita and I can do anything else to make this night special for you, just let us know." Donald's smile was warm and his words seemed sincere. I understood why Miss Page cared so much for him.

"Thank you," I replied.

All the members of the cheerleading team were there, as well as a few of the fellows that attended my school, including Jermaine Powers, the one true love of my life, the boy I'd had a love-hate relationship with since I was twelve. I hadn't said much to him since the incident in the sixth grade, but I was glad that he was at my party, standing before me, showing off his pearly whites.

"Happy Sweet Sixteen, Lanita." He took my hand and kissed the back of it.

"Thanks, Jermaine," I replied, my legs weakening.

"I got something I want to say to you." He pulled me to the side.

Stacia pouted.

"You can have her back in a few," Jermaine said.

We walked over to the lemon tree.

"Listen, Lanita, all this time I've wanted to tell you this, but the timing was never right—and it probably won't ever be. I just wanted to let you know that I'm sorry for dissin' you in the sixth grade. I was young and dumb and just wack," he said, and then grabbed my hand. "I can't make up for the past, but I brought a gift for you. It's over there with the rest of them. I hope you like it." He smiled tentatively at me.

"I'm sure I will, whatever it is," I said, accepting his apology. Now I could love him again. This might have been the best present today.

He stared at me, seemingly at a loss of words. Stacia, who was apparently impatient, interrupted.

"Can we go over to the presents?" she fussed.

"Okay," I said.

She took my hand and we walked over to where the presents were. I hadn't had so many gifts at one time since my birth, and then I had been too new to comprehend even the idea of gifts. It was amazing! Next to the gift table was the wonderful cake with my name on it. There were appetizers and punch too, but I didn't think I could eat—I was filled up with contentment. Aretha walked over to the table.

"Gather around, everyone." She gestured everyone over. "Lanita, go ahead, open your gifts."

I looked at her. We shared a warm smile. Looking around at all my friends, I had everything I could ask for.

"Now?" I wasn't sure.

"Yes, now," Aretha replied.

I sat in the chair beside the gifts. I didn't know where to begin. Miss Page grabbed a box and put it in my lap.

"Start with this one. It's from me."

I gasped for air, then tore into the gift. Inside was a word processor. I couldn't believe my eyes. "Miss Page. This is the bomb!"

Laughter filled the yard.

"It's exactly what I need."

The next gift I opened was from Aretha, who stood back looking proud as I revealed a painting, a replica of the only photograph that she and I had ever had taken by a professional.

"Oh, Momma," I said, taken aback. "Wow."

Aretha grinned from ear to ear.

"How did you get this done?"

"Kevin, who lives in the neighborhood, you know he can paint. He did it in no time at all. I think it turned out great. What do you think?"

"It's amazing," I said.

Oohs and aahs were heard all around.

Everyone eagerly and patiently watched on as I opened every gift. Jermaine's gift was a jewelry box, which I cherished. Stacia's was a T-shirt that read CHEERLEADER on the front and had my name on the back. She said she purchased a matching one for herself. That night I received a watch, a lovely necklace and earring set, clothes, perfume, new music on cassette tapes, a boom box, books, cash, and a host of other goodies.

We partied at least until midnight. I even got to dance with Jermaine. At one point, the entire group formed a *Soul Train* line, displaying their individual dancing abilities as they strutted down the middle of the parallel lines of people. The funniest was Miss Page and Donald doing the bump and Aretha doing the robot. All my friends laughed at their old-school moves. We even did the Hustle. We listened to Kurtis Blow's "The Breaks" and Grandmaster Flash. A few of the guys were pop-locking, but I didn't dare try it.

Everything about that night was special and perfect in my mind, and to top things off, Jermaine walked me home, taking my hand and holding it the whole way. When we got to the door, I stood there staring into his eyes.

"Lanita, I had a great time at your party," he said, sounding shy. "It was the bomb."

"I had a good time too," I whispered, looking at the ground. "I'm so glad you came."

"Word," he said, and then moved closer. "You look so fine in that little skirt."

"You like it?" I blushed.

"Yeah." Jermaine gently but firmly grabbed me around my waist. I held my breath. This was the moment I had dreamed about. I was actually in his arms and he was pulling me closer. Our lips met and we were kissing passionately, intimately. Lost in the emotion of the moment, I closed my eyes as our tongues locked. Then Aretha tapped on the door.

"Lanita, get your fast ass in this house," she yelled, interrupting my first kiss.

Jermaine quickly pushed me away and then whispered, "I'll talk to you later."

"Later," I whispered back. I rushed inside with a feeling of ultimate satisfaction.

Thirteen

After receiving such a wonderful gift from Jermaine for my sixteenth birthday, I hoped that he would eventually ask me to be his girlfriend. I dreamed about us holding hands as he walked me to my classes. I couldn't wait for the day that I would be on the sideline, cheering him on to victory. Then after the game, he'd walk me home and kiss me good-bye at the door again. When he wasn't playing football or basketball, I imagined that he would come over to my apartment on the weekends, and we would make out on the couch in front of the television.

But those things never happened. We talked on the phone a few times at the beginning of our tenth grade year. The possibility of our becoming a couple seemed promising. However, as soon as he was dubbed a high school football star, destined to go on to a great college with the possibility of making it to the pros, an upperclassman took a strong interest in him. Jasmine Ray stole Jermaine's heart and attention completely away from me.

There was no way I could compete. Jasmine was a print-ad model, featured in *Seventeen* magazine more than once. She was the prize, the trophy every hot-blooded Black male at Jordan High School longed to possess, and Jermaine was no exception. When she came knocking at his door, he opened it wide, forgetting I ever existed.

I hoped Jermaine was just a phase Jasmine was going through, but somewhere along the way, they seemed to fall in love. They remained together through Jermaine's and my junior year of high school.

Because I was hopelessly devoted to him, I wasn't able to settle for anyone less. As absurd as it may sound now, anyone who wasn't Jermaine Powers couldn't get my attention. Stacia was always trying to hook me up with some guy or another. I double-dated with her to the skating rink or the arcade, but I was never interested in a relationship. I was holding out for Jermaine.

Both my junior and senior years brought with them disappointing lows and extreme highs, peaks that I'll never forget. It was almost as if the universe was making up for all the bad fortune that had come my way.

I looked forward to receiving letters from Gloria, which came weekly. I hated that she was so far away and was reminded of it every time I addressed my replies. Cheering at the games wasn't as fulfilling as it used to be. I made varsity cheer both years, but Jermaine dominated the football field and the basketball court. There was no escaping him. Yeah, I cheered him to victory, but there was no aftergame kiss to make me float, like I'd dreamed of.

Nonetheless, he was always nice to me. "You look nice," he'd say.

I'd smile, while my heart ached uncontrollably.

Once we even started a conversation, when we ran into each other on the off occasion that he was walking down the hall solo.

"How are things going?" he asked me.

"Pretty good. Pretty good," I repeated.

"I hear you've got a chance of becoming valedictorian next year."

"My grades are good, but you never know . . ."

"Here you are making the highest grades in the school, and I'm just struggling to pass." He seemed ashamed. "Maybe we can study together sometime or something like that."

I was getting ready to tell him that I would be glad to help him, maybe even offer to tutor him, when Jasmine approached like a whirlwind.

"Hey, baby!" She wrapped her arm around his, looking down her nose at me and flipping her hair, ignoring me completely. It was like we were from different planets. "Why are you talking to her?" she asked.

"Lanita's cool," he said.

Jasmine didn't seem happy with his answer—she huffed all the way down the hall.

Devastated, I remembered what my daddy had told me: "When you meet a nice young man—and you will—and you fall in love, make sure that his heart belongs to you, because if he ever expects you to share him with other women, he's not worthy of you."

As deeply as I longed for him, I was not going to share Jermaine with anybody. I could not study with him. I could not tutor him. He belonged to Jasmine; therefore, he was not worthy of any of my time.

I missed my daddy immensely. I felt that if he were in my life, he would have helped me not feel so attached to Jermaine. He would have given me some fatherly advice about relationships from a male point of view. The two men that I longed for so intently were not there for me. Those were some tough times emotionally.

Stacia called me one day with the most incredible news that I'd had in all my years. "Guess what, girl?" She sounded like she could barely contain herself.

"What is it, Stacia?" I asked. It seemed that she always wanted me to figure out what she was calling to tell me. I didn't get excited because most of the time she would generate more excitement around a situation than was necessary.

"Don't guess, because you'll never guess this," she said, sounding overjoyed.

"Tell me already," I said.

"Okay." She took a deep breath and proceeded. "Larry's homeboy is related to the Jackson brothers. By marriage, I think." Larry was her boyfriend. "Anyway, he was able to get us tickets to be part of the audience for the shooting of the new Pepsi commercial they're doing."

"Word?" I could not believe what I was hearing. Would I really get to meet the Jacksons?

"Word. We'll be in the front row during the taping, so there's a good chance we'll be shown in the commercial. Larry says that if that happens, we might be able to get paid more, but that we're going to be considered extras and will make fifty dollars just for going."

I still didn't believe what she was saying. It was too good to be true. "We get to see the Jackson brothers *and* get paid doing it? Just tell me when and where, and I'll be there!"

"Yeah, that's right, we'll be front-row center, and I know that Michael, Marlon, Jackie, Tito, Randy, and Jermaine will all be eyeing me."

"Jermaine. Don't say Jermaine—you're gonna make me depressed." Stacia had spent long hours listening to me bemoan my unrequited love for Jermaine. She knew that just saying that name, even if it was Jermaine *Jackson*, not Jermaine Powers, would send me into a blue funk.

"Don't even start, Lanita," she said. "Jermaine Powers has nothing on Jermaine Jackson. Mr. Jackson is smart, rich, talented, and handsome. He's a man *and* a Jackson. There is no comparison. Anyway, it's next week. I'm not sure which day, but we might have to cut school."

"I'm all in, whatever it takes." I never cut school, but this was an exception.

"I was hoping you'd say that. I'll call you with more details when I get them."

"Cool." I got off the phone and pinched myself. I was about to be close to the Gloved One, Michael Jackson himself, as well as his brothers. The Michael Jackson who had changed the entire music industry with his *Thriller* album, who made Jheri curls cool again and had every high school boy—and even some girls—sporting jackets covered with useless zippers, who invented the mega video. Michael Jackson—I was actually going to see him in person. I would be able to watch the commercial over and over, knowing I had been there. I was so ecstatic I couldn't contain myself.

My only release was to share my news with Aretha.

·　·　·

On January 27, 1984, Stacia, Larry, Larry's friend Cedric, and I entered the set of the Jackson brothers' commercial quite early. Cedric had told Larry that if we arrived early enough, there was a great possibility that we would have the opportunity to meet some, if not all, of the brothers.

We checked in and were promptly escorted through the other audience members, who had gotten there early to ensure they got great seats. The arena was beginning to fill up, but we weren't concerned because we knew we would be front-row center. We followed the stagehand to the back of the soundstage, where the trailers were set up for makeup, costumes, production office, et cetera. Each of the brothers had his own trailer as well.

"So, will we be going to each of their trailers?" I asked.

"No, they're in front of the wardrobe trailer now, taking pictures," said the stagehand, whose name was J.T. "It's a perfect time to meet them."

"Oh my goodness, I am so nervous," I said.

Stagehands were all over the place, messing with props, lighting, and cameras and doing every job in between. A lot of people were dressed in dark pants, jeans, and T-shirts or golf shirts and wearing baseball caps. Although things looked chaotic, everyone seemed to know exactly where he or she was going and what he or she was doing.

"Yeah, what am I gonna do when they say hi to me?" Stacia asked.

"Let me suggest that you try to remain cool," said J.T. "If you become too crazed, I'm going to have to escort you completely off the premises, and you won't get paid or see the concert." He winked at us.

"I'll keep that in mind." Stacia looked a little nervous.

The two of us walked ahead of our dates, eager to get the first glimpse of the Jacksons. Larry and Cedric tried to appear calm, but their eyes gave away their excitement.

"Look, that gentleman over there is Bob Giraldi, the director," J.T. said, pointing him out. "Say hi."

"Hello, Mr. Giraldi," we said in unison.

Mr. Giraldi waved back and continued his discussion with the two people with him.

J.T. had more instructions for us. "Because this is a set and the Jacksons are currently being photographed, we don't want to startle anyone. I can tell that you two are a little excited." He motioned toward me and Stacia. "Let me warn you now because we're getting closer: Stay back when you see them. Be as quiet as you can, and wait until I escort you to them before you speak. Is that understood?"

"Yes, it is," I said.

He eyed Stacia.

"What?" she asked, acting innocent.

"She'll behave," I assured him.

We turned the corner of one of the trailers and saw bright lights shining down on the brothers, who all wore Jheri curls and were dressed in loud, sequined gear or formal military jackets, posing for photos. I gasped and squeezed Stacia's arm to keep from screaming. She did the same to me. I looked behind me. Larry and Cedric had a look of awe in their eyes.

I don't remember breathing for about five minutes. It was magical to see the brothers looking carefree and happy, posing for Pepsi. We watched in utter amazement as they completed the shoot. I tried to take in their personalities—Jermaine's smile, the twinkle in Marlon's eyes, the way Randy's body hit every pose to perfection, how Tito reminded me so much of Joe, how cool Jackie was, and how innocent and almost childlike Michael appeared.

When they were finished, J.T. walked up to a gentleman who was with them and whispered in his ear. The man nodded. J.T. came back over to us, saying, "Take a deep breath, ladies, and do try to contain yourselves. You have just been cleared to meet the Jacksons."

I still wasn't breathing—at least I don't remember doing so—so I did as instructed and took a deep breath.

As we walked up to them, the Jacksons were all smiles. I pulled out a poster I had folded up in my purse.

"Will you sign my poster for me?" I asked, hoping one of them—*any* one of them—would oblige. I don't remember exactly what they said, but I have a definite picture of them painted in my mind. Each brother shook our hands and signed my poster. Everyone else had a crummy piece of paper they wanted signed, but by the time we walked away, I had their autographs on the poster, next to their pictures, to hang on my wall for all eternity.

I was on such a cloud that it didn't matter if we saw the commercial; however, being able to do so was like having a rich frosting on top of an amazing cake. We took our place in the front row before an empty elaborate soundstage, waiting for the Jackson brothers to enter. Bright lights shone everywhere, and a well-lit staircase was at the center of the stage. I wondered what part the staircase would play in the commercial.

"I bet they'll all come down that staircase!" Stacia said.

"Yeah, they probably will!" I agreed.

"Do you think they'll notice us?"

"They might. We're way close, and if we wave out enough"—I stretched my hand toward the stage—"see, like that, we'll draw more attention."

"I want them all to notice me," Stacia said.

"I only want Randy to notice me," I said longingly. "Larry, thank you for the opportunity to meet them. They were great."

"Yeah, Larry, this is the best date I've ever been on." Stacia kissed him dead on the lips.

"I'm gonna have to introduce you to the Jacksons more often," he said.

"Yo, man, I'm so excited I could kiss you myself," Cedric joked.

We laughed.

We were all anxiously awaiting the cue for the brothers to enter the stage. Although everyone in the crowd was supposed to pretend to be thrilled when the Jacksons entered, it was obvious from the anticipation and excitement felt throughout that no one would need to act. The audience was prepared to explode.

The music began before anyone even walked onto the stage. The crowd went wild and edged closer and closer. The four of us were being crowded, just steps away from being trampled, but none of us seemed to mind. We were just happy to be in the front of the action.

Finally the Pepsi theme music began, and the brothers, minus Michael, took their positions on the stage. The audience totally lost control. People were yelling each of their names. Others were screaming at the top of their lungs, "We love you! We love you!" and "Go Jacksons!" Some appeared downright hysterical, especially my group.

The soundstage had been rigged with all sorts of explosives and special effects, which went off as the brothers performed to the music. Suddenly Michael appeared at the top of the staircase. The energy of the crowd increased, if that was possible. I couldn't take my eyes off him. The way he danced down the stairs was unbelievable—he had so much charisma and pizzazz. His movements were so smooth and enchanting that everything and everybody on the set seemed to disappear before my eyes.

I watched him intently, examining his every move, memorizing his actions because I knew I would probably not get another opportunity to see his live performance. I believe a tear even fell from my eyes. I was psyched on Michael. Explosives were going on all around him. Suddenly I thought I saw fire on top of his head. I figured it was my imagination, but then I realized it wasn't.

I yelled, "Michael's hair is on fire!" and I nudged Stacia.

"Oh, my God!" she yelled. "Michael's hair is on fire!"

She nudged Larry, while I nudged Cedric. We were all yelling hysterically and pointing, "Michael's hair is on fire!"

More people around us caught on and began yelling with us. Our screams must have worked because people from the back and sides of the stage rushed toward Michael, who did two quick, beautifully executed spins that seemed to extinguish the fire.

Upon closer examination, his hair was still burning.

Stacia and I had begun to cry, and Cedric and Larry were doing everything in their power to calm us down, but it wasn't working. Finally the fire was extinguished, and Michael was whisked away, rushed to a nearby hospital for treatment. It was a disaster.

Michael was released the following day, suffering second- and third-degree burns on his scalp and neck. The news reported that a smoke bomb had misfired, causing the unfortunate incident.

Stacia and I were upset because of the misfortune Michael had just experienced. Cedric and Larry were bummed out because we were too distraught to spend the rest of the day with them. We needed to go back to my place and mourn for Michael and write him letters about how sorry we were for what had happened to him.

•   •   •

That Pepsi commercial was televised on MTV, who chose to air it for free on February 27 at 10 P.M. Because we felt connected to the broadcast, we decided to make a little party out of it. Aretha had given me permission to ask Stacia to spend the night and invite Larry and Cedric over to watch the sixty-second spot, giving them another opportunity to spend time with us. I made cherry Kool-Aid and hot dogs with all the trimmings, and I popped some popcorn. Once Stacia and the guys arrived, we munched on our snacks and watched the music videos that led up to the commercial.

Larry and Stacia were nearly on top of each other, stealing quick kisses and whispering in each other's ears. The two had talked on the telephone every night since the commercial shoot, but it was the first time that they'd seen each other outside of school since then.

"My mother's in her bedroom, getting some rest," I warned. "Don't get too comfortable. She might have to come out to use the bathroom."

"Chill out, Lanita, we're not doing anything wrong," Stacia argued.

"Believe me, we're only scratching the surface," Larry said, whispering something into her ear.

She giggled.

I rolled my eyes and focused on the television, pretending to be involved in every music video that played, even the songs I didn't like. I was jealous of Stacia and Larry. They had been growing increasingly closer since the day she'd first given him her telephone number. I wanted that same connection, but it wasn't about to happen with Cedric. He was nice and all, but Cedric had the annoying habit of grabbing at his crotch a little too often. It seemed like every time he shifted position, stood, sat, began to walk, or stopped, he was clutching at his manhood. I wasn't comfortable with that. As a matter of fact, I was downright turned off.

"We've got one more minute," Cedric said, looking at his watch. He put his left arm down and then went to his familiar place with his right.

My eyes shifted from him back to the television as quickly as possible. I was beginning to think inviting them over hadn't been the best idea.

When the commercial finally aired, we all seemed to feel the excitement we'd felt the day we'd been in front of the soundstage. We hopped off the furniture, fell to our knees, and surrounded the television. As the commercial progressed, we inched closer, each of us with the same mission—being the first to spot the fire coming off Michael's head—but we didn't see it. The commercial ended as quickly as it had begun.

"That was dope," Larry blurted. "I want to see it again!"

"They edited out the fire," Stacia said, sounding disappointed.

"Yeah, I guess it wouldn't be good for the product if his head were on fire in the commercial," I said.

"Now that that's over, let's continue the party over on the couch." Larry grabbed Stacia's hand.

"My mother is in her bedroom, Larry. Don't disrespect her in here," I demanded.

"You told me once already," Larry said, almost whining. "I'm just gonna hug on my girl for a while and allow her to thank me for making sure she was a part of TV history."

"You sure did, baby," Stacia said, cutting her eyes at me. The two of them got comfortable on the couch while Cedric and I sat awkwardly in front of the television.

"Do you want to play rummy?" I asked, hoping to get him occupied before he'd get any ideas about getting fresh with me.

"I'm not that good at cards," he said.

"I got checkers."

"I don't like checkers," he said.

"Fine, let's not play anything," I snapped.

"We can play 'let's get to know each other better,' " he said. Then he did it again, moved his hand to his crotch, adjusting himself or whatever it was he did when he touched himself. I was disgusted. The party was over.

I announced it, to make it official. "That was fun, but now the party's over."

Stacia looked over at me as if she were in shock. "Why?" she squealed.

I tugged at my ear. "Because Momma told me that everybody had to be out by eleven o'clock," I lied. She had really said midnight, but for me, the party was over.

"But it's only ten forty-five," Larry argued.

"Yeah, but we have to straighten up. By the time we're finished, it'll be eleven."

"Why don't I help you clean things up?" Cedric offered.

Pleading with her eyes, Stacia begged for me to agree. She was my best friend, next to Gloria, so I decided to give her some more time alone with Larry while Cedric and I put everything away and washed the dishes together.

Inappropriate touching aside, Cedric was a very understanding guy. While I complained about a certain somebody I was in love with but who didn't notice me, he listened. I went on and on, and he nodded at all the right places. At the end of the night, he kissed me on my forehead and assured me, "Jermaine doesn't have a clue what he's missing out on."

I blushed. He had known all along that I had been talking about Jermaine.

"Come on, man, let's get outta here," Cedric said to Larry; he had to pull Larry off the couch and away from Stacia. When they got to the door, Cedric waved good-bye and then grabbed at his crotch. I closed the door.

Stacia and I stayed up late that night trying to catch the commercial as many times as we could, until we finally dozed off in the wee hours of the morning. We couldn't get enough of it. After that night, every time that commercial aired, even when I heard the "You're a whole new generation" slogan from within my bedroom, I'd nearly break my neck rushing out, trying to get to the tube just to see the commercial one more time.

Fourteen

Even after Jasmine Ray went away to college, Jermaine was still in love with her. She was attending USC, which wasn't far away. I found out that she and another of her modeling friends had gotten an apartment together near the campus and that Jermaine was over there as often as he could squeeze time from his own schedule. I burned with envy, knowing he was probably spending the night with her.

During my senior year, the few of us at Jordan High who had the grades or were extraordinary athletes were occupied with graduating from high school and getting accepted at good state colleges on scholarship. A few others were trying to get financial aid so they could go out of state, which cost a lot more. I applied to UCLA, Spelman, and Howard, just because my daddy had said I should consider those last two. USC wasn't even an option; that school belonged to Jasmine.

Because we had grown up in Watts, the neighborhood didn't seem bad at all—most of us didn't realize just how poor we were. However, when the subject of tuition became relevant, we all understood how much we didn't have. Larry and Stacia had decided to go to USC. Cedric had been speaking with a military recruiter, while his new girlfriend, Monica, was planning to attend West Los Angeles Community College. I had been accepted to all the schools of my choice and was deciding which would be the best option for me.

In the meantime, everybody was buzzing about the prom and about who was going with whom and what color scheme they'd choose. I didn't have a date, a prospect, or a desire to attend. I was doing everything in my power to get over Jermaine, and there was no way I would go to the prom with the leftovers, those without dates, and watch Jermaine enjoy himself with Jasmine, who was rumored to be his date, even though she'd already graduated.

I was fine with my decision not to attend, and so was Aretha, who was still very involved with her job and with Lester, on and off. Miss Page, whom I visited often, both at her home and at the library, was the only one concerned. She was determined to talk me into going to the prom, a discussion that had begun the previous summer when I worked at the library again.

"Lanita, trust me," she'd say. "You are gonna wake up one day and realize that you didn't go to the prom, and you're gonna regret it for the rest of your life."

Each time she brought this up, my response would be the same: "I've already thought it through and I don't want to go."

That conversation went on throughout the summer, through my senior year, through Christmas, and into the spring. I had been convinced that Miss Page didn't know what she was talking about until a few weeks before the prom, when everybody was coupled up in the lunchroom, making plans.

Groups were getting together, planning to rent limousines; some were talking about renting regular cars. A few girls were having dresses made, while others had saved money all year long to go out and buy them. It was like there was a private club, to which only people going to the prom belonged. They all seemed to be having such a good time making plans; there was even going to be an after-party at a hotel near the airport. I felt left out. For the first time ever, even Stacia and I weren't connecting.

"I don't know why you're not going to the prom," she complained.

"I already explained to you why," I answered, feeling frustrated.

"I can't believe you're gonna let Jermaine and Jasmine cause you to miss out on your senior prom. I know how you feel about him, but he's not worth missing the prom for!"

I thought about it all day at school, and by the time the final bell rang, I realized Stacia was right. Miss Page was right. I wanted to go to the prom badly, but it was too late. I didn't have the money to get a new dress, because I hadn't been saving, and I didn't have a date. There was no one left to go with. I was going to regret for the rest of my life that I hadn't gone.

After school, I rushed to the library, right up to Miss Page, who was helping a patron. I stood by impatiently as she explained to the older lady the difference between fiction and nonfiction, and why although she had seen *Roots* on television, the book wouldn't be located in the fiction section.

My mind was in chaos. I had been so sure that I had made the right decision, and now I was stuck and not sure what to do about it. I figured Miss Page wouldn't be able to fix my situation, but if anybody could make me feel better, she would.

She finally gave up explaining and told the woman to wait there at the desk. She took off down one aisle of books and came back up another one, rushing back to the desk with a copy of *Roots* in her hands.

"Thank you," the woman said. "Can I check that book out?"

Seeing that book reminded me of the family in Fresno I never met. I longed to know them. I missed my daddy.

"Yes, with your library card," Miss Page replied.

"I don't have one of those."

"Do you have personal identification or a driver's license?" Miss Page asked.

"No, I don't," she replied.

"Until you can provide one or the other for me, I can't allow you to check the book out."

The woman just stared at Miss Page. She didn't mutter another word.

I was becoming impatient.

"However, if you'd like," Miss Page continued, "you can come in as often as you want and sit at one of the tables or in one of the comfortable chairs scattered throughout the library and read *Roots* or any other book of your choice, right here."

"Thank you," the woman said, reaching for the book.

"I apologize for keeping you waiting, Lanita," Miss Page said, turning to me. "What's going on? You seem to be upset."

"Upset is an understatement," I huffed.

"Why don't we move to the back of the library, where we can talk in private?"

"Okay." I followed her to my favorite table in the corner of the library.

Before we could even get situated, I blurted, "I want to go to the prom."

Miss Page laughed at me.

"It's not funny."

"I agree with you," she said, trying not to smile. "It's not funny."

"And don't say I told you so," I added.

"I won't," Miss Page promised and laughed some more. Getting hold of herself, she asked, "So what are you going to do about it?"

"That's why I'm here. I don't know what to do about it."

"When is it?" she asked.

"It's in three weeks. I think I've blown it."

"Not necessarily," she replied, trying to sound optimistic.

We fell into deep thought.

"I have a few gowns that aren't that old," Miss Page said. "I bet you can fit into one of them. You might have to have one altered a bit, but they are all still in great shape."

"Okay, so even if your dress works, who am I going to go with?"

"Lanita, I'm sure there are lots of single young men at Jordan who would want to take you to the prom."

"Maybe a month ago, but all the good ones are already committed."

Miss Page looked at me and shook her head. "Why don't we do this? I'll find my dress and have it to you this weekend. I think I might even have pearls for you to wear. Are your ears pierced?"

"No."

"Okay, you'll just have to wear the clip-ons." She thought for a moment. "You call Mrs. Baker and see if she will be able to squeeze your dress into her alteration schedule. And ask your friends and see if there is anyone available for the prom."

I sighed.

"You never know, maybe somebody broke up or was too nervous to ask around. There's gotta be somebody," she insisted.

I agreed hesitantly, afraid of whom I'd get stuck with.

.   .   .

The thought of asking around for a date was not appealing, so I didn't do it. I did pay more attention to conversations dealing with the prom, but there were no leads. Plus, there was nobody I could see myself discussing colors with or making plans with, even Stacia. It all seemed too personal to me. I had resolved to give up until Miss Page brought her dress over to the house at the end of the week, just as she had promised.

Aretha answered the door.

"Hi, Aretha," Miss Page said.

"Hey, Rita. Come on in."

Miss Page walked in. "So, how have you been?" she asked Aretha.

"Just working hard. Trying to understand why my daughter has to go all the way to Washington, D.C., to get her college education."

I walked into the living room when I heard them talking.

"So you chose Howard," Miss Page said when she saw me.

"Yep, I'm going to Howard University. I hope I'll still have my job at the library this summer because I'm going to have to buy a plane ticket and I'll need to ship some of my things."

"Congratulations, Lanita, and you know the job is yours," she assured me.

"I don't know why you're congratulating her," Aretha said. "I don't see why she cain't go to UCLA. There are kids dying to get accepted there, White and Black, and she wanna go to some Black school all those miles away." It had been a point of contention between us for days, ever since the acceptance letter came.

Miss Page had an answer for Aretha. "Howard will offer Lanita the kind of opportunities she won't be able to get at UCLA—smaller classroom sizes, professors who will know her by name, and the ability to connect with some of the most intelligent, most cultured Black women and men in the nation. There is a certain prestige that comes with a degree from Howard." She nodded knowingly.

"There's prestige with a UCLA degree as well," Aretha argued. "Some of the wealthiest White people in the world send their kids there. Plus, it's closer to home."

"I know you're gonna miss her." Miss Page smiled, indicating that she wasn't going to do battle with Aretha.

"She knows I am too," Aretha said. Changing the subject, she asked, "So what do you have there?" She pointed to the garment bag in Miss Page's hand.

"A few of my old gowns. I brought them over for Lanita. I'm hoping she'll be able to wear one to the prom."

Aretha gave me a look. "I had no idea she was going. She don't tell me nothing anymore."

"I'm not going," I announced.

"Nonsense," Miss Page said, handing me the garment bag. "Now go try them on one at a time so that your mother and I can see which one will work best."

"No, really," I protested. "I couldn't find a date."

"What about Cedric?" Aretha asked.

"He has a date. And even if he didn't, I wouldn't want to go with him."

"When did you decide you wanted to go, anyway?" Aretha asked, glaring at Miss Page, who had become flushed.

"I thought I might want to go for a while," I said. "But then I changed my mind again."

"Now it's too late to find a date," Aretha said sympathetically. Then she got on her high horse. "You don't need a man to take you to the prom, you know. Go by yourself."

"I guess I could, but . . ." I knew that there was no way I could get all dressed up and go to that prom alone, knowing Jermaine would be there with a date.

"You're worried about that boy, aren't you?" Aretha said.

"I'm going to go and try on the dresses," I responded, trying to get myself out of that conversation.

"Uumph," she said. She knew better than to continue with that discussion. "Come on, Rita, let's have a seat so we can watch the fashion show. You want something to drink?"

Aretha fixed Miss Page a soft drink. Then they sat on the couch talking while I was in the bathroom, trying to decide which dress to try on first. I could hear them from inside.

"Did you know that Lanita's tuition is paid for to whatever school she chooses to attend? No matter what state in the United States she chooses?" Aretha said, sounding proud.

"No, I didn't, but it doesn't surprise me. She's very smart. I knew she wouldn't have a problem finding the scholarship money."

"Nope, it's not a scholarship, although she's plenty smart enough to get one. This money has been taken care of since her birth," Aretha said proudly. "A Jewish man, probably one of Donald's relatives, set up a trust fund for her when she was born. The girl's lucky, I tell you."

"What makes you think he's related to Donald?" Miss Page asked.

"They're all related—rich and related," Aretha replied.

"Why would you say that?"

"Girl, you're too serious sometimes. You know I'm just playing. It's just a joke. Plus, they always joking about how we all look alike."

"That's the problem with this world—the jokes." Miss Page sounded so dejected.

"You're right." Aretha agreed. "But they could be related, couldn't they? Who's to say?"

I tried on each of the dresses, modeling them one at a time. They were all pretty, all of us agreed. I could have chosen any of them, but I wasn't excited about a single one. How could I be, with no date? After trying on the dresses, I had an even greater desire not only to go to my prom but to go with a date.

Fifteen

One week before the prom, I still didn't have a date. I had chosen a dress from the selections Miss Page had given me and had gotten it altered. Miss Baker had found the time to squeeze my dress in, and Aretha had purchased shoes to match. I didn't want to accept my fate, but I was going to go through with it. If I had to, I was going to go alone.

After school one day I walked over to the library to discuss a work schedule with Miss Page. To cope, I had distracted myself with the thought that soon I would be graduating and be back at the library again. All my worries about the prom would be over, and I would be preparing for college. Then I thought about all the reasons why I was supposed to be happy: I had made the honor roll and was chosen valedictorian of the class of 1984; I was captain of the cheerleading team; I had even been elected to a senior superlative, voted "Most Likely to Succeed." I had nothing to be sad about, but I was still down in the dumps.

When I walked in, Miss Page and I went to our usual spot in the back corner of the library. I sat down and waited to begin discussing the summer work schedule she'd prepared for me. But instead, she pulled a chair close to me and said in a low voice, "I found a date for you."

"What?" I asked, not sure if I had heard her correctly.

"I found a date for you. His name is Todd."

"You're not serious, are you?"

"Yes, I am. The funniest thing happened. I had to go over to the

Beverly Center to pick up some things. While I was there, I ran into someone I hadn't seen in such a long time, an acquaintance named Betty."

"I'm not sure if I can go on a blind date, Miss Page," I said.

"I assure you that you'll have a good time with this kid. I haven't seen Todd since he and his family moved to Los Angeles, but I know you'll like him. Anyway, I don't want to tell you too much about him—I think I should let him do that during your date. But I'll say that he's attractive and charismatic and a perfect gentleman. You two will look good together."

I didn't know what to say.

"You can meet him at my place, and if for any reason you feel uncomfortable, you can just go alone."

I sighed, relieved. "That sounds okay."

"Then it's settled. You have a date for the prom. Now we can discuss your schedule for the summer."

•   •   •

Aretha and I walked over to Miss Page's house. They both wanted to see me off for the prom, so we all decided that I would get dressed over there, and they would help me with my hair and makeup. That way Aretha could meet Todd and give her approval.

The three of us fussed and fussed, changing my hair at least three times until we decided I should wear it up. Aretha put my hair into a bun in the back and formed tendrils of curls framing my face. Miss Page did my makeup and sprayed her best perfume on me. I put on the pearls and sat in a robe while Aretha painted my fingernails and toenails. Miss Page went off to look through her closet to find a purse. Once she'd found the perfect bag, she rushed around the house to fill it with mints, lipstick, and quarters, just in case I wanted to call her or my mother and let them know what a fabulous time I was having.

Once my nails were dry, the two of them helped me step into the hoop skirt, then a powder-pink ball gown that was nicely fitted at the waist. Miss Page zipped me up while Aretha gushed. "My little girl has grown up," she said, tears streaming from her eyes. "Lanita, you look so beautiful."

Miss Page stepped to the side and looked at me with pride. "Oh, I've got to get my camera," she said, rushing off.

"I am so proud of you, Lanita," Aretha said, and then walked over to take both my hands. "I'm happy that you decided to go to the prom and that you will be going away to college. I never got the opportunity to do either. You're changing history for this family. We now have something and somebody to be proud of."

I couldn't believe my ears. This was the first time she'd said anything heartfelt and endearing since I could remember. I reached over to hug her. She hugged back, but retreated quickly. "You look so pretty, and I don't want to mess up your makeup," she said, trying to hide her tears.

We shared a warm laugh.

Miss Page walked in with the camera just as the doorbell rang. "He's here," she announced.

Aretha and I eyed each other. Miss Page was obviously the most excited of the three of us. Momma nudged me, winking, and we followed Miss Page to the door.

A man was at the door, dressed in a dark uniform—hat included.

He removed his hat, bowing to the three of us. "Is this the home of Miss Rita Page?"

"Yes, it is," Rita said. She was as giddy as, well, I should have been.

"Thank you, ma'am," he said and walked back to a limousine parked out front.

I took a deep breath and prepared for the worst, praying Miss Page hadn't let me down, that my date would be someone with whom I would be proud to walk in. I was so nervous that I grabbed and squeezed Aretha's hand.

She squeezed back. "Limousine," she commented. "Nice touch."

We glanced at each other and smiled.

The driver opened the door and my date stepped out.

I couldn't see him well, but he looked familiar.

He got closer to the house.

"He's cute," I whispered to Aretha. "He kind of looks like . . ."

"Todd Bridges?" Aretha said.

"Todd Bridges!" I yelled.

"Todd! Hey!" Miss Page said, rushing out to meet him in the middle of the yard.

My legs felt like jelly. My breathing became faint. I was speechless. I squeezed Aretha's hand even tighter. I couldn't move.

"Rita," he said, giving her a hug.

"It's been so long. I've had to watch you grow up on the television," she said. "Come on and let me introduce you to your date for the evening."

Todd smiled and followed her to the door. His smile brightened up the entire neighborhood, as far as I was concerned.

I squeezed tighter.

"Lanita, you're gonna have to calm down. He's a human being just like you and me. So calm down or he's gonna feel uncomfortable." Aretha peeled my hand off hers. "Now smile and say hi," she ordered.

"Todd, meet Lanita, the young lady I was telling you about," Miss Page said.

"Hello, Lanita," he said behind his huge smile.

I reached out to shake his hand. He took it with both of his and gently brought it to his lips, kissing me on the back of my hand.

The jelly legs returned. I took a deep breath and smiled.

"And this is her mother, Aretha," Miss Page said.

"Hi, Todd, we love your work. Me and Lanita are big fans of *Diff'rent Strokes*," Aretha said. Then she reached up to fix her hair.

"Let's go inside," Miss Page said. "I'd like to get pictures of the two of you before you get out of here."

We all went in. As Miss Page walked by me, she winked.

I winked back. The smile that came over my face remained plastered throughout the entire night.

•   •   •

When we finally got into the limousine, Todd turned to me and said, "Lanita, you look amazing."

"Thank you," I said, blushing.

"You don't have to be shy around me," he said, holding my hand. "I'm just an ordinary guy who just so happens to have a TV show that airs once a week."

"You're anything but ordinary," I said with a dreamy tone. I tried to stop it, but I couldn't. "You're the flyest brother on television."

"You think so?" he said, arching an eyebrow.

"I know so. As a matter of fact, I can't even think of a White actor who's flyer than you. That means you're the flyest." I was babbling, but I didn't care. I was too happy.

He laughed.

"So, how long have you been acting?" I asked.

"I made my first TV commercial when I was six," he said. "It was a Jell-O commercial. My entire family was in it."

"I bet that was fun."

"Yeah, it was, but my brother and I ate so much Jell-O that I was sick of it for a while."

He was a mild-mannered, calm guy, and I felt special just being in his presence.

"What else did you do?" I asked.

"Well, I played on *The Waltons, Little House on the Prairie, Barney Miller, Fish.*"

"I remember seeing you in most of those. What else?"

"We can go on like this if you want, Lanita, but those are the kinds of questions most people ask. Don't you have anything different to ask me?" he said. "Better yet, why don't I ask you a few questions?"

"Okay," I said.

"Why is it that a pretty girl like you didn't have a date to the prom?"

"That's complicated," I said just as we pulled into the school parking lot. Couples were all over the lawn, dressed in matching color schemes, and other cars and limos were lined up.

"It'll be a while before we're in front of the door, and even if you're not finished by then, they'll just have to wait, right?"

I smiled.

"Go ahead and tell me," he pushed.

"I couldn't go with Jermaine, the one guy I'm in love with, so I didn't want to go at all—until the last minute, and then it was too late to get a date," I confessed.

"Are you sure it's love, Lanita?" he asked.

"I think about him all the time, so it has to be love," I replied.

"It doesn't sound like love to me. More like longing."

"What do you mean, longing?"

"You know how you go to a mall and see something you like, but you don't have enough money to afford it? Then you see it on TV, and then you see it in a magazine or a newspaper and it's on sale, but you still can't afford it. The more you see it and can't have it, the more you think about how much you want it. You don't love it, you just long for it. That's what I mean by longing."

"You've got a good point," I admitted, thinking about my feelings for Jermaine in a whole new light. "I guess I'm not in love with him. In a weird way, that's a relief to know."

"I felt the same way when someone explained it to me," he said. "So what if I had said no to taking you when my mother asked me? What would you have done then?" he asked.

"I would've gone by myself," I replied with confidence. I looked out the window. I noticed Stacia and Larry walking in with Cedric and Monica. Cedric was entertaining himself with his favorite pastime, grabbing his crotch.

"That's a good thing," Todd said. "In that case, I'm really glad that I'm going with you. But why couldn't you go with the dude you wanted to go with?"

"He has a girlfriend," I explained. "Plus, he doesn't even notice I exist."

"After he sees you in your gown tonight, two things are going to happen," Todd said.

"What?"

"One, he's gonna notice you, because you look absolutely fine. Two, he's going to wish he'd paid you more attention."

"You think so?"

"Oh, I know so!" he said.

Our car was at the front of the entrance.

"Shall we go in?" he said.

"Yes, we shall," I replied. My face hurt from grinning.

The driver parked the car and opened the door to let us out. Todd was closest to the door, so he exited first and held out his hand for me. I felt like I was dreaming.

At the entrance, we had to fill out a card with our names so that we could be announced when we entered. As we walked through the door, we heard over the intercom, "Mr. Todd Bridges and Miss Lanita Light-foot."

Whispers flooded the gym. Todd locked his arm in mine and led me to the dance floor.

Stacia and Larry rushed over to us. "Lanita, why didn't you tell me that Todd Bridges was going to be your prom date?" she asked.

"I'm sorry. I guess it slipped my mind," I said nonchalantly.

"So are you gonna introduce me?" she pushed.

"Yeah, Todd, this is my good friend Stacia. Stacia, this is Todd."

"Hello, Todd. I'm a big fan. You are so gorgeous," she said all in one breath.

Larry nudged her.

"Oh I'm sorry," Stacia said, flustered. "Todd, This is um . . . um . . . um . . ."

"Yo, Todd, man. My name is Larry," he jumped in. They shook hands.

Before the night was over, nearly everybody in the gym, teachers included, found a reason to introduce themselves to my date. He was gracious and polite, still finding the time to be courteous and attentive toward me. We received glances all night; even when we went to take pictures, we had a crowd around us.

A beautiful girl I had never seen before walked up to Todd after we had our picture taken together. "Hey, handsome," she said, pouting. "Can we go back over to the backdrop and take a quick shot together?"

"I'm sorry, I don't mean to be rude, but I'm only taking pictures with my date tonight," he said, as nice as you please.

The girl looked over at me, rolled her eyes, and walked back over to her date, who seemed to be trying to figure out where she had been.

The night was going fine until Jermaine and Jasmine Ray showed up, an hour and a half late. She walked in with her nose in the air, with him following behind her like a little puppy dog.

"That's Jermaine," I whispered in Todd's ear. We were sitting at a table with Stacia and Larry, taking a break from the dance floor.

"Oh," he said. We watched them as they walked in.

The band played a ballad, and Todd stood up, holding out his hand. "Would you like to dance?"

"Of course," I replied.

We walked out to the floor, Stacia and Larry right beside us.

"Are you having a good time?" Todd asked.

"The best." I was. "This night is better than I'd ever dreamed."

"That's good to know," he said, "because so am I."

I closed my eyes and let Todd lead. I was preparing to write this down as the best night of my life when Jasmine Ray interrupted our dance.

"Todd Bridges?" she said, looking surprised. "Hi, I'm Jasmine Ray. I'm a model and aspiring actress. You might have seen me in *Teen, Seventeen,* or *Young Miss.*"

"No, I don't read those," Todd said.

"I'm sorry to interrupt, but I just had to meet you."

"Well, I'm in the middle of dancing with my date," he said politely.

"I know, but I just need a moment of your time. I'd like to give you my telephone number. You can call me anytime. Maybe we can discuss the business, if you know what I mean." She winked and gave him a slip of paper, just like the ones my daddy used to receive.

I was hot, I mean *on fire.* I wanted to punch her right in the face.

By then Jermaine had walked over to us. "I'm getting tired of this," he huffed. "Everywhere we go, it's like this. You're always trying to step to another brother."

"Calm down, Jermaine. You're making a big deal out of nothing," she retorted.

"Oh, am I?" he yelled, and then turned to Todd, who was looking at me with a blank face. "Man, did she slip you her number?" Before Todd could answer, Jermaine continued. "You don't even have to answer, man. I already know she did, because that's what she does."

"Excuse me, bro, but I'm just trying to enjoy my evening with my lovely date," Todd said, motioning toward me.

"My bad, man," Jermaine said, and then looked in my direction, seeing me for the first time. "Oh!" he said.

I smiled awkwardly.

"Oh, Lanita. I didn't mean to . . ." He stopped speaking and stared. "You look great . . . I'm so sorry," he said and began to walk off.

"Just where do you think you're going?" Jasmine yelled, following him.

"I'm not dealing with this tonight," he yelled without turning to look at her. "As far as I'm concerned, you're on your own."

"Fine!" she said, but continued right behind him.

There was a drumroll and everyone's attention focused on the stage.

Pevis Dulin, the president of the student council, stood at the microphone.

"It's now time to announce this year's prom king and queen."

Todd squeezed my hand. "Who do you think will get it?"

"Probably Jermaine and . . ." I began.

"This year's prom queen is Lanita Lightfoot," Pevis announced.

The audience began clapping and turned to me.

"Come on up, Lanita, you are Jordan High School's 1984 prom queen."

I stood speechless.

"Go on up there," Todd urged, kissing me on the cheek.

Pevis crowned me, then turned back to the microphone.

"The prom king is Jermaine Powers."

Jermaine looked as shocked as I felt when they called my name. Jasmine jumped up and down, clapping hysterically. She attached herself to him and escorted him to the stage.

"We only need the king," Pevis announced to her.

Jasmine rolled her eyes and frowned up her nose while Jermaine stepped next to me.

"Congratulations," he said.

Pevis crowned him.

"I present to you Jordan High's 1984 prom king and queen, Jermaine Powers and Lanita Lightfoot." He looked at the two of us. Someone took a picture. "Please honor us with a dance."

I gulped. Never in a million years would I have imagined receiving such an honor, much less sharing it with Jermaine. I was floored.

"Baby Come to Me" by Patti Austin and James Ingram played through the loud speakers.

"May I have this dance?" Jermaine asked.

"I guess so, if we must," I replied.

He led me to the dance floor. Wrapping his arms around me, he pulled me close. I felt sick with worry and stiffened up. I wondered if Todd was okay with my dancing with Jermaine. I wondered if Jasmine Ray would cause a scene.

"Loosen up, Lanita. You are the queen over the entire school, so have fun with me just until the end of the song. I'll get you back to your date as soon as the dance is over," he whispered in my ear.

We giggled.

Once I took his advice, I enjoyed my opportunity to be close to Jermaine. However, I wasn't disillusioned. I was well aware that he was not my prize for being crowned queen, that this was a temporary situation. Nonetheless, I enjoyed our dance, feeling good about my real date.

Before the night was over, Jasmine Ray and Jermaine had made up and were on the dance floor in each other's arms. Todd and I walked right by them on our way out, shaking our heads. At the trash can near the exit door, Todd stopped, lifted the lid, balled up the slip of paper Jasmine had given him, and threw it inside.

I felt warm and safe, just like I had when my daddy was around.

Later that night, we went to an all-night spot in Hollywood, where we got shakes and chocolate cake for dessert.

"I haven't been to Hollywood since my daddy brought me here," I said, remembering. "When I was a kid, we ate at a little restaurant similar to this one." I sat for a moment, lost in the memory of my parents and me walking to Grauman's Chinese Theatre after eating and then driving around Lake Hollywood, through a hilly neighborhood, to get as close as possible to the Hollywood sign.

"Is your dad dead?" Todd asked me, interrupting my moment.

"No, I suppose he's in Las Vegas. I haven't seen him since I was in the seventh grade."

"That's a long time. You miss him." It wasn't a question.

"Too much. When I was twelve, my daddy just showed up in our apartment, out of the blue. Sometimes, on my way home from school, I hold my breath as I walk through the door, hoping he'll be sitting on the sofa, just as when I first met him, and tell me he was back for good." I dropped my head, embarrassed at my silliness. "I know it sounds dumb."

"No, it doesn't." I could tell by the way that he looked at me that he meant it.

Feeling more secure, I continued to discuss my father, and he told me his stories too. I enjoyed talking with him, so I told him about my plans to move to D.C. at the end of the summer to start school. He must have felt the same way; he discussed his personal life and the things that he was dealing with, with his family. By the end of the night, I understood what he meant when he said that he was an ordinary guy who happened to be on TV once a week. Like me, he had dreams and goals, failures and successes.

When we finally got back to my apartment, he walked me to my door.

"I'll never forget this night," I said.

"Neither will I. This has been the best date I've gone on in quite a while," he said.

"You're just saying that."

"Why would I do that?"

"You're not just saying that?"

"Lanita, you're attractive, intelligent, and fun to be around—and you like dessert. I rate this evening a ten plus."

"Thank you for everything," I said.

"You're more than welcome," he replied, putting his arms around my waist. Mine went around his neck, and we shared a nice, soft kiss. I didn't want it to stop, but the porch light came on, followed by Aretha with her camera. Her hair was done up and she was neatly dressed.

"I've been waiting for y'all all night. Here, Lanita," she said and gave me the instant camera. It was brand-new. "Take a picture of me and Todd."

We all laughed.

We used up the entire pack of film she had purchased, taking serious and silly shots. Todd even called his driver over to take a picture of the three of us. Then Aretha and the driver took a picture together.

When the film was gone, our date had officially come to an end.

"Good night, beautiful ladies," Todd said.

Aretha blushed, giving Todd a picture of the three of us. The two of us waved good night to him. I couldn't wait to write to Gloria and let her know every little detail.

Sixteen

Jimmy Choo spun Lanita around in the chair and presented her with a view of his creation. She stared at herself in the mirror and then got out of the chair to take a closer look.

"Jimmy, I love it. I look fabulous," she said. "Check me out. I'm bouncing, I'm behaving, and I'm chic. Halle Berry, eat your heart out!"

"Yet another satisfied customer," Jimmy bragged, patting himself on the back. "So, did your mother have your hair looking this good when she hooked you up for your date with Todd Bridges?"

"For the eighties, I was looking fly—but not nearly as good as now."

"You know, it's such a shame what happened with all those kids from *Diff'rent Strokes*. I mean, with Gary Coleman being charged with assault after punching that poor fan who was trying to get his autograph, and Dana Plato dying from a drug overdose, it makes you wonder if being rich and famous is all that it's cracked up to be," Jimmy said.

"I know, and poor Todd. Through the years he went through his own share of woes, with being arrested for allegedly stabbing a boarder at his home, suspicion of cocaine possession, and allegedly shooting at a man at a crack house in LA. Then there was the drama with his cars. He had been arrested for ramming a friend's car with his own over a videogame dispute, allegedly skipped out on a five-hundred-dollar auto-repair bill, and was hit with suspicion of reckless driving. Then he pleaded no contest to the charge of making bomb threats against an auto detailer." I shook my head, wondering what had gone so wrong with my prom date.

"You've been following your high school sweetheart, haven't you?" Jimmy joked.

"As a matter of fact, I have. But things happen, and Todd seems to have pulled himself together. He's married, and he and Dori have a child. He's a working actor again—he was cast on *The Young and the Restless*—and he's a motivational speaker."

"I see he's still got a cheerleader in you," Jimmy said.

"I will always have a warm place in my heart for Todd," Lanita replied.

"I just bet you will." Jimmy smiled.

"So where am I headed to next?" Lanita asked.

"I'll walk you to the receptionist area, where Natasha is. She'll be able to direct you to your next appointment."

"Sounds good," Lanita said, following Jimmy to the front desk, where Natasha was serving drinks to a handful of customers sitting in the waiting area. She walked back over to the desk, where Jimmy and Lanita were standing. Natasha whispered, "As you can see, we have a full schedule today. From right to left is Kobe Bryant's mom, Tracy Edmonds's mom, and Mary J. Blige's sister."

"Whoopee," Jimmy said sarcastically.

"By the way, your next appointment just called from her cell phone. She's just around the corner and will be parking her car shortly."

"Must be Shirlene," Jimmy said, seeming unsurprised.

"Yeah, Shirlene," Natasha confirmed.

"It figures. She's always about fifteen minutes behind schedule." He turned to me. "Shirlene is Vivica A. Fox's aunt's best friend. For that reason alone, she demands the attention of an A-list star. We treat her accordingly, but only because she's a good customer overall."

Natasha nodded in agreement, raising a finger. "Also, Tracy Edmonds is on her way. But don't stress, she and her mother are beginning with massages, so you have time to get Shirlene out of the way before you tackle them."

"Good deal," Jimmy said calmly. "So where does Lanita go next?"

"She's scheduled for a facial with Miss Lina, who is waiting for her."

"Since Shirlene is running behind, why don't I help you out and walk her back to meet Miss Lina?"

"You don't have to—"

"I insist," Jimmy said, putting his arm around Lanita's shoulder.

"Just give me a minute." He walked over to the ladies sitting in the waiting area, greeting each of them. Then he came back over to guide Lanita to her next appointment. "Lanita, I just wanted to say thank you for sharing your story with me," Jimmy said. "You've inspired me in ways you'll never know. It's been a hectic week, and you're the brightest ray of sunshine to sit in my chair in some time. You have such a positive attitude about life." Jimmy stopped just outside of the door of the esthetician. "Miss Lina is a really nice older lady, and she knows skin. She'll have you glowing when she's done with you—and she'll be able to tell you how to keep your glow until you can get back to see her again."

"Okay. Sounds good."

Jimmy knocked, and Miss Lina came to the door. She was a short, small-framed, older Italian woman. She gave a big smile when she saw Lanita. "You must be Lanita," she said.

"Hello, Miss Lina," Lanita replied, extending her hand.

"Let's get started," Miss Lina said.

Jimmy stayed behind, looking puzzled, as Miss Lina and Lanita walked into the room.

"One more question," he said.

Lanita smiled and turned to look at him.

"What I don't understand is why you're just now getting your degree. Didn't you say you chose to attend Howard? Plus your education was paid for, right? What happened?"

"Good question."

•   •   •

It wasn't until after I had filled my boxes, shipped them, and purchased my plane ticket that reality set in for Aretha. She cried for days when she finally accepted that I was really leaving. She had done everything in her power to stop me, but once she saw that I was determined, she gave up and began to support me, saying that other than for Christmas—and maybe in the summer, if I didn't take classes—she didn't want me to come home again without my degree.

Aretha and Miss Page took me to the airport to see me off. That was back when people could see their loved ones off at the terminal. We sat waiting until it was time to board. Aretha was a ball of nerves, which in turn made me nervous. Miss Page was there to ease the mood.

"Although I love traveling by train, there's nothing like boarding planes and flying off to faraway destinations," she said, trying to fill the silence with chatter. "My favorite flight was to Hawaii, but my longest flight was to New York. That's a six-hour flight from here. You'll be flying about the same distance, Lanita."

"That's a long time to be in the air," Aretha complained.

"They'll show a movie and she'll get dinner," Miss Page assured her.

Aretha continued as if she hadn't heard a word Miss Page had spoken. "What if something were to happen to you once you get to D.C.?" Aretha said. "How am I supposed to get to you, Lanita? I don't fly, and I don't have a car to drive across the country. Even if I did, it would take me three or four days to get to you. By then it might be too late."

"Momma, you're overreacting."

"Aretha, she's gonna be just fine," Miss Page promised.

"Momma, Gloria Mack is going to start school there as well. I'll have her with me, to look out for me." I smiled at the thought that Gloria, whom I had kept in touch with over the years, would also be attending Howard.

"Gloria is as young as you." Momma wouldn't leave off with the worrying.

"You have to calm down, Momma," I begged.

"I'll calm down once you call me and tell me you've made it to your dorm room." Aretha grabbed her purse, which was quite large, and started rummaging through it. "Better yet, I'll calm down once you come home with your degree and move close enough so that I can get to you if I need to," she said. "I don't care if you move to the Valley, the Bay Area, San Diego, as long as you're in the state of California."

They announced boarding for the flight. Aretha pulled out a box that was nicely wrapped with a bright yellow bow. "I brought something for you." She handed the gift to me.

I was speechless when I pulled out a Walkman, two cassette tapes, and three packs of batteries. I had asked for a Walkman for the last few Christmases, and I guess she had listened. It wasn't even Christmas, which made the gift even better. "Momma, you didn't have to—"

"Oh, yes I did. That's a long flight, and I don't want you to get too bored up there. Plus, if you get scared, you can just listen to those cassettes and think good thoughts."

Aretha and I hadn't hugged much, but that day at the airport, right before I boarded the plane, I clung to my mother and held her as tightly as I could for as long as I could. Tears rushed from my eyes, and I didn't even try to stop them. I was fighting another battle, between feeling good thoughts toward my mother and wanting to say the words "I love you." I suppressed the urge. Saying "I love you" made my leaving seem too permanent, but the tears I allowed to fall.

"Tell Gloria I said hi," Aretha directed. "She was always a good little girl. And make sure the two of you look out for each other."

"Yes, ma'am," I managed to utter.

I stood there until the final boarding was called, and then I pulled away.

Before I left, I hugged Miss Page.

"Go and make us proud, Lanita," she said. "If you need anything, just give me a call."

I turned and walked over to the boarding area. I was the last person in line. Aretha and Miss Page stood there, watching me, until I got to the agent and handed her my ticket. She returned my stub, and I took one last look at Aretha and Miss Page, both waving and wiping away tears. I waved one last time and turned to face my destiny, inhaling deeply. When I released my breath, I was releasing the past and embracing my future, which I knew I could not experience unless I walked down the jetway and boarded the plane—so that's exactly what I did.

I took my seat between two men, neither of whom seemed happy that the seat between them was going to be occupied. By their expressions, I knew there wouldn't be a conversation between any of us for the duration of the flight. I immediately pulled out my Walkman and tapes. Aretha had gotten me music by Run-DMC and Andraé Crouch.

Rap and gospel? Aretha had never been into either. I smiled when I thought about what she might have been thinking while she was searching to find the right music to give me. Not only did I play both cassettes throughout the entire flight, I all but wore them out during my freshman year. When I needed a boost, I put on Run-DMC. When I needed a spiritual lift, I put on Andraé Crouch. Both albums were inspirational. That must have been what Aretha had been trying for.

Seventeen

When Gloria and I reunited at Howard University, we picked up right where we had left off all those years before. Only now we were young women, not little girls, anxious to explore this new planet on which we had landed. It was a wonderful life. I felt free yet protected within the confines of campus. Our parents weren't there to supervise us. We were on our own, becoming educated and meeting other like-minded young African-American women and men with high aspirations. Plus, a Howard student had the opportunity to explore the many sights and sounds of D.C., Virginia, and Maryland, all of which were nearby. I absolutely fell in love with Howard and Washington, D.C. I couldn't imagine being anywhere else.

It was 1985. Ronald Reagan was president of the United States, Rock Hudson died of AIDS at the age of fifty-nine, and most people were grooving to Madonna's "Like a Virgin." Although I missed Aretha and became homesick on many occasions, I had Gloria—we were a tight twosome. Also, every time I spoke to Momma on the phone, she had a way of straightening me out. She'd say, "Lanita, don't you be up there acting like you can't make it without me. You're a grown woman now. I did my part in raising you the best I could. Now it's your turn to stand on your own two feet."

We took the advice Gloria had given me during my freshman year of high school and joined organizations immediately. I became a cheerleader and Gloria took up band, playing the flute. In the fall we traveled to football games, entertaining the crowds. In the spring, we supported the basketball team. In between we spent countless hours at the library, studying.

We met several young men and women who came from upstanding family backgrounds. Through them I was introduced to the joy of vacationing. Spring break was approaching and the campus was buzzing with discussion of whether to go to the Gullah Islands, near South Carolina and Georgia, Oak Bluff on Martha's Vineyard, Virginia Beach, Miami, or Los Angeles. Neither Gloria nor I had any extra cash floating around, so we didn't make any plans.

One day I was leaving my dorm room headed for the library when I ran into my neighbor, Shelia, an extremely nice soft-spoken freshman from Chicago whose older sister had gone through Howard, taking it by storm. Shelia lived in the shadow of her sister and hadn't quite found her own voice. She rushed by me in tears.

"Whoa, slow down. What's wrong?" I asked.

"It's nothing. I'll be okay," she sobbed.

"I'm sure you'll be fine, but I'm here right now—that is, if you need someone to talk to. I've been told I'm a good listener," I said. I hated to see her upset and wanted to help her out in any way I could.

"Well, I don't want to talk in the hall, but you can come in," she said, motioning to her door.

"Okay," I replied, following her inside her room.

Shelia flopped on her bed and let me know exactly what her problem was. "I begged my parents all year long to pay for a weeklong rental for my good friend Carla and me to stay in for our spring vacation." She reached for the desk beside her bed and found a Kleenex. "And now that we're a week away from the break, Carla informs me that she won't be able to go because her grandmother is sick and she is going to go home to Atlanta to visit with her."

"That's too bad," I said sympathetically.

"I'm not mad at Carla. She's my best friend. I'm just disappointed because there's no way my parents would allow me to go to Martha's Vineyard alone. They don't trust me driving by myself."

"What about your sister?" I asked.

"She's going to Niagara Falls with her boyfriend. She's always too busy for me," she said, tears falling again. "This was going to be my first vacation without my parents and now it's not going to happen."

"Why don't you ask someone else to go with you?"

"I've asked all my friends and everyone already has plans. After my parents set me up in Oak Bluff, if I change my plans I'll probably never persuade them to do anything else like this for me."

"I don't have plans," I offered. "Neither does Gloria."

"Are you serious? I just assumed the two of you would be headed back to California."

"No, we're staying here."

"And you wouldn't mind going with me?" she asked.

"We would love to!" I said, speaking for Gloria. "Wait a minute. How will we get there?" I realized that neither of us could afford a plane ticket even if the lodging was paid for.

"Oh, we'll take my car," Shelia said, sounding relieved. "This is going to be my best vacation yet. We are going to have the time of our lives."

.   .   .

We loaded our luggage into the trunk of Shelia's 1984 Mercedes-Benz 190 and took off on our nine-and-a-half-hour road trip to Martha's Vineyard. We drove through Pennsylvania, New York, Connecticut, Rhode Island, and Massachusetts to get to Cape Cod, where we had to take a ferry over to the island. But once we were on the ferry I knew it was well worth the journey. Martha's Vineyard was a hidden treasure waiting for me to discover.

"Wow!" I screeched.

"You should see it in the summer," Shelia said.

"You have?" I asked.

"Yes. My family has come here every summer since I can remember."

"I bet you loved it," Gloria said.

"I did most of the time, but as I got older, I wanted to experience it through my own eyes. Not as dictated by my parents. That's why I wanted to come for spring break this year."

What a wonderful week the three of us had, biking along paths, walking through the town, going in and out of boutiques, taking midnight walks on the beach discussing Howard and the differences between Shelia's world and Gloria's and mine. We found out that Shelia's father was a corporate attorney and that her mother's father was a judge. Her mother was a homemaker who remained active in numerous social organizations.

When speaking about her childhood, Shelia said, "Growing up, I was in Jack & Jill. So was Carla. We met right here in Oak Bluff."

"Well, Gloria and I went to day camp at the park in our neighborhood in Watts, but we met in school."

"Our meeting wasn't as glamorous as yours and Carla's, but we remained friends after I moved away to Oakland," Gloria said.

"It doesn't matter if you never came here before, you're here now," Shelia said. "Plus meeting in Watts and remaining close is just as special. The important thing is that you're friends, right?"

"Right," we agreed.

We cooked most nights to save money, because Gloria and I had very little, but went out to eat at the end of the week at Lola's Southern Seafood restaurant. The place featured live music and was decorated with animal prints and elegant lighting. We ate stuffed jumbo shrimp, blackened catfish, and seafood étoufée.

We visited the Flying Horses Carousel and both the East Chop and the Aquinnah Cliffs lighthouses. We enjoyed the experience of following the African American Heritage Trail. When we left the grave of Captain William Martin, the island's only African-American whaling captain, Shelia said, "My parents wouldn't bother taking me here, so I'm glad you two came with me."

We smiled back.

"No, thank you for bringing us," I said.

While walking down Myrtle Avenue, we came to the home of Dorothy West, a writer and the last surviving member of the Harlem Renaissance. That's when I got excited.

"She's an actual published writer?" I asked Shelia.

"Yes, she is. She wrote a book titled *The Living Is Easy.* It was originally published back in the forties. Plus she once owned a magazine. I think it was named *The Challenge,* and Richard Wright worked with her."

"I have to get her autograph," I insisted. "I've met one author and didn't get his. I won't let this opportunity get by me again."

"I don't think that would be such a good idea," Gloria said. "We can't just knock on her door and say hi."

"Why not? My parents know her well," Shelia said, walking toward the door. "You're just going to love her, Lanita."

Before Shelia could begin knocking, the door opened. An elderly woman who appeared to be in her late seventies came out, looking at us like we were long-lost relatives.

"Hello, Miss West," Shelia said. "Do you remember me?"

"Of course I do. You're Milo and Alberta's youngest."

"That's right."

"I thought you were my friend. I'm headed out for lunch," she said.

"Hello," I said, waving eagerly.

"Miss West, this is Lanita Lightfoot," Shelia said.

"How do you do?" she said, extending her hand to shake mine.

"Excited about meeting you."

"And beside Lanita is Gloria."

"Pleased to meet you," Gloria said while shaking her hand.

I was beaming, wondering whom she would be dining with and where inside of her house she wrote, or if she went to the beach or any of the many shops in town to become inspired.

"I don't mean to be forward, Miss West, but may I please have your autograph?" I asked.

She smiled warmly at me. "Of course you can."

Her ride pulled up. "I'll be just a minute," she said to the well-dressed lady.

"Excuse me," she said, walking back into her home.

She came back with a copy of her novel *The Living Is Easy*. She pulled out a pen and personalized it for me right there on her front porch.

After receiving the book, I hugged her. "I will cherish this for the rest of my life," I promised.

"Just enjoy it, and if you like it, tell somebody else to go out and buy it."

"Okay, I will."

We walked her to her friend's car and helped her in.

"Are you working on anything else?" I asked.

"As a matter of fact I am," she said, "I'm thinking about calling it *The Wedding.*"

"When it comes out, I'll be the first to read it," I said.

"Have a good day, Miss West," Shelia said.

"It was a distinct pleasure," Gloria added.

We waved good-bye to Dorothy West and continued with our stroll.

Back when she was an editor for Doubleday, Jacqueline Kennedy Onassis encouraged Dorothy to finish *The Wedding* and it was published in 1995. Oprah Winfrey produced a two-part TV miniseries adapted from the book. It aired in February 1998. Miss West died later that year, in August, a few days after my birthday. She was an incredible woman linked to icons and I met her.

.   .   .

We returned to school refreshed and ready to continue studying like there was no tomorrow. Gloria and I agreed that if we graduated from college and built substantial careers, vacation destinations such as Martha's Vineyard would be in our future. At the end of our freshman year, we both had above-average grades and were looking forward to returning for more in the fall.

Eighteen

It was 1986, our sophomore year, and we were unstoppable. Martin Luther King Jr. Day had finally become a recognized national holiday early that year, after which Gloria and I *knew* we were unstoppable. We knew the ropes and were better equipped, more knowledgeable, savvier pros at navigating our way through school. There was no end to what we could achieve. We felt bold, and we were ready to move forward. Gloria and I even discussed moving off campus and renting an apartment together.

So we got jobs. That summer I had begun working at the campus bookstore and Gloria worked at a record store near campus. We hoped that by the end of the summer, at the beginning of our junior year, we would be ready to move into a two-bedroom apartment together. We had each enrolled in two summer courses and would meet every day after work and walk to the library to study. The summer semester was more intensive than regular semesters, so we crammed as much information into our brains every evening as we could manage.

But the summer of 1986 was not all work and studying. There was also a lot of hanging out, having fun, and partying, especially on the weekends. Because Gloria worked at the record store, people were always coming in and dropping off flyers for parties. One Howard student in particular, a popular, busy DJ, always came in to purchase the latest albums. He went by the name DJ Jammin' and had a crush on Gloria, so every week—even if he wasn't purchasing—he'd fill her in on the most desirable and exclusive parties, mostly private, that were going on in the area. If she and I felt we had studied enough, we'd dress up and go out on the town. That summer we partied all over, from downtown to Georgetown, from Virginia to Maryland. We had found our new pastime—drinking and occasionally snorting a line or two. Some of the parties we attended offered all the free liquor you could drink and all the cocaine you could fit up your nose. It all seemed like harmless fun, so we indulged with little hesitation. At the time I distanced the kind of drinking that I was doing from Aretha's alcoholism. She drank by herself, alone in her own depressing world, while I drank with friends in a festive and social setting. I convinced myself that what I was doing was acceptable, fun.

The first time I did powder coke, I was left with a high I'll never forget. I was at a party at a senator's son's house and someone invited me to do a line or two. Not knowing much about what I was in for, I accepted the rolled-up hundred-dollar bill that was handed to me and following the lead of everyone else I had seen snorting, I leaned over the table, placed the bill to my nose, and inhaled the line of powder. It stung going up, and I felt like I was having a severe sinus headache.

"Why would anyone want to do this?" I complained, frowning, angry that I had been foolish enough to indulge. Soon my frown turned into a smile as the high began to hit me. I felt like I wanted to dance, and dancing made me feel even better. I felt so good that I found myself on top of the table, rolling my hips and touching my body, dancing in a way I'd never before thought myself capable of.

Several guys surrounded me and started throwing money my way. Being the center of attention seemed to increase my high, so I kept dancing and began picking up money. I became part of a taboo fantasy, which was suddenly okay to experience. I felt like anything that I felt like doing I could and would do. As I picked up the money I felt the urge to undress. I couldn't tell you why, but I followed my impulse. Even if I wanted to stop myself, I don't think I could have. I began taking my clothes off without a care in the world. First I removed my blouse. I was irrepressible, my hand moving next to my skirt. I stepped out of it, twirled it over my head, and threw it—I have no idea where it landed—unfazed by the fact that I would have to face some of these same people at school at the beginning of the week. I had stripped down to my bra and panties before Gloria came running around the corner to drag me off the table and out of the party. She gathered my belongings and shoved me toward the door. I didn't want to leave because I *was* the party.

"What were you thinking, Lanita?" she demanded as she draped a jacket over me. "What are you going to do when this gets back to the people on campus?"

"I don't care about them. I am having a ball!" I threw my hands out as I exited the front door. The jacket slipped off me. "I'm on top of the world!"

Gloria quickly bent down to pick the jacket up and shoved my arms into the sleeves. Then she buttoned me up. "We're leaving now!" she demanded. Heedless of my protests, she flagged down a cab and we went back to campus.

I sat in the cab, singing and dancing in my seat all the way back. I felt damned good. I was in such a state of euphoria that I was convinced that if I had tried to walk on water, I wouldn't even get wet. "Let's go to Washington Harbor!" I kept yelling.

After experiencing this amazing euphoria, I revisited it whenever the occasion arose. I can't say that I was addicted, but the pleasure I experienced from cocaine seemed to continually bring me back to it.

All of that changed on June 19, 1986. This was the night that forced Gloria and me to realize that a little harmless fun could prove deadly. I'll never forget Gloria's banging on our room door. She had just gotten off work from the record store and I was relaxing, having just gotten off work myself. I had been preparing to take a nap so that if we decided to hit the town, I would be rested enough to stay out late without pooping out. I quickly slipped my pajama shirt over my head and rushed to open the door.

Gloria bounced in all happy, wearing her dual-colored jeans. The fronts were light and the backs were dark denim. "I forgot my key," she confessed.

"Oh." I was still sleepy.

"You're never going to guess where we're going tonight!"

"Where?" I yawned.

"To a party out in Cherry Hill!" she said, excitement in her eyes.

"Okay," I responded dryly, wondering what the big deal was.

"Not just any party in Cherry Hill—*the* party in Cherry Hill."

"Sounds good. I'm about to get some rest so I'll be energized for the evening." I jerked the covers back on my twin bed and got in, pulling them over me and snuggling in. "What time do we need to be ready to leave?" I asked. "Is Jammin' picking us up?"

"You're not listening to me," she fussed.

"Yes, I am."

"Guess who's going to be there?"

"Uh, I don't know."

Gloria sighed from frustration. "Who do you love?" she asked.

"Uh, I don't know what you're talking about, Gloria."

"Who have you been dying to meet since your freshman year? Whose games do you watch, even if you have an exam the next day? Who is it that you gave up on meeting because you thought you didn't have a chance because he attends the University of Maryland and you attend Howard? Who just got drafted by the Boston Celtics only a few days ago? Who—"

"Oh my God! Are you serious?"

"Yes, I'm serious."

"Don't play with me, Gloria."

"I'm not playing, Lanita. Jammin' told me that Len Bias is coming back into town tonight and will be stopping by the party."

I jumped out of bed. "What am I going to wear?" I rushed to the mirror. "My hair—what am I going to do with it?"

"I figured you'd be pretty excited." She looked smug.

"Excited? I can't breathe! I can't think . . . I'm going to be in the same room as Len Bias, the greatest basketball player *ever*."

"Well, you've got until seven to be ready. We have to leave early because we're riding with Jammin', and we don't want to make him late because he has to be on time to set up. The party begins at nine."

"I hate it when we have to be there so early." I always felt overeager, even though there was a perfectly good reason for our early arrival.

"Cherry Hill is much too far for us to get there any other way."

"I know."

"We can do our hair and makeup when we get there, if you want. I'm sure there will be a bathroom we can steal."

"You're right." I looked through the closet to see what I could throw together. "I guess this means a nap is out."

"It looks that way," Gloria said. "It's already after six. You sure you wanna go?" she teased.

I shot her a look. "I might be tired, but how many chances will I ever get to meet Len Bias?"

.   .   .

The party at Cherry Hill wasn't what we expected. First of all, DJ Jammin' didn't have to set up his equipment because it was just a small gathering. The guy who'd hired him to come out only wanted to use his music, so they forfeited putting up the subwoofer speakers and opted just to use the very nice entertainment system that was already there. Jammin' pulled out several mixed tapes, and the setup was complete. We didn't complain, however, because we were going to meet Len Bias.

While Jammin' was talking to the host, we got dressed. After sitting around and waiting for the guests to arrive, we became bored, so we convinced Jammin' to take us to a fast-food restaurant to get something to eat. With our rushing to get to the party, we had failed to nourish ourselves. We left and went to find a place close by, Jammin' flirting with Gloria the entire trip. As usual, she didn't seem to mind. After we devoured our food, we stayed for a while and chatted about Len Bias. Of course I began the conversation.

"Do you think Len is really going to show up?" I asked Jammin', who was sitting across the table from me, next to Gloria.

"He's supposed to be stopping by—at least that's what I was told. Word has it he's supposed to be flying in from Boston this evening with his father. He should be over shortly after that."

"I am so excited," I gushed. "Do you know if he has a girlfriend? Do you think he'll be interested in me?"

"I don't know much about him—I only met him once."

"You did? What kind of person is he?" I was out of control with excitement.

"Chill out, girl. I told you I only met him once. He seemed like a nice guy."

"Well, let's hurry up and get back so that I can make sure I don't miss him."

Jammin' scooted close to Gloria. "I'm feeling kind of cozy sitting here next to this bad fly-ass woman. Do you think I'm in a hurry to move?"

"Duh, you'll be sitting beside her in the van," I said. "Now let's go before I miss out on meeting the man destined to rock my world."

We drove back over to the gathering, but no Len. We socialized with the people there, but I was bored stiff. I didn't want to be there, but I kept reminding myself that it would be worth suffering through a wack party in order to be in the presence of Len Bias.

The night dragged on, and there was still no sign of him. Gloria had been ready to go hours before, but I insisted it was too early. Then finally, a little after 2:00 A.M., we both had become weary. We approached Jammin' to see about our options.

"Listen, how much longer are you required to stay here?" I asked.

"Yeah, Jammin', we really ought to be leaving soon," Gloria said.

"Y'all are ready to go? That's cool. We could have left a long time ago. I've been paid, and I'll just swing by here tomorrow and pick up the cassettes. I thought Lanita here was dying to meet Len, so I didn't say anything."

"Well, it's already after two," I said resignedly. "It's become painfully obvious that I'll never meet him."

"If not tonight, maybe you'll have another opportunity," Jammin' said.

"I doubt it. He's going back to Boston. If he doesn't come tonight, it's over for me."

"I'm sorry, Lanita," Gloria said. "I know this meant a lot to you."

"Don't worry about it," I replied, glum but accepting of my fate.

We headed for the door, with me leading the way. When I opened it, he was standing there, Len Bias, looking startled that the door had opened before he'd even knocked.

I gasped.

So did he.

We laughed.

"Are you leaving?" he asked.

"Uh . . . no. I'm just coming out for a moment to get some fresh air," I lied. Then I stood there in front of the door staring at him. I was rendered speechless.

Jammin' came to my rescue. "Hi, man, I'm a big fan. I met you before, but it's been a while. My name is Jammin'."

"Oh, I know who you are. You're only one of the most-talked-about DJs in D.C."

"I just put the work in and spin the wax," Jammin' responded humbly.

"Word," Len said.

"The two lovely ladies with me are my true love, Gloria . . ."

Gloria didn't correct him, but just held out her hand and said, "Hi. It's a pleasure to meet you."

". . . And this is her best friend and probably one of your biggest fans, Lanita."

I was uncouth, I'll admit, but I just followed my feelings. I stepped into his space and hugged him, laying a kiss right there on his cheek.

"Thank you, Lanita. It's nice to meet you too," he said, being a good sport.

After I released him, I stood there, just looking at him.

"Is it okay if I come in?" he joked.

I realized I was preventing him from entering. "Oh, my bad," I said, embarrassed. I stepped to the side, and he walked in, just as tall as I had expected. He had such manly features and seemed to be a gentleman. I loved him even more.

"Don't worry about it," he said.

"Hey, Lenny, back here," someone yelled from inside.

"Lenny?" I said under my breath, giggling.

He walked right past us, and then stopped short and turned around to face the three of us, standing there awestruck.

"It was a pleasure meeting you," he said, and then continued inside.

I grabbed my chest and sighed. I was in a state of elated bliss.

"Can we go home now?" Gloria said.

"I'm afraid if I leave I might miss something."

"Why don't we go chill in the truck, Gloria, so that we can have the opportunity to talk alone. Then when you're ready to leave, Lanita, just come out," Jammin' suggested.

I was so starstruck I didn't move.

They didn't wait for an answer. Before I could blink, they were out the door.

There was no alcohol being served, so I went in and grabbed a soda. Keeping my distance, I mildly stalked Len for the rest of the evening, my eyes watching his every movement. Cordial and cool, he said hello to most everyone there. I watched everything about him—his mannerisms, the way his lips moved when he talked. He seemed a bit tired; yet he was lively. I was just glad to be in the same room with him.

By 4:00 A.M., the gathering was beginning to fizzle. I felt it; I'm sure Len and everyone else felt it too. I convinced myself that I had obsessed over him enough for one night and decided to bring it to an end. I slowly and reluctantly headed for the door. He was leaving at the same time.

"Lanita," he said.

"Yes," I gulped.

"Thanks for the hug and kiss. They were nice." He smiled.

"You're welcome," I replied. My cheeks were stinging from the grin planted on my face.

"Good night," he said.

"Good night," I replied.

I walked over and got into the van. He got into his car, a shiny new Nissan 300ZX.

·   ·   ·

Gloria and I slept in late. Once we finally got stirring, she turned on our dorm room television to help get our minds going for the day. She was flicking through the channels to see if anything interesting was playing when she passed a special news bulletin.

"There's a picture of Len on the screen, behind the newscaster," I said. "Go back!"

The news anchor spoke: "University of Maryland all-American basketball player Len Bias collapsed in his dormitory suite early this morning. Two hours later, he was pronounced dead of cardiac arrest at Leland Memorial Hospital in Riverdale."

"What?" I yelled.

"This can't be right," Gloria said.

The commentator continued: "Evidence of cocaine was found in a urine sample taken at the hospital as an emergency medical team labored from six-fifty to eight-fifty A.M. to revive him . . ."

"Turn it off," I demanded.

"What?"

"Turn it off. It's not true. I refuse to believe it. I just saw him last night. Didn't I, Gloria? He was okay then, wasn't he? Gloria, there was no cocaine at that party. Why are they saying he's dead?" I buried my head in the pillow and sobbed in disbelief.

Gloria came over and wrapped her arms around me, but I was not comforted. We both spent the rest of the day in shock. Everywhere we turned, they were reporting that Len Bias had died from a heart attack due to the use of powder cocaine.

I didn't want to accept it, because the Len Bias I had just met was going to go away to Boston and play professional basketball—surely he couldn't be dead. There was *no way* he could be dead.

.   .   .

As the days went by, I was forced to face the truth. Len Bias was in fact dead. According to the report, that night after I had met him at the gathering in Cherry Hill, he had gone back to his dormitory suite, collapsing some time after 6:00 A.M. while talking to his teammate and roommate, Terry Long. Len had lain back like he was going to sleep, and instead started having a seizure. Terry tried to administer CPR until the ambulance attendants arrived at his dorm at 6:36 A.M.

Len Bias had been unconscious and not breathing all that time, and he never regained consciousness or breathed on his own again. At the hospital, he had been given five drugs in an attempt to revive him: sodium epinephrine, which is basically adrenaline; sodium bicarbonate, to stabilize the acidity in his bloodstream; lidocaine, to regulate his heartbeat; calcium, to stimulate the heart muscle; and bretyline, which was also used to control his heart irregularity. A pacemaker had been implanted to try to get his heart beating again, but that failed too. Just as my meeting him was brief and fleeting, so were poor Lenny's life and professional athletic career.

Neither Gloria nor I ever touched cocaine again.

Nineteen

It seemed that after Len Bias died, so did so many wonderful elements of my life. Gloria and I registered for classes our junior year and paid a security deposit on our new apartment. After the events of the summer, I became even more determined to buckle down and get serious again about my life. Both Gloria and I had cut down on the number of parties we attended and had become focused on school.

For my twenty-first birthday, instead of partying all weekend, I planned to get baptized. I chose to do so because as a child I wanted so badly to be a part of a Christian family, one that attended church on Sundays, listening to the choir sing and hearing good preaching. Because I was turning twenty-one, I was becoming an adult with the ability to make my own choices regarding my life. Choosing to get baptized was my statement of independence from Aretha. I still loved her, but it was time that my successes and failures be a result of my own decisions, not hers. I was saying, "If I have the choice, I want to be a Christian."

Gloria helped me invite several of our close friends on campus to church that Sunday for my birthday celebration.

Dressed in a white gown, I stepped into the freezing water. While I walked toward the pastor, who had on rubber-boot pants, I looked out at the congregation, seeing a cluster of about ten of my friends, including Gloria and Jammin'. I smiled when I saw the enthusiasm on their faces, especially Gloria's. She had been baptized when she turned twelve and thought it was a great birthday gift to myself.

The pastor put his arm around my back and raised his right hand to the sky. "Lanita Lightfoot, I baptize you in the name of the Father, the Son, and the Holy Spirit!" He placed his hand and mine over my nose and then proceeded to lay me out in the water.

As my body lay submerged in the water, I became light. An elation surged through me that surpassed even the high I'd experienced with cocaine. I felt clean and genuinely happy. I came out of the water smiling, filled with joy.

The pastor said, "Lanita, this is the beginning of a spiritual journey. As a Christian, you're not perfect, and being baptized doesn't mean you won't stumble or fall. It just means that now you have Christ in your corner, and with Him, there is nothing you won't be able to overcome."

After the service, our group went out to dinner, where they showered me with birthday presents. It was apparent by the gifts I unwrapped that everyone knew the space I was in: I received a Study Book Bible, a journal, several jazz and gospel cassettes, and Christian and inspirational books. It wasn't the kind of twenty-first birthday I had always dreamed of, but it was exactly the one I needed, a celebration that was healing for my spirit and my soul.

· · ·

With the first semester of my junior year behind me, I looked forward to going home to spend time with Aretha during the Christmas holiday. It was the first time since I had been away at school that I felt homesick, and I longed to be with my mother. We talked on the phone once every two weeks or so, but I missed seeing her face and just being around her.

Once I got off the plane and picked up my luggage, I stepped outside the concourse into the beautiful California winter weather. I closed my eyes and breathed in the smoggy air that meant I was home, appreciating every breath of it.

Miss Page and Donald were right outside in his car, waiting to take me home. I was surprised to see them out in public together—surprised and glad.

"Hey, Lanita, welcome home." Donald embraced me. "You're looking good. Seems that college life is working well for you." He popped the trunk and began loading my luggage.

Miss Page was right behind him. She wrapped her arms around me and squeezed me tight. I didn't think she was going to let go. Just when it seemed she would release her grip on me, her hug intensified.

"Have I been gone that long?" I asked.

She wiped the sparse tears falling from her eyes. "You look so good, Lanita."

We got into the car and pulled off, bound for Watts.

"How was your flight?" Donald asked.

"Fine, thank you. We experienced a lot of turbulence going over Texas, but once we got over New Mexico, it was smooth sailing."

I was beginning to feel uneasy. Miss Page was at a loss for words, which was unusual, and Donald was leading the conversation—another red flag.

"So, what am I missing?" I asked.

"What are you talking about?" Miss Page said, her voice shaking.

"I mean, it seems like there's something you're not telling me."

"Well, Lanita, actually—" Donald began.

"I'll tell her," Miss Page interrupted.

"What is it?" I demanded.

"Lanita, we weren't trying to hide anything from you. I was just waiting for the best time to tell you," Miss Page said.

"What is it?" I braced myself for the worst.

"It's your mother," Miss Page said.

"My mother?" I wasn't prepared for news about my mother.

"Aretha is in the hospital. She just went in last night."

"I talked to her yesterday," I said, confused. "She was fine."

"Aretha has been sick for quite some time," Miss Page said softly. "She got really bad last night, so she had to be admitted. We stopped by the hospital before we came here."

"We spoke to her before coming to get you, and she's doing fine," Donald added.

"What's wrong with her?" I asked, tears beginning to flow.

Donald grabbed Miss Page's hand.

She answered. "She has cirrhosis of the liver."

"Isn't that supposed to be fatal?" I asked.

"It can be, but according to the doctor, they caught it in an early enough stage," Donald said. "If she follows the doctor's orders, there is a good chance she will heal."

• • •

When I walked into Aretha's room, the first thing I noticed was that she had lost a lot of weight. She was asleep and I didn't want to wake her. Miss Page and Donald dropped me off at the hospital, saying they had something they needed to do, but promised they'd be back within the hour.

I sat down in the chair next to the bed and watched her sleep. She had always been a pistol, and it was difficult to see her on her back in a hospital bed, defeated by a disease. I felt helpless. There was nothing I could do for Aretha except hope the doctors were knowledgeable enough to treat her properly. I needed to talk to someone to get a better understanding of what was going on with my mother. I left her room and went down the hallway to the nurse's desk.

"May I help you?" the young Black nurse offered.

"Yes, I'm Lanita Lightfoot, Aretha Downs's daughter. I would like to speak with someone about her current state," I said.

"Okay. If you'd like to go back to her room, I'll have a doctor who is familiar with her chart come and speak with you as soon as possible."

"And just how long will that take?" I asked.

"It shouldn't be any more than five to ten minutes."

My first inclination was to take my frustrations out on the nurse, but I got hold of myself and took a deep breath to calm down. "Thank you," I said and returned to the room.

Someone was in to see me sooner than I expected. It was a doctor, an older Black gentleman. I hadn't seen many Black doctors in my time, but I was glad to have a brother on the job.

There was a light tap at the door as he came in.

"Miss Lightfoot?" he whispered.

"Yes, I'm Aretha's daughter, Lanita." I stood and reached out to shake his hand.

"Do you want to step out with me for a moment?"

I followed him out the door, looking back to make sure Aretha was still sleeping. When we got into the hall, he introduced himself. "Hello, I'm Dr. Stanley Robinson. I'm one of the doctors caring for your mother."

"Nice to meet you," I said.

"I met your mother's friends earlier, Rita and Donald."

"Yes," I replied.

"They tell me that you're in school at Howard."

"Yes, I am." I waited for him to get to the point.

"I have several friends who are Howard alums. It's a great school," he said. "I attended Berkeley for undergrad and UCLA for grad."

I interrupted him. "Doctor, how is my mother doing?"

He sighed. "I apologize. I'm sure you're worried about her. Aretha's doing as well as can be expected under the circumstances."

"I understand that she has cirrhosis," I said.

"Yes, she has alcoholic cirrhosis, which we're working to treat. We caught it early enough, although her liver is in bad shape. But it can repair and rehabilitate itself if she changes her lifestyle once she has been released."

"What do you mean by change her lifestyle? Does she need to move?"

"Not necessarily. By change her lifestyle, I mean that she must totally abstain from alcohol from this point on. She's got to watch what she eats and make sure her diet includes foods rich in protein, and she needs to be sure to supplement her diet with vitamins. If she does those things, she'll be on the road to recovery."

"What if she doesn't?" I asked. Momma had never been very good at taking care of herself, and I was worried that she wouldn't start now, even if it meant life or death.

"Right now, her abdomen and her ankles are swollen. She has lost a lot of weight and is generally fatigued. Because cirrhosis is a degenerative disease, if she continues to drink recklessly and refuses to change her diet, she'll more than likely develop jaundice and will possibly begin vomiting blood, resulting in irreversible damage and the collapse of her liver."

"Does that mean that she will die?" I didn't want to know the answer.

"It means she would possibly need a liver transplant, and a further diagnosis would have to be given at that time."

"Oh," I said, feeling small.

"Lanita, the main thing is to make sure your mother lays off the alcohol and eats healthy; then you won't have to worry about the worst-case scenario."

"I can't watch my mother, Dr. Robinson. I'm all the way in D.C. She lives here. What am I supposed to do?"

"I do apologize. You're right. Those things are your mother's responsibility. I guess what I'm saying is be sure to encourage your mother toward a path of recovery."

"I'll do my best," I said.

We stood in a brief, awkward silence.

"Is there anything else that I can help you with?" he asked.

"Yes. How much longer is she going to be here?"

"Well, I estimate that we'll need to keep her for at least three more days. She should be free to go right before the Christmas holiday."

"Thank you very much, Dr. Robinson," I said.

"No problem, and if you ever have any questions, don't hesitate to contact me," he said and handed me his card. "We'll do everything in our power to make sure that your mother is healed and rested enough to return home for the holidays. In the meantime, you keep a positive attitude and encourage her to change her lifestyle. Okay?"

I returned to the room and sat next to Aretha. I put my hands together and said a short prayer: "Dear Lord, my mother is sick, and this is serious. Please heal her, and please help me to help her the best way I can. Dear Lord, please allow her to be well in time for Christmas, and help her to do right when she gets out of the hospital."

I just hoped my prayer would be answered.

.　　.　　.

Aretha awoke a few hours later. Miss Page and Donald had come back and left again to get me food when I told them that I was going to stay with Aretha. Miss Page offered to pick me up first thing in the morning, so I could go home for a while to get some rest.

"Lanita, you made it," Aretha said weakly.

I immediately woke up when I heard her voice. "Yeah, Momma. I'm here."

"How was your flight?" she asked casually, as if we were not in a hospital and she were not a patient.

"It was fine," I said. "How are you feeling?"

"Girl, I'm just fine. You know me. I'm gonna be all right. Just got worn out from work and my stomach blew up like a balloon, that's all."

"You do know why you're sick, don't you?" I asked.

"Yeah, they tried to tell me I have cirrhosis, but I think they don't know what they're talking about." She was the same old Aretha.

"That's what they get paid for, Momma, to diagnose and treat diseases and ailments. I think the doctors know what they're talking about."

"The doctor I've seen the most is Black," Aretha complained, sounding almost peevish. "I really would prefer a White doctor. You know, White people get a better education than Blacks."

I was appalled. "That's not true, Momma. I can't believe you said that." I was angry with her, but I tried to keep my tone calm. "Plus, Momma, Dr. Robinson attended UCLA Medical School. He was educated by the best and the brightest. The man knows what he's doing."

"I've never had a Black doctor in my life. How am I supposed to trust that he knows what he's doing?"

"Momma, please don't be like that," I begged. I couldn't believe I was having such a discussion.

"I'm sorry, Lanita, but I just don't want to be here. If you say so, I guess Dr. Robinson knows what he's doing."

"He does," I assured her, thanking God I was a part of a generation that wasn't as narrow-minded as Momma's.

"I'm hungry," she said. "Do you know when they're going to feed me?"

"The nurse said someone would be by with your dinner in the next thirty minutes or so."

"Have you been over to the apartment?"

"I'm going to stay here with you until you can leave, but I'll be stopping by the apartment every day. Miss Page is going to pick me up in the morning."

"Rita's so nice," she said. "But you don't have to stay here with me. I'm gonna be just fine. I already told you that."

"I know, but I came home to visit you, and that's what I intend to do. You're here, so that's where I want to be." I smoothed her unkempt hair.

"You're such a good girl, Lanita. You always have been," she said. "Now tell me about everything that's been going on in D.C."

That evening I filled Aretha in on my baptism and my meeting Len Bias. I told her about all the interesting classes I had taken and the students who attended Howard—that although most of them were Black, they were diverse, from varied backgrounds. I described all the new places I had visited in D.C. I expressed how much I loved Howard and how I looked forward to her one day getting on a plane to visit me there so that she could see it through her own eyes.

She agreed that it would be a wonderful trip.

"So tell me about Martha's Vineyard again," she requested.

"Okay," I replied, recapping my trip to Massachusetts with Gloria and Shelia. I would never forget being on that island.

After eating her dinner and taking her final meds for the evening, she dozed off as I continued to go on and on about everything D.C. I'd had a long day, so I wasn't far behind her. I curled underneath a blanket I'd gotten from one of the nurses and dozed off, hoping she'd be ready to go home soon.

Twenty

After covering her eyes with something cold and stimulating and applying a mask to Lanita's face, Miss Lina walked around to the small sink that was in the corner of the room. Washing her hands, she said, "Alcohol and drugs are beasts. Both have wreaked havoc through my family line for years."

"You don't say," Lanita said.

"Drugs had my brother and alcoholism had my father and still has my youngest sister."

"I can't say that I know anybody who hasn't been affected in some way," Lanita said, thinking about the lives she knew had been affected, especially her own.

Miss Lina walked to the edge of the table. Standing over Lanita's head, she began massaging Lanita's upper back, shoulders, and neck. "Must have been a tough holiday season for the two of you."

Lanita took deep breaths, helping release the tension Miss Lina was loosening with her massage. "We made the best of the situation. No matter what came our way, we strove to survive, but my momma's illness caused a chain of actions that tested my faith."

Twenty-one

Aretha was allowed to check out of the hospital the morning of Christmas Eve. Prior to that, every day I had left the hospital, I'd spent time cleaning the apartment and going through her mail. It was then I realized just how bad things had gotten since I'd left.

Apparently, Aretha's illness had caused her to miss several days of work. She had just been fired the week before she had been admitted into the hospital, and because she had missed so many days without informing her boss that she was ill, she had gotten two months behind on her rent. She would be three months behind by January and would be evicted. She was in a lot of debt, and she didn't have insurance, so the hospital bills were going to have to be paid out of her pocket—or someone's. The necessary medications, vitamins, and healthy foods meant she'd need a hefty amount of money, money she didn't have.

Putting aside the financial strain Aretha had been under, I attempted to bring some joy into her life. I decorated the apartment so it would have a festive feel when she could come home. I didn't do it alone, however; I enlisted some help from Stacia, whom I'd been so glad to see, and Miss Page and Donald, who had already done so much for Aretha. When I asked if they would pick up a tree, they brought one over, along with some old decorations Miss Page had Donald bring down from her attic. They stayed and helped us decorate the apartment. I was pleased with the outcome and couldn't wait until Aretha would be home and able to enjoy it.

I didn't want to think about where the money would come from.

. . .

We stood in front of our apartment door while I attempted to unlock it. I opened it wide so it would be easy for Aretha to walk in. She smiled at what she saw: a nicely trimmed Christmas tree, garland all over the place, and little red bows stuck on everything. I had left Christmas music playing to help set the mood. It worked.

"When did you ever find the time?" she asked, marveling.

"I have my ways," I replied.

We walked in and sat down on the couch.

"The doctor said that you would need to continue getting some rest, so I'll roll the television into your bedroom for you whenever you're ready to lie down," I said. "And I'll be preparing a healthy meal for lunch and dinner."

"Thank you, Lanita," she said. "I don't know what I'd do without you."

. . .

It was a different kind of Christmas break for Aretha and me, but we made the best of it. I wanted to talk to her about her outstanding bills, but we never had the kind of relationship in which I could just talk to her about money, so I pushed the conversation off, thinking that I would wait until after Christmas to bring it up. Meanwhile, I found myself monitoring her to make sure she didn't find a way to have one of her friends sneak over some alcohol.

Lester came by on Christmas Day. He walked in and saw Aretha sitting on the couch in her pajamas.

"How you feeling Aretha, baby?" he said, slurring his words.

I couldn't believe he'd already been drinking this early, and on Christmas Day.

"I'm fine, Lester," she said, looking straight ahead at the television.

He tried to whisper, but because he was drunk, he was loud. "I paid one month of rent for you, but baby, I can't come up with enough money to take care of two more months. At least you're only two months behind now, so they won't evict you."

Aretha gave him a dirty look. "Lester, didn't I tell you before that this conversation needed to be between the two of us and the two of us alone?"

"Well, baby, I'm trying to whisper. What's the problem?" He staggered closer to Aretha, sitting down next to her. He held a bottle of Jack Daniel's in front of Aretha's face. "I brought good cheer."

I rushed over to the couch. "Excuse me, Lester, I don't know if Momma told you or not, but she has cirrhosis of the liver, derived from drinking alcohol. If she wants to live, she won't be drinking anymore, so please don't bring any more liquor over here ever again."

"Aretha, is she telling the truth?"

Momma sighed. "Yes, Lester, she's telling the truth. So why don't you go on and leave," she said. "You talk too much, anyway."

"But Aretha, baby, I want to be here for you." He wobbled where he was sitting.

"Lester, just leave," she insisted.

He left that night, and I didn't see him through the rest of the holiday.

After he left, Aretha and I had a heart-to-heart about her financial situation. It was as bad as I'd expected. She insisted that I not worry and assured me that everything was going to be just fine. Somehow I couldn't accept her words and continued to worry about her well-being while trying to figure out what I could do to be of help.

We went to Miss Page's annual Christmas party on Christmas night, but other than that, I didn't hang out with Stacia much or sit around in my pajamas, catching up on all the television I'd been too busy to watch while away at school. A lot needed to be done for Aretha. I used most of the extra money I had saved to help out, shopping for groceries. I prepared healthy meals for her every day and made sure that she took her vitamins. During the evenings, I'd read to her from pamphlets and books I had found at the library about cirrhosis and the importance of her taking care of her body.

My time at home flew by quickly, and New Year's Eve came before we knew it. I still hadn't come up with a way to help her out financially, but I was still thinking about it.

"You are going out tonight, aren't you?" Aretha said.

"No. I figured we could chill out here, eat popcorn and bring in the New Year with Dick Clark."

"I'm not having that," she said. "You have been cooped up in this house during your whole break, taking care of me since you got here. I want you to have some fun tonight. I'll be just fine."

I thought about it. As much as I knew I needed to get out, I didn't want to leave her. Going out would have been a refreshing change of pace, and it would have been good to see some of my old classmates, but I had only one mother and wanted to keep her company.

Aretha continued to push. I continued to decline.

"If you don't get out of this house, girl, I'm gonna get a belt to you," she joked.

Eventually she convinced me she was in good spirits and really didn't need me there. I decided that I would go out for at least one evening, even if only for a few hours.

I called Stacia to find out my options.

"Lanita, I can't believe you finally called. I didn't think I'd hear from you again until next Christmas. As a matter of fact, I called Christmas night, but nobody answered."

"We were at Miss Page's."

"Oh. So what's going on? How's Miss Aretha?"

"Momma's doing much better. I'll tell her you asked," I said. "I called to find out what's going on. What are your plans for New Year's Eve?"

"I haven't decided yet. I hear that Jermaine is having a party, but I'm sure you wouldn't want to see him."

"Why not? I've been over him for some time now. Plus, I think it would be good to see him and Jasmine arguing for old time's sake."

"I heard through the USC grapevine they broke up," said Stacia, who attended USC.

"Oh, really? Well, in that case, it's decided. We're going to Jermaine's party for sure."

I got myself dressed and met Stacia at her place. We walked over to Jermaine's apartment together. The closer we got, the louder the music we heard echoing from his building. My stomach began to churn. I was anxious about seeing him. What would we say to each other? Would he have another girlfriend there with him? Would I still be attracted to him? Would he be attracted to me?

We tapped on the screen door, and Jermaine pushed it open. "Happy New Year!" he yelled.

Stacia and I were startled. Jermaine was ecstatic.

"Happy 1987," Stacia said.

I smiled.

He gave me a second look. "Lanita?"

"Happy New Year, Jermaine," I said calmly.

He hugged me and I hugged back. He smelled so good.

Then he hugged Stacia. "What's up, Stacia?"

I peeped inside and noticed that people were already scattered throughout his family's living room and kitchen.

"Nothing much, boy. What you got to drink in there?" she asked.

"We got a little something for you in the kitchen," he said. "Go on inside. My brother Calvin is back there. He'll set you up."

"Oh, he's cute," Stacia said, rushing past us. "I'm gonna go see what Calvin has for me."

Jermaine and I stayed out on the porch.

"Lanita Lightfoot," he said, sizing me up.

"In the flesh." I smiled.

So did he.

"So how's D.C. treating you?"

"It's wonderful. I love D.C."

"So, are you gonna stay there when you graduate, or do you think you'll be moving back here?"

"Here meaning good ol' Watts, or LA in general?"

"Either." He stepped into my personal space and focused on my eyes.

He was still as handsome as I remembered. The old feelings returned. I didn't want them to, but there they were. "I haven't decided yet," I said. "Momma's been sick. If her health continues to decline, there's no way I can live that far away from her after graduation."

"I hear you." He stepped back.

"So, are you keeping your grades up?" he asked. "Wait a minute, I'm talking to Lanita Lightfoot. You probably have a 4.0 GPA," he said, chuckling.

"My grades are good." I laughed along with him. "So what about you. How is USC treating you?"

"I'm not there anymore."

"Why not? What happened?"

"I haven't been at USC for almost a year now. I had to leave after my sophomore year."

"Why? I thought you were there on a football scholarship."

"I was, but I lost my scholarship when I got a hip injury and could no longer play. When they couldn't use me anymore, they cut me from the team." He rested on the rail behind him. "Man, I was so down when I got cut that I did miserably during finals and didn't make the grade, so I had to leave school altogether."

"I'm sorry to hear that."

"Yeah, but things happen for a reason," he said. "It turned me into a man."

I took a step toward him. "Is that right? So what are you doing now?"

He sighed. "Manual labor, something I hoped I'd never have to do. It pays okay." He pepped up. "But I will be going back to school," he said definitely.

"That's good."

He changed the subject. "So, when are you going back to D.C., and when will you be back here?"

"I'm leaving out on the fifth. I'll be back next Christmas."

"Christmas, huh. That's a long time away."

"That's the way it's been for the past few years."

"That should change," he said, stepping into my space again.

"Why?" I challenged him.

He blushed. "Well, because I'm sure your mother wants to see you more." He moved closer. "But she's not the only one. I'd like to see more of you too, Lanita."

His words didn't move me the way that I would have expected them to years ago. I didn't believe him. When I wanted his attention from elementary through high school, he wasn't available. But once I had become unable to see him, he had finally chosen to express an interest. Well, it was too late. My life was now in Washington, D.C., not Watts, CA. It was just too little too late for us.

"That's nice of you, Jermaine," I said, "but I visit once a year. That's how it is. It's what my mother and I agreed on."

"I see." He leaned back against the rail again. "Hey, it's New Year's Eve, and this is supposed to be a party, right?" He stood and threw his arms out. "I'm crushed, I'll admit it, but I understand." He grabbed my hand and kissed the back of it, just like he'd done during my sixteenth birthday party.

I became flushed.

"Listen," he said, "I understand that you might not be interested in coming home to visit me, but while you're here, would you at least be interested in dinner and a movie one night before you leave?"

"Yeah," I smiled. "I would like that."

"Then it's a date." He smiled shyly. "Let's go inside."

.   .   .

Jermaine picked me up for our dinner and a movie on New Year's Day night. We drove into Hollywood and went to Grauman's Chinese Theatre. Afterward, we walked across the street to have a bite to eat at Hamburger Hamlet.

I'll never forget how nervous I felt, being that close, that exclusive, with Jermaine. He held my hand as we crossed the street, his grip firm, manly, yet gentle and comforting.

While we waited to be seated, he continued to hold my hand, neither of us speaking. We were shown to our seats. There was an anxious energy between us as we browsed through our menus. The waiters took our polite orders and our menus, and we were left to face each other.

First there was an awkward silence. I stared at him. He stared back. I smiled, and so did he. Our smiles transformed into giggles, and then the giggling became all-out laughter. We were behaving like kids.

"I guess you're as nervous as I am," he said.

"I'm not nervous," I replied. "Well, maybe, kind of, but why should we be? We've known each other since elementary school."

"You're right, but I just can't believe that I'm finally out on a date with *the* Lanita Lightfoot."

"Why are you frontin'?"

"I'm not frontin'. You don't know how long I've waited for a night like tonight, to sit across the table from you, to gaze into your eyes, to really get to know you," he said, grinning all the while.

I didn't believe him. I was overwhelmed with excitement just to be there with him, but I didn't buy his enthusiasm or his supposed sincerity. I overlooked his comment as if he'd never made it, changing the subject. "Have you ever been to D.C.?" I asked.

"The only traveling I've done was with the USC football team and we never played there, but I would love to go to D.C. to visit you. How long a plane ride is it?"

Why was he blowing smoke? I thought. My mind drifted to my daddy and how much being in Hollywood reminded me of him. The images of us there together weren't as clear as the longing to feel the way I had when he was alive and in my life. My heart ached. My daddy had left me, and so had Jermaine, right after my sixteenth birthday. I was resigned that I would not fall into the trap of surrendering my feelings to him, only to have him disregard them and turn away from me as if nothing had ever happened. I was much too smart for that.

"D.C. is about a six-hour flight away," I responded dryly.

I spent the rest of the evening talking about how great D.C. was. I embellished my encounter with Len Bias. I made the District of Columbia sound as if it were the greatest place to live on American soil. I'm sure I wore him out with my detailed descriptions of all the monuments and museums and the White House and the restaurants and the parties and my church and Gloria and Jammin' . . . and of course, Howard itself. I just kept talking. I intended to control the conversation and prevent the possibility of exposing what I truly felt about him.

That evening, after our date, I went to sleep convinced I had properly handled my date with Jermaine. With the fortress I had built around my heart, he couldn't hurt me.

My heart would be safe.

Twenty-two

I slept late the day after New Year's, finally awakened by Aretha cussing and fussing. A representative from the gas company had been sent over to turn off the gas because the bill was several months behind.

"You better not turn off my gas," Aretha was yelling. "I've been paying my bills on time for more than ten years, but finally I have a few bad months, and this is how you treat me?"

"I'm sorry, ma'am. I'm only here doing my job," he said.

"Well, you need to do your job elsewhere because you're not about to turn off my gas."

"Ma'am, you owe seventy-five dollars to the gas company. If you just pay me thirty, I'll be able to leave the gas on for you."

"I don't have no thirty dollars, you ugly, big-belly, big-nose, sawed-off sucker!"

I threw on my robe and rushed out of my room and to the door as quickly as I could. I felt partially responsible because I should have been more on top of what was owed and when.

"Excuse me, sir," I said, adopting a tone meant to make up for my mother's insults. "My mother has been extremely ill. I'll take over from here."

"No, Lanita, this doesn't concern you," she said.

I ignored her. "What seems to be the problem?" I asked.

He took his time and relayed to me everything he had already explained to Aretha.

"I'll give you the thirty dollars, sir," I said. "Just give me a moment."

"Lanita, it's my bill, and I don't want to take your money," Aretha said.

"Momma, unfortunately you've been sick, and you don't have the money right now." I tightened the knot of the belt around my robe and walked back to my room to get my checkbook.

The guy took the check out of my hand and wrote me a receipt. "I'm sorry I had to do this," he said, "but I'm just doing my job."

"I just bet you are," Aretha said, rolling her eyes.

He handed me the receipt and walked away.

"I cain't believe they had the nerve to try to cut off my gas," she said, huffing.

"Momma, the man was only doing his job. Plus, if you're late, you're late." I walked over to the drawer where she always kept her bills. "Now, let's sit down and see what you owe and try to figure out what we need to do to catch you up until you're able to work again."

We sat down at the table and spent the afternoon going over her expenses. Aretha was thousands of dollars in debt, including her rent, utilities, and medical bills. We decided to go one step further and try and figure out how much a month it would be to add in her medicine, vitamins, and groceries, coming up with an additional expense of $250 per month.

Aretha put her head down and began to sob. Apparently she had never taken the time to realize just how far in debt she had become.

"What am I going to do?" she asked.

"I don't know." I sat there, staring at the magnets on the refrigerator, wondering how my mother was going to dig herself out of her hole. I was going to be away at school, and she still hadn't recovered enough to go back to work. We were in a bind, and I had committed myself to helping her make it through this crisis, no matter what it took.

I said what I had been considering, but had hoped I wouldn't have to do. "Why don't I sit out this semester or go to school here in the city as a visiting student? People do it all the time. That way, I can get a job and help you catch up on your bills. I'll stay through the summer, and then I'll return to D.C. in the fall."

"No. Oh, no." She was instantly angry. "I am not going to be the cause of you messing up your career. This is my problem, Lanita. You are going back to D.C., and that is my final word. I'll think of something." She walked back to her room.

I sat there, praying for a miracle, but in the back of my mind, I had already accepted the inevitable. There was no way I was going to leave my sick mother stranded, one step from being evicted, to go back to my carefree life in D.C. If I couldn't visit a local college I would be just one semester behind when I returned, and she was worth the sacrifice.

Besides preparing meals for Aretha, I spent the rest of the day preparing to make drastic changes to ensure my transition would be as effortless as possible. My first step was to contact Gloria, who was still in Oakland, and inform her what had been going on and why she would need to try to get a new roommate.

"It's a good thing we've already paid for January's rent," she said.

"Yeah, that gives you a full month to find someone to take my place. And Gloria, when you get back, I'm gonna have to ask you to ship some things here to me."

"Whatever you need, but are you sure this is what has to be done?" she asked.

"Do you have any other suggestions? I'm open to anything."

We sat in silence.

"Well, I'll make sure that whoever moves in understands that she'll have your room only through the summer, and that you'll be back in the fall."

"Exactly. Surely by the end of the summer, everything will be caught up enough that Aretha will be on her own until I graduate and move back home."

"Lanita, I'm really proud of you," Gloria said. "You're doing the right thing."

"Thank you so much, Gloria. I needed to hear that."

I was nearly moved to tears, but I stopped myself. A tough exterior based on a "whatever it takes to make this work" attitude took over, and I was able to push forward.

Next, I contacted both Howard and UCLA to get information on the appropriate steps to be a visiting student for the semester. Both schools promised to put the necessary forms in the mail for me.

Aretha yelled in to me, "Lanita, let me use the phone when you get off."

Even though she told him to leave her alone, she called Lester for more money, but they ended up arguing. Aretha slammed down the phone and rushed to the bathroom.

I knew my mother was hurting. So was I. I reassured myself that it was a temporary situation, that we would be okay. If only I could convince her of the same.

I tapped on the bathroom door. "Momma, there's no use in crying about it. It won't change a thing."

"I know, Lanita, but why is it that life is so damned hard?"

I thought about her words, and she was right. Life was harsh. It had a way of throwing curves that stole all hope. But I was not going to give up. I intended to meet this battle head-on.

I encouraged Aretha to get some rest and not worry about it. Then I got back on the phone.

I contacted Miss Page and informed her of my plans.

In true form, she offered her full support. "If there is anything that I can do, just let me know."

"We need to get at least one more month paid on the rent as soon as possible. It'll take some of the pressure off. And all the utilities are behind. If you could let me borrow five hundred dollars, I'll pay every penny of it back to you," I promised.

"You got it, Lanita. I'll have it to you by the end of the week. In the meantime, I want you to call everyone she owes and try to make some sort of payment arrangement. That way, you won't lose any of your utilities or get put out until you can get caught up."

"Thank you so much, Miss Page," I said. "I don't know what I'd do if God hadn't placed you in my life."

"I love you like the daughter I never had, Lanita. I only wish I could do more."

We hung up the phone, and I commenced calling and making payment arrangements for all of Aretha's bills. After I made the last call of the day, I felt like I could at least breathe again.

The phone rang.

I picked it up. "Hello," I said.

"Hey, Lanita, this is Jermaine."

"Oh, hi, Jermaine. How are you?" I said, trying to remove any tension that remained in my voice from the calls I'd just made.

"I've been thinking about you ever since I saw you last night. Really, I'd been thinking about you since you left Watts."

I took a deep breath, then slowly released it. "What were you thinking?"

"Well, I thought about all the things you told me about your life in Washington, D.C. Then I wondered what would have happened between us if I had found the guts to pursue you after your birthday party."

It was the wrong time for nonsense. I was not going to let him play games with me, so I called his bluff. "How could you have pursued me when you and Jasmine Ray were such a hot couple?"

"I was with Jasmine because *she* pursued *me*. I didn't have to do anything. She made all the moves. It was easy. If you recall, she and I were mismatched. We spent more time arguing than anything."

"Why did you stay?"

"Young and dumb. But I'm a man now, and I would never put myself through that kind of a relationship again."

"Oh," I said, still unconvinced.

"Back in high school, I was scared of you. You're a piece of work. I was crazy about you, but I wasn't ready for you. Lanita, you were a real woman, even back then, and I wasn't mature enough to step up to the plate."

"What makes you think that?"

"You were always the smart girl. A beauty with brains. You had the option to go to any school you wanted, plus you were a cheerleader. Jasmine was only outer beauty. There wasn't an intelligent bone in her body. I don't know, I guess I could say that I was intimidated by you."

"I had no idea, Jermaine." The wall I'd put around my heart was beginning to crumble.

"Plus, I've always admired you, the way you went from being the girl in class who no one wanted to associate with to becoming one of the most popular girls in school. It says a lot about you. I only wish that instead of falling for the peer pressure of the other dudes when I was young, I would have defended you back then."

In some twisted way, Jermaine's words were sweet, but I still wasn't sure how sincere he was being with me.

"So, when do you think we can get together again?" he asked. "I was thinking that Saturday night would be best. What do you think?"

"I'm not sure, Jermaine. I have a lot going on right now. I'm gonna have to get back to you on it."

"I knew it. You haven't really cared for me much since sixth grade. Did I ever tell you how sorry I was?"

"Jermaine, listen. It's in the past. You were young. Plus, I forgave you when you apologized the first time, remember, at my sixteenth birthday?"

"Ah, yeah. I remember. We kissed on your porch. I even brought you a gift."

"I still have it."

"Really?"

"Yep."

"So why don't you want to go out with me again?"

"Jermaine, I'm dealing with some things that are going on with Aretha and with school. I don't know if I'll be able to see you any time soon. But I'll get back with you," I promised.

"Okay, but remember that it's my treat again. And you can choose wherever we go. Maybe that'll help you while you're deciding."

"Thanks, Jermaine."

When we hung up, I went to the bathroom, ran a tub of hot water, and submerged myself in it to soak away the worries of the day. I had no idea what kind of job I would be able to find, but I was optimistic that everything would work out.

I took a moment and closed my eyes and prayed: "Dear Lord, this is Lanita. I don't understand what you're up to, but I pray that everything will eventually work out."

I sat back in the tub and trusted that He had heard me.

Twenty-three

Miss Lina executed the final step in Lanita's facial, rubbing moisturizer over her skin.

"Your face is good and clean now. All the dead skin has been removed. You now have the gentle radiance of a well-pampered woman," she said. "You can go over and look at yourself in the mirror if you'd like."

Lanita, who had gotten quite comfortable lying back on the table, got up and went over to the mirror. She looked at her face, which was glowing back at her, and smiled as she removed the satin scarf Miss Lina had used to protect her hair. She ran her fingers through her hair, her smile growing wider.

"I look damn good," she said.

"You sure do."

"Thanks so much, Miss Lina," Lanita said.

"It was my pleasure. It's not often that someone as sweet and selfless as you visits me. Thanks for sharing your story with me. I can relate to the pain you felt back then and I'm glad to see you've apparently overcome."

"Yes I have. Believe it or not, there was a time you wouldn't have viewed me as sweet or selfless. But thank God our past doesn't define our present."

"You can say that again." Miss Lina smiled, falling into her own thoughts.

"So where is my final destination?" Lanita asked.

"I'll walk you over. You'll be seeing Deidra Michelle, our nail tech, who does an incredible job. She's located at the end of the hall."

Miss Lina walked Lanita down the hall. "Hello, Deidra. How's it going?" she asked.

"Today is a good day." Deidra was a young, hip Black woman with great taste and style, as evident in her chic jeans and cute baby-doll T. She wore her curly hair parted down the middle, flowing to just below her ears.

"Good for you," Miss Lina said. "It seems I'm passing another client over to you. Deidra Michelle, this is Lanita."

"Hello, Lanita," Deidra Michelle said, smiling. "You can go ahead and have a seat so we can begin," she cheerfully instructed.

Lanita sat down.

"Lanita is graduating from college today," Miss Lina said, waving good-bye.

"Oh, congratulations."

"Thank you. I'm leaving from here to go directly to the school. My husband is meeting me over there."

"Really," Deidra replied. "Excuse me, Lanita. I'm gonna go prep for your pedicure."

She raced off and returned with a foot bowl. She plugged it in and placed it at Lanita's feet. As she turned a knob on the top, bubbles began to form. "Hop in," she said.

Lanita removed her sandals and submerged her feet in the bowl. "Ooh, that feels good."

"It's the simple pleasures in life that excite," Deidra Michelle said with a giggle.

"You're right about that," Lanita replied.

"If you don't mind me asking, how old are you?" Deidra walked around to the other side of the manicurist's table and took a seat.

"Oh, not at all. I'm thirty-eight."

Deidra took Lanita's hands in hers and began rubbing them.

"You're aging well, if you don't mind my saying so. I hope I look as great as you when I'm thirty-eight."

"It's not me," Lanita said, blushing. "It's the facial Miss Lina just gave me."

Deidra placed Lanita's hands flat on the table and went to work. "Yeah, maybe, but I see a lot of women come through here. I've come to realize that you either age well or you don't, no matter how often Miss Lina exfoliates your skin."

They both laughed.

"So you're thirty-eight and you're married. What did you do before you decided to get your degree?"

Lanita took a deep breath and began to explain to Deidra Michelle just why it had taken her so long to graduate.

. . .

After completing two and a half years at Howard University, I planned to be a visiting student at UCLA for one semester, with hopes of returning to Howard the following fall. But the problems continued to mount. I found out that it was too late to apply as a visiting student, that they weren't accepting any more for the semester. I wasn't able to get into any other schools for the same reason.

I accepted that I would still be returning to Howard in the fall, just one semester behind. I didn't mind much because I had taken summer courses every year so I would have been able to have a lighter class load my senior year. I would just have to carry a heavier load than I had expected.

On top of the bad news about school, it took me three weeks to get my first job. I was finally hired as a customer-service representative for an insurance company, making $7.50 an hour. I woke up at around four-thirty every morning, got dressed, and then rushed out to catch the bus to downtown Los Angeles. After work, I'd rush back home and prepare dinner for Aretha and me. In between, I would run any necessary errands. On Sundays we would go to church at my insistence. Aretha resisted initially, saying, "I haven't been to church in this long. Why should I start now? I'm a sinner, Lanita, God won't forgive me for staying away from Him for all these years."

"No, Momma, it's not like that. God doesn't care what you did before you came to Him. No matter what kind of person you are, He's always waiting for you with open arms to come to Him so He can heal and protect you."

"How do you know that, Lanita?" she asked.

"That's what the preacher said at my church in D.C. And I believe him. Also, you got a second chance. Your cirrhosis could have wiped you out. Aren't you thankful you survived?" I asked her.

"Some days," she responded dryly.

Aretha must have taken my words into consideration because after much discussion she decided to give the "church thing" a try.

I continued at an exhausting pace through the spring and well into the summer. As it began to get close to the time I'd been planning to return to D.C., it became painfully clear that I hadn't raised enough money to get Aretha in the proper position to be left alone. Nor did I have enough money to fly back and begin again in D.C.—not to mention that I still hadn't repaid Miss Page. As the summer turned into fall, it became obvious that my plan to get back to D.C. was failing.

Once I realized the severity of my situation, I panicked. Somewhere deep down in my heart, I lost faith. I gave up. Yet I continued floundering through my days, feeling disillusioned and depressed. It seemed that there was no way Aretha and I would ever get caught up. I became overwhelmed with my new responsibilities and didn't have much of an outlet.

I didn't want to be seen out in too many places because subconsciously I was hiding from Jermaine. I didn't want him to know that I hadn't returned to D.C. I never called him back like I'd promised, and I wasn't prepared to run into him. I would have to explain why I was still in town.

One evening Stacia came by. We sat in my bedroom listening to the radio, while Aretha, who seemed to have gotten used to having me around, sat content in front of the television, which had become one of her favorite pastimes since she had taken ill. Fatigue kept her stationary; however, that didn't change the mouth she had on her.

She was fussing at the contestants on *Family Feud* so loudly that we could hear her over the music. "You flimsy fool, how you gonna say that a way to make a baby stop crying would be to lay it down alone in a bassinet? That would make a baby cry, not stop it. Dumb. Dumb. Just plain dumb."

We continued our conversation.

"You remember that girl Jackie?" Stacia asked.

"You mean Jackie Miles, the quiet girl whose clothes were always too tight for her?"

"Yeah, her."

"What about her?" I asked.

"Somebody told me that she's changed a lot. She's probably still wearing clothes that are too tight, but now she's taking them off."

"What are you talking about?"

"I'm saying she's shaking her moneymaker. Jackie is working at the local strip club, clocking dollars."

"No way. She was always so quiet!"

"Yep. Everybody's been talking about it. She's only been there about two months, but I hear she's already driving a hot ride and dresses in designer wear from head to toe."

"She's making good money, huh?" I asked. "I've been wondering what I could do to make some big money, so I can get out of the rut I'm in."

"Well, she sure figured it out."

"Would you ever do it?" I asked Stacia.

"Girl, I thought about it. It's not right, but what broke woman hasn't considered stripping?"

"Would you ever do it?"

Stacia sniffed. "I never followed up with my thoughts for two reasons. One, haven't you noticed how much weight I've picked up since we graduated from high school? The other reason is that every man in this neighborhood goes down to that strip joint. I wouldn't be able to deal with all them knowing what my body looks like. Being the talk of the town like Jackie—no, my reputation is much too valuable."

"I know what you mean," I sighed. "That's why I've been staying in this house. All I do is go to work and church on Sundays."

"Trying to hide from Jermaine? Girl, he knows you're still here. Watts ain't but yea big."

I knew she was right, but I still didn't want to run into him. I switched back to our first subject. "If you could be a stripper outside Watts, would you?"

"The only way I would is if I found a discreet club in West Hollywood or somewhere like that, where the brothers out here would never dream of going. But even then . . . I don't know. What about you?" she asked. "You thinking about it?"

"Stacia, the thought never once crossed my mind until now. You know I'm still a virgin, but I feel like my prayers aren't being answered, like God doesn't want me to get back to D.C. Girl, I'm so desperate for money that anything that's going to get me ahead is enticing. Yet I'm with you—I couldn't imagine everybody seeing me naked, especially when I'd have to turn around and face them in church or at the grocery store the next day."

"I would prefer to be a cocktail waitress at one of those spots," Stacia said. "They still get paid pretty good, but they're not performing, and all those eyes wouldn't be on you because the customers come to see the strippers."

"How do you know so much?"

"Oh, a couple of girls at USC work as cocktail waitresses to help pay their tuition. They seem to like their jobs."

I made a mental note to check into becoming a cocktail waitress. I didn't share my aspiration with Stacia because in case I did find a job, I didn't want the news to get back to Jermaine.

"Yeah, life's a trip," I sighed.

"That it is," Stacia agreed. "You know, you need to face Jermaine."

I snorted. "I don't intend to do that any time soon."

"You're insane. You've been crazy for him since you can remember, and he expresses an interest finally, and you turn and run in a different direction?"

"I've got too much going on to go and fall in love right now, Stacia. What if he doesn't have my back just when I need him the most? Plus, being in love might alter my plans."

"What's wrong with that?" Stacia asked.

"I have to get back to D.C. fast."

"Why? What's so great in that city that you don't have here?"

"I just have to get back there," I said. "You wouldn't understand."

"Maybe I wouldn't," Stacia said, rolling her eyes, "but I also know that if a good man were after me, I would stand up and take notice."

We sat in silence, listening to "I Wanna Dance with Somebody" by Whitney Houston on the radio. It was one of those moments when Stacia saw things one way and I saw them another. Neither of us would be swayed in our opinions; therefore nothing else needed to be said.

Twenty-four

I walked into the dark, smoky, nearly empty room. I was extremely nervous, but I'd convinced myself to continue. The music was blaring through the speakers posted next to the stage, and two men were sitting at a lone table in the corner, one smoking a cigar and the other speaking intensely. The guy with the cigar kept nodding periodically, and both had serious faces.

I carefully watched them before slowly approaching.

"Excuse me," I said.

They continued their discussion. I knew I needed to speak up, but I hoped I wouldn't have to say it again.

I walked a bit closer. "Excuse me." I increased the volume in my voice.

The guy who had been doing most of the talking looked up, scanning me from head to toe, and said, "Well, what do we have here?"

"I apologize for interrupting your conversation, but my name is Lanita Lightfoot and"—I swallowed—"I am interested in being a cocktail waitress at your club."

"We're not looking for any new waitresses," the guy with the cigar barked.

"Wait a minute, Ronnie. Isn't Dominique supposed to be moving back to D.C. in two weeks?" the other said.

I took that information as a good sign. Dominique, whoever she was, had apparently saved enough money to get back to D.C. Maybe I could do the same thing.

"I didn't know she was leaving, Dave. Why is this the first I've heard?" Ronnie placed his cigar in the ashtray.

"I was just getting ready to tell you, but I thought the other thing was more important."

Ronnie grunted. "So, what's your name again?" He squinted at me through the smoke.

"Lanita L—"

"That won't work. Can you dance?" he said.

"Oh, no, I don't want to dance. I just want to be a waitress."

"There are no positions available, but we do need a new dancer, and you look like you might have what it takes," Ronnie said.

"You're right," Dave said, eyeing me. "She's cute enough."

"Yeah, she's cute. But cute doesn't sell drinks. It helps, but I need to know if you can move," Ronnie said.

"I'm sorry—stripping, that's not me," I said and rushed out the door past two casually dressed young ladies who were coming in.

My heart was pounding in my chest, and I was shaking. I fell back against the wall of the club. I couldn't believe they had asked me to dance. Every bone in my body said stripping was not the right road for me. I was a Christian, and showing my body would clash with my every belief. It was bad enough that I was choosing to work in such a sinful environment, but being the main attraction would send me straight to hell.

I had taken the bus from work to West Hollywood with that one strip club in mind. There was another one a few blocks away. I would have to walk to it, getting up my courage to begin again.

Just then, the door flew open. It was Dave. He was a tall, lanky, near-White-looking Black guy dressed in an expensive yet cheesy suit. He seemed hyper—I would bet he had a cocaine habit.

"Hey, Lanita, Ronnie would like to talk to you about the cocktail waitress thing."

I stared.

"Come on in. It's just a conversation," he insisted.

I reluctantly followed him back into the club, holding on to the hope that they would work something out with me. I was so focused on getting back to D.C. and completing what I had begun that I was willing to listen to anybody who was talking about putting some money in my pockets. The more money, the sooner I could get back to my normal life.

"Lanita, come and have a seat," Ronnie said, his voice deep and raspy.

I sat, and Dave took the chair on the other side of me. He wrapped his arm around my chair, his finger tapping the back of my seat. I tried to ignore it.

The houselights went down, and the music played louder.

"So what are you drinking?" Ronnie politely asked. He was a broad Italian guy with a round nose and wavy coal-black hair. His glare was intense, and he looked like he didn't get enough sleep. He was well dressed and his fingernails were better-kept than mine.

"Oh, I don't drink," I replied timidly. My stint with cocaine had left me clean and sober, and Momma's current condition was enough to dry out anyone.

"How about a Shirley Temple, honey?" he suggested. "It's non-alcoholic."

"Okay, that's cool," I replied.

After a moment, a scantily dressed waitress walked over and gave us our drinks.

"So you want to be a cocktail waitress?" Dave tapped on my chair some more.

I turned in his direction, "Well, I'm thinking about it, if the money's right." I took a sip of my drink. "This is good. What's in it?" I asked the waitress.

"Sprite and grenadine," she replied. She was cool.

Ronnie leaned in close to me. "Tish here makes three dollars and fifty cents an hour, base. She gets about two, three, and, on an exceptionally good night, maybe four hundred in tips."

Tish smiled and walked away.

Ronnie continued. "With the way our schedule works, she's required to work five nights a week, with no exception. If she misses one night, she goes on probation. Once she misses two nights, her hours are cut drastically—she becomes a substitute. If she misses another night, she's out of here permanently. We have a waiting list a mile long for cocktail waitresses to fill her shoes, chicks who won't miss any days."

"I consider myself reliable," I said confidently.

"I'm sure you are, and the money's pretty good, right?" Ronnie fired up another cigar.

"The money sounds great," I said optimistically.

"Well, check this out," Dave said. Now his knee and his finger were hopping.

A spotlight hit the stage and a new song played from the speakers. One of the two women who had walked past me earlier, a Puerto Rican girl, came from the wings, dressed as the sexiest nurse I'd ever seen, and began dancing seductively. She was beautiful.

My eyes widened.

"That's Carmen," Dave said with a huge grin.

"Okay," I said, trying to seem unfazed.

"Carmen is required to dance only three nights a week, and she makes roughly a grand a night. On the really good nights, she's been known to clock anywhere from fifteen hundred to three thousand dollars."

My jaw dropped. I never would have imagined that kind of money could be made in one night, even stripping. Carmen continued to move, dancing around the pole at the center of the stage. She peeled off the uniform and walked with confidence down the catwalk in a sequined bra and a G-string.

I couldn't take my eyes off her. The figures Dave had run down were racing through my mind. What she was doing didn't seem all that difficult. She didn't even have to remove her bra.

Once the two saw the look in my eyes, they knew they had my attention.

"That's enough, Carmen," Ronnie said.

She winked and blew a kiss at him, strutting off the stage and picking up her costume along the way.

"What would your daddy say if he knew you stripped?" Ronnie asked.

"Why would you ask me a question like that?" I replied defensively.

The volume of the music decreased.

He calmly replied, "Well, that's usually the girls' major concern, how their fathers would take the news of their stripping."

"Oh, I'm not concerned about that. I haven't seen my daddy since I was twelve. I just don't think stripping is for me."

The waitress walked back over to the table. "Excuse me, Ronnie, but there is an important call for you."

"Pardon me for a moment," he said and followed her to the back of the club.

Dave turned to me. "What a shame," he said sympathetically.

I thought he was talking about me not wanting to strip, but his next words proved otherwise.

"I know how that feels—my daddy walked out on my mother and me when I was born. I never knew the bastard," he confessed.

"I'm sorry to hear that," I replied.

"See, that's what's missing in this society—loyalty. So I try to give that to my girls." He pulled his seat closer to me. "My girls feel safe here. I think some of them even look at me as their daddy."

I was skeptical, extremely skeptical.

"I see to it that the club runs smoothly so the girls make plenty of money every night. I take money from my profits to have bodyguards available at all times to walk the girls to and from their cars—and they all drive nice cars. And if any of them are going through anything or are having any problems, no matter what, I have an open-door policy. They can always come to me. They even have my home number. What other employer gives his employees his home number?"

"I just assumed Ronnie was the owner."

"Well, he is, but I manage this spot. I feel attached to it. We're like one big family here. In the seven years I've been managing this joint, I have never walked out on these girls. I'm constant. A pillar," he said.

"So are you interested?" Ronnie chimed in, taking his seat on the other side of me.

•   •   •

I went back to my customer-service job. The entire day I scrutinized everything about my job. I was frustrated with the seven-fifty an hour I was making; by my small, empty cubicle; by the strict policies of the office, which included no phone calls that weren't work related; by the thirty-minute lunch breaks; and by the other girls in the office, who had no aspirations or goals in their lives.

My conversation with Dave played in my head all day. I clung to his words. He was a bit highstrung, but he had reached out to me and shared an intimate piece of his private life that I completely connected with. I decided that I trusted him. It seemed that I would be safe dancing as long as Dave was there. Plus, it would only be temporary.

The moment I left work, I phoned Dave and asked for a private audition. We set up a time.

That weekend, I went to a video store and looked through the X-rated section for anything centered around strip clubs. I watched the girls dance and practiced in the mirror every night after Aretha went to sleep.

I put a tape in the tape deck, stood in front of the mirror, and began swaying from side to side. The sight of me trying to be erotically appealing was ridiculous. I bowed over in laughter. Once I got my composure, I turned away from the mirror and concentrated on synchronizing my body movements with the music until I no longer felt awkward.

Eventually I became reasonably comfortable with my sensual side. My comfort turned into fright. My integrity was challenged. I wasn't just dancing for enjoyment, I was preparing to step into the immoral world of adult entertainment.

Aretha called to me. "Lanita."

I quickly turned off the music and rushed to her room.

"Lanita, can you bring me another blanket?" she asked.

"Sure. Are you cold?"

"No, it's just that I've had this same mattress since before you were born. The springs are coming through. I don't know how much longer I can take it."

To know that my mother was not only ill but also uncomfortable was tough to take. "Why don't we switch mattresses until we can afford to get you a new mattress."

That night we switched mattresses, although mine wasn't in much better shape than hers.

I went back to the club, ready to audition.

"We normally have an open call for new dancers," Ronnie said, "but since my friend here seems to be pulling for you, here's your chance. If we like you, we hire you. If you're no good, I'm gonna have to ask you to never come back."

Ronnie looked over at Dave, who was grinning from ear to ear.

"Are any of the girls here?" Ronnie asked.

"Yeah, Carmen and Tina," Dave said. "They're preparing the schedule for next week."

"Okay, have them come up so that we can have an audience."

"Follow Dave," Ronnie ordered.

I followed him behind the stage and down a short hall to the dressing room. Before tapping on the door, he looked at me and said, "Don't you worry about a thing. You're gonna do just fine." He squeezed my shoulder and smiled.

"Hey, Dave," said a skinny blue-eyed, big-boobed, blond-haired chick I later learned was Tina.

"This is . . . well, Lanita, but not for long." He laughed. "Anyway, she needs to get outfitted for an audition."

"Since when did we start doing things like this?" said Carmen, the girl I had seen perform a few days earlier.

"Today," Dave said. "Find her something to dance in. Then Ronnie wants you two to come out with us and watch her."

He walked out.

"You must be pretty special to get a private audition," Tina said as she went through some costumes hanging in a portable closet against the wall.

"Yeah, I wonder who she had to fuck," Carmen said, eyeing me with obvious distrust.

"I didn't fuck anybody," I boldly replied. I stared at Carmen, silently informing her that I wasn't there to play games with her.

"Oh, don't mind Carmen," Tina said. "She's our only exotic, and she just fears the competition."

"Fuck both a y'all!" Carmen said and walked out.

"Exotic? What do you mean by that?" I asked.

"Well, out here in West Hollywood, anyone who isn't the typical White girl next door is considered exotic and taboo to our main customers, who are wealthy, White, and Jewish men out to have a good time. If they're not in love with my type, the White man's treasure, and if you're good, they'd tip a beauty like you well to keep their laps happy. Right now, Carmen is our most attractive and well-paid exotic."

"Oh." I didn't know how I felt about being an exotic, but if it meant more money, I didn't care.

"Are you good?" Tina asked.

I was honest. "I don't know."

"Well, before you step out on that stage, you'd better think you're the best gift God ever put on this earth—and you'd better know that every person in that audience, man or woman, would spend his entire paycheck to get next to you."

"Why is that?" I asked.

"It's called an air, and you want that to exude from your very being," Tina shared.

"Thank you," I said.

"I don't mind sharing with you because I already know that no girl who walks into this club will ever be better looking, more desirable, or better paid than I am." She smiled. "You look a little tense. Why don't you have a drink?"

"I don't drink," I said.

"You'd better start, because if you get chosen to work here, you're gonna need some kind of vice to remain sane, and the girls who choose sex never make it very far."

I took the glass that Tina offered me and chugged down its contents, which made me gag. "What is this?" I asked.

"It's pure grain, straight."

"Damn."

I changed into my outfit as quickly as I could. My high hit just in time for me to get on the stage. The music started, and I worked my body like I had been dancing for money all my life. I strutted down the catwalk and began to seductively remove articles of clothing, piece by piece. I moved like I owned the stage, all the while convincing myself that I was the sexiest, most desirable woman in the world. In order to keep up the facade, I pretended that while I was dancing, Jermaine was the only person in the audience. The more clothes I removed, the more he wanted me. Only he couldn't have me because there were bars between us. I escaped into my fantasy world, trying to convince everyone at the table that I was the one for the job.

The music stopped abruptly, and I was a deer caught in headlights.

"Get down here, Destiny," Ronnie said.

"Excuse me?"

"That's your new name, Destiny."

I got off the stage, and Ronnie and Dave advised me of the ins and outs of the job.

Ronnie cleared his voice, but it was still raspy, "First things first. You need to go downtown and get a license in order to work."

Dave added, "There is a charge for that, but you'll get that little money back in no time." I nodded. Dave wrote down the address on a piece of paper and handed it to me.

The shocker came when Ronnie casually added, "Make sure that you get as comfortable in the nude as you are with your breasts covered."

Dave added, "There's no bigger turn-off than a girl who seems confident, but loses it when her bra comes off."

"I have to remove my bra?" I asked.

"Yeah, everything comes off except the G-string," Dave replied.

Ronnie looked at me as if I should have expected it.

"After seeing Carmen dance, I'd been under the impression that I would stop at my bra."

"Nah Kid, it don't work like that," Dave said and continued to go down the house rules before I could digest this new information.

A lot of rules were surprising: for example, boyfriends were not allowed in the club. But there were others I was grateful for, especially the one that said I wasn't allowed to have sex with any of the customers, and the other that said that customers could look but not touch. It was good to know that even though I'd be sinning, I wouldn't be getting touched by any of the other sinners.

Twenty-five

With the help of Dave's comforting words, I got used to the idea of removing my bra. I was disappointed at myself in my quick acceptance of drinking to release my tension. I never would have imagined I would have felt the need to drink in order to make it through a workday or, in the case of a dancer, a worknight. It was the one thing Aretha would have bet I would not have done, the one thing I was sure I'd never do, especially after the way it had messed up Aretha's liver. I began to drink pure grain alcohol—and I had a partner in Tina, who swore by the stuff.

Once I began dancing, time managed to get away from me, and before I knew it I had been seductively removing my clothes three to four times a week for nearly a year. The money was as good as they promised. It was 1988, and so much about me and my surroundings had changed that nothing made sense. Prozac was introduced as an antidepressant. Minister Jimmy Swaggart admitted to being with a prostitute. Actress Robin Givens filed for divorce from Mike Tyson, and entertainer Sonny Bono became mayor of Palm Springs. Strangest of all, I was stripping to make money.

I repaid Miss Page the five hundred I had borrowed from her. I caught up on Aretha's expenses and the doctor bills and got us both new mattresses and a new sofa. She had regained her health and started back working again.

But me, I was so ashamed of my occupation and the fact that I hadn't finished school that I had gotten out of the neighborhood as quickly as I could. I went back to visit Aretha and bring her money.

Once she asked, "Now that we've caught up the bills, when you going back to D.C.?"

"I'm working on it." I responded.

Another time she asked, "So, what kind of job do you have, Lanita? It seems that things are going pretty good for you."

I replied, "It's no big deal, just a little something to make ends meet until I can get my degree."

"Speaking of degree . . ." she'd begin.

"Oh, Aretha, I hate to, but I really gotta go. I've got a lot to do. I'll come by to see you next week."

"I'm sick of all this secretiveness, Lanita." She'd follow me as I rushed out the door as quickly as I'd come in.

No one in my new circle knew me as Lanita. I had become Destiny, the exotic Black chick who shared an overpriced two-bedroom apartment in West Hollywood with a White blonde named Tina. I was driving a brand spanking new sports car and dating some of the wealthiest men in Hollywood.

I had somehow become caught up in the game of receiving whatever I desired, just for making my beauty available to the men who paid big money to see it. As long as I continued to dance and believed that men would do anything for an encounter with my beauty, they did just that. A wealthy widower who threw parties on his private yacht once a month had given me my car. I had agreed to spend the night with him—one night. We didn't even have sex. He just kissed on my breasts all night until he fell asleep. The next morning he asked me what kind of car I wanted, and I had it by the end of the week.

Tina and I became quite a pair. We were more than just strippers; we had dubbed ourselves "ladies of leisure," sleeping until noon, dining in the best restaurants, and shopping on Robertson Boulevard and Rodeo Drive. Then we'd dress for the evening to hit Sunset Strip, drinking and barhopping as part of our mission to meet wealthy men.

When we were invited to private parties, we'd charge. Our presence alone at exclusive parties garnered a couple of grand each, and we didn't even have to strip. We spent time at mansions in Beverly Hills, Hollywood Hills, and Woodland Hills, but the ultimate was when we were invited to meet Hugh Hefner at the Midsummer Night's Dream party, his annual event at the Playboy Mansion.

Tina and I were so excited. We planned for days, including a visit to the spa and salon and a shopping spree to buy the sexiest pajama ensembles we could find. Tina's goal was to be featured in *Playboy* magazine. Mine was to make money, as always.

The closer we got to the date at the mansion, the more I realized what I had been suppressing since I had begun to dance—that I was living out Tina's dream, not mine. In truth, the only reason I continued to dance was that I was scared to go back to D.C., especially since Gloria had already obtained her degree. But who could I share that information with?

Fear had me trapped in a lifestyle that—although at times it seemed exciting and glamorous on the outside—was eating away at my soul. I no longer stood for anything. I couldn't remember the last time I had gone to church or even prayed to God to help me change. I had no goals. I didn't want to be featured on the cover of *Playboy* or anywhere in its sheets. I was just living day to day, taking whatever men chose to throw my way, fighting to hold on to the one thing that kept me sane, my virginity.

The irony of it all is that I was a twenty-three-year-old virgin, making a living selling the illusion of sex. Since I had been back in Los Angeles, I hadn't dated a man I liked—I mean, *truly* liked—and I spent a lot of time thinking about Jermaine, from whom I had run. My life made no sense.

While we were getting ready for the party that night, Tina's eyes were beaming. This was the night that she had been working toward.

"Destiny, look at us. We are so hot!" she said. "We are going to turn heads left and right when we walk into that party."

I smiled back at her and continued to get dressed.

"And once Hugh gets a load of these, he's going to beg me to pose for his magazine," she said, grabbing her pumped-up breasts. "Wouldn't it be cool if he chose both of us or asked us to move into the mansion?"

"I wouldn't want to," I said as I patiently applied my false eyelashes.

"Why not?" she asked and began harping on her philosophy of men. "Hugh loves to have beautiful women of all kinds around him. He is the epitome of what I've been trying to tell you about men from the beginning. Hugh, just like every other man in this world, is not capable of being monogamous. That's why I don't want to settle down with just one man—at least not while I'm still young. I'm not ready to get my heart broken."

"So you're going to remain single?" I asked.

"Of course not. I'll eventually marry an old rich fart who'll be twice my age and can barely get it up. Once we have one or two kids, I'll have an affair with some young, virile guy who'll be at my beck and call. Because even though the old fogy would more than likely be impotent, he'll still be out chasing women every free chance he gets."

"You're twisted, you know that?"

"Maybe so, but that's why I'll never be without."

I changed the subject. "I wonder who's going to be at the party tonight?"

"Everybody who's anybody will be there tonight."

"So what time will Peter be here?" I asked.

"He should be here in about thirty minutes."

"That gives me time to have a drink. Do you want anything?" I asked.

"Yeah, Destiny, whatever you're having," she responded.

I went into the kitchen and fixed us a couple of cocktails, bringing them back to her room, where we finished getting dressed.

"By the way, the mail came," she said. "You might want to check it out. It looks like there's an invitation for you."

I walked over to the counter, where Tina always put the mail, and sorted through the envelopes. I pulled out a wedding invitation. Upon closer examination, it was an invitation for the union of Miss Page and Donald. I smiled big. Either society had definitely changed or Donald had finally found the courage to stand up to the world and proclaim his love for Miss Page. Either way, their union was now going to be legit and would have to be acknowledged by his friends and family, just as it had been by Miss Page's. I felt nothing but pure joy for the two of them. It had been a long time coming.

As much as I wanted, I couldn't show my face at their wedding. I felt too ashamed, too dirty to subject them to my presence. I was elated for them, but I didn't have the courage to join them in their celebration.

Moved by their newfound strength, I did something I hadn't done in quite some time. I prayed. "Dear God, help me find the strength to stand up and make some changes in my own mess of a life."

The words of the preacher who'd baptized me back in D.C. came to mind. "As a Christian, you're not perfect, and it doesn't mean you won't stumble or fall. It just means that now you have Christ in your corner, and with Him, there is nothing you won't be able to overcome."

I hoped that what he said on that day was true because I had dug a deep hole for myself and had no clear way of getting out.

.   .   .

Peter, a cool British guy who frequented the strip club where we danced, often bringing celebrities, picked us up. We hopped into his Benz and made our way to the Playboy Mansion.

Once we pulled up to the carport, Tina nearly leaped out of the car before we could get to the valet. "I'm so excited," she gushed.

"So am I. This place is gorgeous," I said. The mansion was huge and beautiful.

"I don't understand why you wouldn't want to live here," she said. "I would do anything to call this place home."

One of the valets opened the door to the car, and Tina, Peter, and I got out. When I stood, I realized I'd had just a little too much to drink, but I composed myself as best I could as we walked through the foyer, down the hall, and into the ballroom.

The music was cranked way up, and people were partying like there was no tomorrow. Everyone was dressed in his or her sexiest lingerie, moving around either on or near the dance floor, mingling or grooving. The three of us immediately joined in.

Those who weren't dancing lounged on a sea of colorful satin pillows, while others munched on the spread of delectable foods.

"There's Hugh," Peter said, pointing him out.

We looked across the floor and spotted Hef, sporting an elegant smoking jacket over silk pajamas, with a pipe between his lips, flanked by several women in fewer clothes than Tina and I.

"Can we meet him now?" Tina begged.

"Of course, anything for you," Peter replied. He took us each by the hand and walked us over to Hugh Hefner.

Peter shook Hugh's hand. "Ladies, I'd like to introduce you to one of my favorite people, Mr. Hugh Hefner." Peter turned to Tina. "Hugh, meet the tempting Tina . . ." He then turned toward me. ". . . and the dynamic Destiny."

Hugh reached forward and kissed us on the lips.

"Mr. Hefner, you have a lovely place," Tina said. "I would love for you to show me around if you get a free moment this evening."

"We might be able to arrange a tour for you," he said.

"That would be awesome," she gushed.

"So are you ladies enjoying the evening?" he asked.

"We just got here," I said.

"Well, stick around and make yourselves comfortable, because you are in for the party of a lifetime," he said. "Things will only get better."

Hugh and his entourage strolled around the party, continuing to mingle with the other guests.

"Destiny, do you think he liked me?" Tina asked.

"It's hard to say," I replied. "But he probably does because every girl he has draped on his arm looks a lot like you."

"He did say he would give me a tour," she mused.

"Wouldn't that be nice."

"Yes. And it is going to happen. By the end of the night, he will show me around," she shot back confidently. Then she put her arms around Peter. "Peter, you will arrange for me to get a tour with Hugh, won't you?" she pouted.

"Of course, Tina, anything for you," Peter said. "In the meantime, would you ladies like a drink?"

That evening, we danced the night away with celebrities and Hollywood heavy hitters. We were in the midst of hedonism at its best, where anything and everything was accepted. It was the wildest, most outrageous party I had ever attended. I had a ball, but not nearly as much fun as Tina did.

Peter stepped away and had a private conversation with "Hef," as all his friends called him.

He returned. "Are you ladies ready for your tour?" he asked.

"Sure," we said in unison.

Peter took us by the hands and led us to Hef who graciously escorted us throughout his estate.

"You've gotta see this," he said, leading us to the infamous grotto, the steamy cave into which the pool leads. There were more cushions and pillows covering the rock ledges surrounding the water's edge. This area was a love scene waiting to happen. And from what I hear, happened again and again that night.

We went from there to the mansion, past the fountain, circular drive, manicured hedges and limousines, to a small building a few hundred yards away down a little path. That building was the game room, people were actually in there playing the games.

"Just off the game room is what I like to call the 'in here' room," Hef said. We followed him into a room that had padded carpet and plush earth-tone pillows. The walls and ceiling were covered by mirrors, which reflected the image of pillows being everywhere.

"I can understand why you call it that," I said, wide eyed.

As we continued around the grounds, we took the time to look at the iguanas, monkeys, and peacocks, all of which were in cages.

"When there are not so many people around, I like to let the peacocks walk around freely," Hef explained.

"I bet that would be cool," Tina said. I agreed.

"So what do you think about the place so far," he asked.

"I love it. I want to stay," Tina said.

"You never know," Hef said.

He was charming and sexy. Tina appeared mesmerized. I was taken aback myself. I understood why women flocked to him. He was protective, yet gentle.

"Let's go inside," he said. We followed along.

By the time we left the party, Peter had negotiated opportunities for both Tina and me to send in test photos taken by photographers affiliated with the magazine, for consideration for a magazine shoot. Tina was well on her way.

I was living out someone else's dream and worlds away from my own.

Twenty-six

Everything had fallen into place. Tina and I had appointments for the photo shoot that could potentially change our careers, taking us out of stripping and into the even more lucrative business of posing for the camera.

Every day Tina talked about leaving the club, about how she couldn't wait until the last day she'd have to strut down its catwalk. In the midst of those conversations, I finally realized that behind her tough exterior and facade, deep down, Tina was as miserable as I. Only she was hoping she'd find more pleasure making love to the camera instead of to the laps of strangers.

I was miserable because I felt like a fish out of water.

I was good at entertaining; however, inside, I knew that the lifestyle I'd become involved in was not what my life was meant to be. I found myself dreaming about Howard's campus and all the beautiful Black people walking between classes and working to educate themselves. I imagined Gloria walking across the stage and accepting her degree. When she looked in the audience, there was always an empty seat with my name written on it.

"Destiny, you're up," one of the girls called to me as she entered the dressing room to change outfits.

I got out of my chair and made my way to the stage as the DJ introduced me. "If you want to know what's in store for you in your near future, direct your eyes to the stage and prepare to meet your Destiny."

My music was cued, and I sashayed out on the stage, dressed as a genie. As I usually did when I needed help feeling sexy and seductive, I imagined that Jermaine was sitting center stage, the only one in the club, and that I was dancing for him. I sauntered down the catwalk, gyrating my hips seductively. I threw my hands above my head and rolled my upper body and torso. Destiny was performing for Jermaine, who was sitting center stage. And I knew he wanted me.

I looked off the stage to get a look at him, but my fantasy would not take. I could see everyone in the audience, and none of them was Jermaine. As I danced, my eyes scanned the crowd. I removed my first article of clothing, a top with puffy sleeves, while trying to go deeper into my fantasy. Suddenly I was there, but instead of Jermaine being alone, center stage, he was sitting stage right with a group of five or six other guys, and everyone in the club were still there too. My fantasy was changing.

I continued to dance, waving my arms down to rip off my puffy pants, which were Velcro-rigged so they would tear off immediately with a single tug. Once I had them off, I looked up at the audience. Jermaine was standing right in front of the stage, just as I had always fantasized. Only this time, he was yelling at me instead of sitting back watching in contentment, and two bouncers were headed his way.

I hadn't been dreaming. Jermaine Powers was actually there, and he was yelling at me. "Get off the fucking stage before I come up there and get you off myself."

I stopped in the middle of my routine and watched as the bouncers took him away, cussing and screaming. The rest of the guys with him, none of whom I recognized except his brother Calvin, got up and followed him out. Calvin looked back at me and shook his head, and then turned and left.

I walked off the stage and rushed back to the dressing room.

Dave came in behind me. "Excuse me, ladies," he said as he rushed past the other dancers, who were at various stages of getting dressed and undressed. He followed me to my dressing table. "What is the meaning of this?" His voice was deeper than usual. He was pissed. "I told you from day one, don't have any jealous boyfriends coming in here, interrupting business—and the last time I checked, this was still a business."

"He is not my boyfriend, Dave," I said.

"Oh, so he was just some crazed customer who just took it upon himself to demand that you get off the stage."

"He's an old friend. I haven't seen him in at least two years."

"Well, make sure you have a talk with him and let him know he's never welcome in this club again," Dave said, laying down the law.

"I'm taking the rest of the evening off," I said, burying my face in my hands. "This has been too stressful for me."

"You do what you need to do. Just handle your friend and make sure it never happens again."

"Okay, Dave," I promised. "Everything is cool." I was stunned, embarrassed, and angry.

I dressed in my street clothes and gathered my things. I wanted to get out of that place as quickly as I could. I rushed out so I could get to my place to bury my head in my pillow and cry away the blues of the evening. I didn't even remove my wig or take off my makeup. I just jetted out in haste.

Whenever we left the club, it was customary to have a bouncer walk us to our cars. Because I wanted out fast, I didn't ask for an escort. I rushed to my car without getting my keys out. When I got to the door, I opened my purse and fumbled through for them. While I was doing so, a thin, pale White man walked up to me.

"Destiny," he sang.

I didn't look back, but kept rummaging for my keys.

"Destiny, you didn't finish my dance," he said in a low, even tone.

I found my keys and reached for the door to unlock it.

He grabbed my wrist, and the keys fell to the ground.

"I came all the way out here from Pasadena to see my Destiny. You let me down."

My voice trembled as I tried to take control of the situation. "I'll be back to the club tomorrow night. You can check out my performance then."

"I want my performance now, Destiny," he said and whipped me around so I was facing him. He grabbed my face and squeezed my cheeks, forcing a lip-lock. His breath tasted like cigarettes.

I pushed him away and grabbed for my keys.

"You're not getting away from me, Destiny. Not until I get my dance." His gaze was intense, heated, depraved. He drew his hand back, opened his palm wide, and rapped it across my face. My cheek stung. I was in shock, not believing that I could experience such wrath from a complete stranger.

I screamed at the top of my lungs, "Help me! Help me! Somebody, please help me!" I didn't see anyone nearby and feared that my yelling was in vain. I was so frightened. It became clear to me that if I didn't do something quick, I would become the city's next rape victim. I kicked him in the groin, and he bent over to comfort himself. Seeing an opportunity to escape, I fumbled through my key ring to get my car key, but I was so nervous that they all looked alike.

Just when I found the right key, he had recuperated from the blow. "I only wanted to see you dance, and now you've pissed me off." He hurled his body against mine, pushing me against my car. The keys fell from my grasp.

"Get off me," I yelled, trying to push him away.

He stuck his tongue in my mouth, but somehow he was flung off me. I looked up and saw that Jermaine had thrown the man to the ground and was banging the man's head with his fist. Each time he made contact with that man's face, blood gushed from his mouth and his nose, and then his eye.

"Jermaine, that's enough," I yelled. "You're going to kill him."

Calvin had pulled up in a car filled with the other guys they'd been with in the bar. "Let him go, Jermaine. We're in the wrong neighborhood for this, and as you can see, she ain't worth going to jail for." He looked me up and down, a sneer on his face.

Jermaine let go of the man. Breathing ferociously, he eyed me, disappointment in his eyes.

As soon as my attacker became partially coherent, he jumped up and ran off.

"Get in the car," Calvin demanded. "He might call the police."

Jermaine remained focused on me. "Are you all right?" he asked.

I nodded yes, and the floodgates opened. I began to cry the tears I had been holding back since I had first stepped foot on the stage.

"Jermaine, get in the car. We gotta get out of here."

"Don't worry about me, man. Go on. I'll catch up later."

"You're making a big mistake, man," Calvin shot back.

"Don't worry about me." Jermaine gave Calvin a look.

Calvin shook his head and peeled off in anger.

"I'm gonna drive you home and make sure you get there safe," Jermaine said, reaching over to pick up the keys.

I didn't argue. He walked me over to the passenger side of the car and opened the door for me. I climbed in clumsily. He shut the door, taking his time, and walked over to the driver's side of the car, letting himself in.

"The last time I checked, this city looks a whole lot like Hollywood. I'm going to have a tough time navigating from here to D.C., so I'm gonna need you to show me where you live," he said, turning the key in the ignition.

I shot a look at him. He gazed at the rearview mirror to see what was behind him.

"Go straight out of the parking lot and then take a left," I managed to mumble.

Jermaine didn't say another word. He never once made eye contact with me while we were in the car. I leaned against the door and reflected on what Jermaine must be thinking of me. All the way to my apartment, he kept his eyes focused on the road, and the only words spoken were my directions.

We pulled into the lot at my place. I pointed out my assigned space and Jermaine pulled into it.

"How long have you been living here?" he asked.

"About a year."

He turned the key and placed it in my lap. After that, he didn't budge. Neither did I.

His thumb began tapping against the steering wheel. He sighed, and the pace of the tapping increased.

"Go ahead and say whatever it is you need to say," I blurted.

"That's just it. I don't know what to say to you, Lanita. Or is it Destiny?" He swung his head in my direction and peered into my soul.

I immediately jumped on the defensive.

"I'm not going to sit here and allow you to judge me. Yes, I have been stripping for over a year. Yes, I have been living in West Hollywood for quite some time. No, I never called you to fill you in on the change in my life plans. And no, I didn't go back to D.C. Now what, Jermaine?" I shot him back a similar look.

"What's going through your brain, Lanita? You're too smart for this," he insisted.

The sound of my birth name coming from his lips struck me to the core. He forced me to face myself. I couldn't pretend with him—Jermaine knew the real me.

"Surviving," I shot back.

"It seems to me that you're doing more than just surviving. How much are you paying in rent on a fancy place like this?"

"None of your business," I snapped. "As a matter of fact, you can just leave."

I pushed the passenger door open, jumped out of the car, and began walking toward the door that led to the interior of my apartment building.

"Wait just one motherfuckin' minute," he yelled, slamming the driver's side door closed. He rushed over to me. "So it's like that. You don't have to explain yourself to nobody. You're just a happy whore, living the high life, getting paid off sharing your body—and you don't give a damn what people think."

I turned in his direction and slapped him as hard as I could. "I am not a whore. And no, I don't give a damn about what people think—not the men who come into the bar, not your brother Calvin, and especially not you."

I was afraid he would retaliate, so I rushed to the door and pushed it open.

Jermaine followed me inside.

"What do you want from me?" I yelled as I pushed the Up button on the elevator. "I was just nearly raped and my nerves are shot. I don't have time for this."

"I want to talk to you. I want to understand what went wrong, because right now, I'm lost." He cornered me near the elevator. "And not just about you. I want to know what went wrong with me. We both had so much going for us. Why have we failed?"

He grabbed my hands. "Lanita, I am not judging you. But I do want to blame somebody or something. How can this world be so twisted that two of the most promising students who graduated from Jordan High ended up doing the exact opposite of what they dreamed of, what they prayed for?" he asked.

My head dropped.

The elevator opened.

"I don't know what to tell you, Jermaine. Maybe we weren't meant to be much better than we already are." I stepped inside the elevator.

"I don't believe that, and neither do you," he said, holding the door open.

"What are you trying to say?" I asked. Even though Jermaine's words weren't making sense, they were a place to start, a thing to hold on to, a reason to listen.

"I think there's a better way," he replied.

He took my hand again.

My heart softened.

"Just talk to me, Lanita," he said.

Tears formed in my eyes. I squeezed his hand. "What about?"

"Anything."

I squeezed tighter.

"Does this mean I'm invited up?" he asked. He appeared confused.

I nodded yes.

"Are you sure?" he asked.

"Yes," I whispered.

Jermaine squeezed back and stepped on the elevator with me.

We rode up to my apartment.

"You can have a seat in the living room," I said, and then excused myself to the bathroom to remove any remnants of Destiny: hair, makeup, and all. Then I looked around and realized that all of my surroundings were by-products of Destiny.

I walked into the living room and sat next to Jermaine, who wrapped me in his arms and passionately, thoughtfully, and tenderly kissed me as though our lives depended on it. Maybe they did. He placed my cheeks in his hands to make sure he had my full attention. "Do you want to continue dancing?"

"No."

"Then stop," he said.

"How am I going to continue to help Aretha out and afford my lease?"

"Are you that attached to this apartment?" he asked.

"Well, I—"

"Walk away from it," he whispered and kissed me with the same passion as before. He said it again. "Walk away."

He squeezed me tighter.

I squeezed back.

We kissed again.

"You are all that I've thought about over the past few years," he confessed. "I've played it over in my mind, again and again, what I'd say to you when I saw you next. I didn't know what had happened to you. I thought I'd lost you forever."

"Are you serious?" I couldn't believe what I was hearing.

"Yes, I am," he said. "I want to make love to you so bad, but I don't want you to view me like you do all the other men."

"What other men?" I said, on the defensive again.

"The other men you've slept with."

"Jermaine, get it straight. I strip. That's all that I do. I have never . . . I don't have to defend myself to you." I pushed away from him.

"I'm sorry, Lanita. Maybe I'm just naive. I just assumed . . ."

"So you *do* think I'm a whore."

"No, it's not like that. I'm just saying that I assumed you hooked up with some of your customers. Isn't that what goes on at strip clubs?"

I didn't answer.

"Isn't it?" he questioned.

"Well, yeah, sometimes, but not with me."

"So you never hooked up with any of your customers?"

"Yes, but not like that. And not that it's any of your business, but I'm still a virgin. I have not given myself to any of my customers—or to any other man, for that matter."

"You don't have to lie to me, Lanita."

"Get out!" I yelled. I could not take this from him.

"What?" His jaw dropped.

"You heard me—get out of my apartment."

"You can't mean that."

Folding my arms and rolling my eyes, I stood firm. "If you don't get out, I'm calling security."

"I'm sorry, Lanita . . . I didn't mean—"

"What reason do I have to lie to you?" I asked.

"None, but understand where I'm coming from. It's hard to buy."

"Well, maybe I'm an anomaly."

"Anomaly?"

"Yes, Jermaine, maybe I'm an exception to the rule. Could that be possible?" I glared at him.

He put his arm around me. "I don't care."

"About what?" I tried to push away.

"I don't care if you're a virgin or not. I don't care if you've stripped. I don't care if you quit school. The only thing I care about is you and how you feel about me—and where we can go from here. I want you, Lanita. I want to take care of you. I want to see you finish school. I'm not perfect and I definitely can't house you in a place like this, but I can treat you with respect and dignity and love."

I sat there, flabbergasted. I was sure that he was concerned for my well-being, but I didn't really believe the depth of his affection. It was too good to be true.

"Lanita, if you're willing to give up on all of this"—he looked around the room—"then I would like to see what we can build together."

As much as I cared for Jermaine, and as much as I wanted to fall into his arms and allow everything to instantly become better, I couldn't. He meant well and I was going to give him a chance, but it was something I would need to ease into. I didn't want to get hurt again. Nonetheless, I wanted to feel the touch of a man who wasn't captivated by the fantasy Destiny provided.

I moved close to him and rested in his arms. He wrapped himself around me and we continued to talk about the events of the evening, about what the future could look like. In that time and space, his arms and chest and comforting words were exactly what I needed to shed the blues of the evening and of the past few years, just the medicine I needed to believe there was a possibility of hope for a more suitable future, a future in which I could be proud of myself again.

Twenty-seven

After filing Lanita's shabby nails smooth, Deidra Michelle used a huge brush to remove the debris. "I'm finding it difficult to believe you once were a stripper."

She took Lanita's right hand and dipped it into a tub of paraffin wax, lifted and dipped again. "But then again, this is LA and you never know what you might find yourself caught up in." She covered the hand with plastic bags, then cotton gloves. Then did the same with the left.

"You're right about that," Lanita said, thinking about the many girls she met while dancing at the strip club. Some wanted to be there, embracing the life and all the negative elements that came with it, while others fought their involvement the whole way.

"The interesting thing that I found was that while all the strippers I met, me included, could tell you why they first got involved, most couldn't give a reasonable explanation as to why they stayed. I fell in that category. I shouldn't have been there. But just like I heard so many times in Hollywood, I was caught up."

"But you got out. That's major," she said.

"I got out, but the funny thing about getting out is that there are side effects to ever having been involved."

I had given up stripping. Everything that happened the night when Jermaine came back into my life gave me the courage to let it go forever. I thanked God because I felt He'd been listening to me when I reached out to him that night before going to the Playboy Mansion.

Tina was perturbed when I told her I was moving out, but she got over it because she managed to do exactly what she set out to do: By the end of the next year, she had been invited to do a spread in *Playboy* and eventually moved into the mansion. She even adorned a cover for the magazine.

Two years flew by. I had moved back in with Aretha, who was happy to have me back home. We never discussed my previous occupation, but gossip gets around Watts. If she didn't know before the night that Jermaine found me there, she knew afterward. The only comment she made regarding my having been away so long was "Lanita, I hated you being out there in West Hollywood. It was too far for me to get to you if I needed to."

I guess me being anyplace that wasn't home was too far for Aretha.

After being back home for a while, I went through a period of depression. Being *Destiny* was bad enough, but going back to being Lanita was tougher. Lanita was intelligent, virtuous, voted "most likely to succeed" by her peers. How was I going to be able to step back into such exemplary shoes? I had seen too much, experienced too much. I would never be that version of Lanita again. I often sat in my bedroom staring at the wall, wondering who I was, really.

Just when I thought I had a grip, I was struck with the urge to drink. At odd times, I'd sneak away and find myself at a liquor store in Long Beach, Carson, or Inglewood—anywhere that I wouldn't be identified.

I came up with excuses to drink. At first I was celebrating being away from the strip club. Every weekend that I didn't spend with Jermaine I had a private drunken ceremony commemorating the new me. Only the new me was becoming more dependent on the bottle. Drinking daily crept up on me.

Jermaine and I talked on the phone almost every night. When we were together I tried to refrain from drinking. Our conversations provided a ray of hope, but I was so far gone that I had a hard time believing his vision for us.

He'd say, "Lanita, I believe in you. I know things are tough right now, but we'll get through this."

"I don't know, Jermaine."

"We have a plan. It's gonna take us a while, but we're gonna come out on top. And if we work hard and save money we can move to D.C. together and finish school at Howard."

"Sure," I'd respond, trying to believe, but knowing I didn't.

Aretha and Jermaine worked during the week and weren't always available for me to lean on. I got lonely and bored. Sometimes after I was good and drunk I'd walk over to visit with Stacia in the middle of the day.

Happy to have me back in Watts, she promised it would be like old times. We spent a lot of time together initially. I didn't have a job and she was in school part-time finishing up her degree in social work. She had coupled up with a guy from the neighborhood named Bobby and they had moved into an apartment together. She was three months pregnant. They were talking about marriage, but had yet to set a date.

I was naive enough to think she didn't know I had been drinking. She was kind enough to overlook my erratic behavior. Some days we'd laugh; others I'd cry. We'd talk about life and just how hard it sometimes was to maintain our spirits on a daily basis. We joked about the good ol' days. She'd let me go on and on about D.C. Initially it was refreshing to be around her. I found hope in her perseverance. She had only one semester left and Bobby had moved up to assistant manager at the car wash. They were doing well.

One day we sat on the steps of her porch to enjoy the nice weather. Our conversation was all over the place. I was working to cover up my drunkenness. To do so I talked, a lot.

"I can't believe you ended up hooking up with Bobby of all people. Can you believe my good friend Gloria had a crush on him back when we were in the seventh grade? But you didn't know Gloria, did you?" I closed my eyes and smiled at the thought of Gloria walking across the stage at Howard and shaking the dean's hand.

"It's amazing how life works that way. You never know who you're going to end up with," Stacia replied.

"She's so smart. I bet if Bobby saw her now, he would forget he was committed to you."

"Lanita . . ."

"Girl, don't pay me any attention. Plus Gloria wouldn't give somebody like Bobby the time of day. After all, he works at the car wash. I'm sure she's dating government officials and doctors." I didn't know for sure, because I didn't have the guts to call her since I had begun stripping.

"Lanita you're drunk!"

"So what if I am," I retorted. "I'm telling the truth."

"What are you doing?" she rolled her eyes. "You could've had it all, but now look at you. You're a drunk just like your mother used to be."

"Shut up, Stacia," I demanded.

"And why, because you couldn't go back to D.C.?" She grabbed the rail and pulled herself off the steps. She looked down at me. "Life didn't stop when you left D.C. You gave up."

Stacia turned her back to me and went into the apartment.

The truth stung. I sat there unsure how to react, but I knew I wasn't going to take her insults. Reluctantly, I stood up, but I didn't want to leave because it meant I would have to go back to the apartment alone. But I knew I had gone too far. Upset with myself, I took it out on her.

"I don't need you, Stacia. I went to Howard University, had a 3.75 GPA. I'm smart. I can get my degree if I want to. I drive a bad-ass sports car. What do you drive, Stacia? Nothing. You don't have a car. I don't need you, Stacia. Just stay out of my life," I yelled.

. . .

One night while Momma was at work, I wanted to surprise her, so I purchased groceries along with a bottle of gin for myself. I'd planned to cook sirloin steak, green beans, and mashed potatoes. After placing the lightly oiled pan on an eye, I turned the temperature to high. Then I pulled out a pot to boil the potatoes. Once I got dinner started, I turned on the radio. Mariah Carey's "Vision of Love" was playing. I closed my eyes as her beautiful voice sang in my ears. Then I brought out the gin, sitting in the same chair that I had watched Aretha sit in for years. I poured a glass full, on the rocks, and sat back listening to the music while trying to lose myself in the melody. I was pathetic, lost, scared.

By the time I came to the end of the bottle, I found myself in a drunken stupor, totally forgetting that I was supposed to be cooking.

Aretha came in and found me, passed out.

"Lanita!" she yelled.

I heard the hysteria in her voice. "What?" I said, oblivious to the fire that was beginning to overtake the kitchen.

"You're gonna catch the house on fire," she yelled, grabbing the extinguisher that had sat in the corner but had never been used. Then she fought to extinguish the fire.

Coughing, I managed, "What's going on?"

"Child, what are trying to do, kill yourself?"

"What are you talking about, Aretha?" I said, slurring my words. I saw the flames but hadn't realized the severity of the fire.

"Lanita, if I hadn't come home early you would have burned up in here." White material flew out of the extinguisher, smothering the flames.

"So!" I said. The thought of those words frightened me. Had I allowed myself to get so deeply depressed that I didn't care if I lived or died?

With the fire extinguished, Aretha rushed around the house opening windows, freeing the smoke. She came back into the kitchen. I remained sitting, coughing, and thinking about how pitiful I was.

The smoke was thick. She came back in with an album cover, fanning. Realizing that the smoke wasn't going anywhere, she shook her head and helped me up, walking me outside. She set me down on a step.

"After all we've gone through, why would you choose to become everything you ever despised about me?"

"What?" I lifted my head as if nothing she said meant anything to me.

Even though I was drunk, I got the message loud and clear. I got it when Stacia delivered it days before. I didn't want to become her. And even though I said I didn't care, I wasn't ready to die. A neighbor came out of his apartment. "Do you want me to call the fire department?"

"I don't know, I guess," Aretha said. "But the fire is out."

"I'm sorry, Aretha," I said, crying. "I'm so sorry."

"Just stop, Lanita. You deserve better than this," Aretha said, wrapping her arms around me; she hugged me tightly as I cried in her arms.

I couldn't go on like this.

I knew something had to change.

.　　.　　.

I gave up drinking, going cold turkey. Initially stopping wasn't easy, but I fought against the urge daily. Every time I thought about the fact I had nearly died, I resisted.

It was time to face life and the mess I had made of it. I had to do something to move me out of my rut. With time and support from both Aretha and Jermaine, I decided that my new vice would be improving my life.

I set out to reestablish my relationship with God and began to get to know Him better. I began to read again, self-help books and Christian literature. I even picked up on my summer reading list. I set a goal to read ten books, but I outdid myself and completed my usual fifteen. The classics on my list that year were James Weldon Johnson's *The Autobiography of an Ex-Colored Man*, Ralph Ellison's *Invisible Man*, and Gordon Parks's *The Learning Tree*. My contemporary selections were Gloria Naylor's *The Women of Brewster Place*, Jamaica Kincaid's *Annie John*, and Joyce Carol Oates's *You Must Remember This*. I also picked up *Mama* by a new author, Terry McMillan. I finished the summer reading everything I could find by Nikki Giovanni.

Twenty-eight

I put together a résumé and went job hunting and eventually found a job as a receptionist at an advertising firm, a bustling Hollywood corporation filled with advertising executives, most of whom were condescending and loved to appear busy and important.

After working there for more than a year, I had become quite familiar with the ins and outs of the business. Two executives in particular, Bill and Doug, were the company's go-to guys. If the two of them couldn't close a deal, no one could. They had come up with the cleverest ideas for advertising campaigns for beer, cereal, baby food, cars, and sporting apparel. They were the kings of advertising. There was an ongoing joke in the office: "Bill and Doug could sell an air conditioner to an Eskimo—and would sell their souls in the process, if it would help close the deal." The saying was true.

The year was 1990, Debbie Turner was crowned the third African-American Miss America, South Africa finally freed Nelson Mandela, August Wilson won his second Pulitzer Prize for his play *The Piano Lesson*, and Sammy Davis Jr. passed away. Closer to home, Bill and Doug had been hard at work bringing to life a new campaign they'd come up with for a toothpaste account they'd landed. Although they were considered brilliant, Bill and Doug were notorious for their condescending behavior. I often experienced it firsthand and was not amused. Every time they stopped by my desk and asked for their messages, they had a way of not looking at me. They often defined the simplest words to me, assuming I didn't know their meaning.

Bill would say, "Lanita, could you please call the caterer to double-check that we have hors d'oeuvres for the reception?"

Doug would follow up with "Yes, it would be a shame if the trays of appetizers don't show up."

"No problem," I'd respond, cringing. Like I didn't know what hors d'oeuvres were!

On Secretary's Day, the office sent me a fruit basket. Doug said, "Lanita, make sure to store the fruit in a cool area so it won't perish too soon."

"Yes, Lanita, we wouldn't want your fruit to go bad," Bill chimed in. They were aggravating, but it paid to be in their good graces.

The big deal for the toothpaste ad was to find the all-American girl to promote the toothpaste to women between the ages of twenty-one and thirty-five. The duo debated which of the casting agencies they normally used would be the best to find the new toothpaste girl. The casting agent had to be flexible because, although they would be used to narrow the search, the president of the toothpaste company wanted to make the ultimate decision.

Once they made their decision, they approached me.

"Lanita, could you please contact Lisa Nealson Casting and set up a two-thirty P.M. meeting for us on Wednesday or Thursday? And please inform her that we'll go with her preference," Doug instructed.

"Yes, please tell Lisa we'd be glad to meet with her on whichever day works best for her," Bill clarified.

"No problem," I responded. My skin crawled.

I called and set up the meeting. Lisa preferred to meet on Thursday, so I booked her for that date.

The week had been a hectic one. Bill and Doug were preparing for the commercial shoot and print campaign. Most of the junior executives were working to assist in any way they could, hoping that something they contributed would allow their stars to shine brightly enough to eventually be considered for a shot at removing the "junior" from their titles. Although my job description as receptionist was to answer phones, take messages, maintain a manageable filing system, and make coffee, I was also expected to chip in and assist whenever necessary.

On Wednesday night, I was asked to stay late to help out in any way that I could. I found myself doing odd jobs, like making last-minute photocopies of documents and playing gofer. We had worked so late that everyone got hungry.

"Lanita, would you happen to have a car?" Bill asked.

"Yes, I do," I replied.

"That'll make this request a lot easier," he commented. "We'd like you to go to the deli at that grocery store that's located a block down on Santa Monica and pick up cold-cut subs, chips, and cold drinks."

"Okay."

"The company will reimburse you for your gas expense," he said.

And of course Doug was there in case I didn't understand. "Yeah, Lanita, we'll pay you back for the gas you use to get there."

"No problem," I replied. I wanted to puke.

"The cash I'm giving you comes from petty cash, so be sure to keep the receipt and bring it back with you," Bill said.

"Okay," I replied, masking my annoyance with his failure to realize that I understood how the office's petty cash system worked. I had been with the company for nearly two years, after all.

I was presented a list of items that I needed to bring back and a wad of cash, and I was off. When I pulled up to the grocery-store lot, I saw a well-dressed man and his daughter get out of a new E-class Mercedes-Benz. It seemed that the little girl, who looked like she was about six years old, was running her father with the way she was tugging at his arm as she led him down the parking lot toward the store.

I laughed, put my car in park, and got out and stretched. I was a bit worn out from the long day. Inside, I stood in front of the large glass displays at the deli and carefully detailed each order to the lady behind the counter. I had to ensure that each person's order was just as he or she had requested or I'd catch hell back at the office.

The little girl I had seen in the parking lot slowly walked around the corner, looking frantically all around, getting more anxious when she couldn't find what she was looking for. She made her way to the middle of the deli and turned around in a complete circle once and then once again. The second time she turned in my direction, tears were racing down her fear-filled face. I looked around to see if her father was nearby. He was nowhere to be found.

My first instinct was to go to her and make sure she was okay, so I rushed over, knelt down in front of her, and put my hand on her back.

"What's wrong?" I asked.

She put her head down.

"Are you lost?" I asked her. "I'll help you find your father."

"You will?" she asked through her tears.

"I sure will," I promised. I turned to the lady at the deli. "I'll be right back."

I took the little girl by the hand and walked toward the customer-service desk. "What is your name?" I asked her.

"Sarah," she said.

"Hello, Sarah, my name is Lanita. I'm gonna take you over to customer service, and we're going to have them page your dad so that he'll know where you are. What's his name?"

"Martin," she said.

We turned the corner and saw that the gentleman I had seen with her earlier was at the desk.

"Daddy!" she yelled, running into his arms.

"Sarah," he said. "I was so worried."

"Daddy, this is Lanita, and she helped me find you."

I smiled to see the two back together.

"Hello, Lanita," he said. "I was just getting ready to have someone at customer service page Sarah. She's so active that it's sometimes difficult to keep up with her."

"Yeah, we were headed to do the same thing," I said.

"Great minds think alike," Sarah said.

"You're right, sweetheart. They do," Martin said to his daughter.

I smiled.

Martin picked up Sarah as if they were going to walk away. Then he gave me an awkward glance. He put her back down at his side and placed her hand in his, and then he walked closer to me.

He stared.

"What did you say your name is?" he asked.

"It's Lanita."

"And what do you do, Lanita?"

I got a little nervous because I wasn't sure if maybe he had remembered me from when I was Destiny. "I'm a receptionist."

"Are you sure you're not an actress or a model?" he inquired.

"No. I'm a receptionist, but I'm going to be starting back at school to complete my degree next spring."

"But you don't model?" he said.

"No, sir, I don't." I had begun to feel uneasy, and the feeling wasn't letting up.

"Would you be interested?" he said.

"I'm not sure. What are you asking me?"

He laughed. I guess he could see the discomfort in my face. "I don't know much about modeling and acting, but I know the look that I'm searching for when I see it."

I was still confused.

"My toothpaste company is looking for a new spokesperson for a huge advertising campaign that we're getting ready to launch in the next few days. I'm working with a top-notch ad agency, which is setting up casting for the commercials." He stepped even closer. "I made it clear to them that I wanted to have the final approval, and I approve of you. I don't need to see anybody else. You should do the commercial."

Everything began to make sense. I realized that I was being offered the job my very own company was planning a search to fill.

"They want to bring in a casting agent, but I say, why bother when we have Lanita? Would you be interested?" he asked.

"Sure," I said, "but I've never acted before."

"But you're a natural. I can tell by looking at you. You'll do just fine," he assured me.

Martin handed me his card and told me to contact his office the first thing the next morning.

"My secretary will set everything up for you."

I said good-bye to him and Sarah and went back over to the deli to finish getting late-night snacks for my soon-to-be-former coworkers. I was sure that if Doug and Bill had anything to do with it, I would be fired before they would allow me to be featured in that commercial.

Twenty-nine

To Bill and Doug's chagrin, but just as Martin had promised, I was selected to be the spokesperson for the toothpaste company.

I remained an employee at the ad agency, but they gave me leave time for the commercial and photo shoot. My face and pearly white smile were displayed in a television commercial that ran for several months, several times each day, and in a print ad campaign in which my face was plastered on billboards and in major magazines throughout the country. Also, I received a hefty paycheck of $50,000, including royalties, just because I had smiled at a few cameras and proclaimed how much I loved using the company's toothpaste.

The money was right on time because even though Jermaine and I hadn't moved away to D.C. as we'd hoped, we'd followed our schedule and had begun taking classes at USC the spring of 1991. We wanted to stay around to see if I could book more commercials. We had both applied as part-time students, carrying one class each, working through the week and studying together at night. It was tough at first, because we'd be extremely tired at the end of a workday and our brains seemed unable to consume much more. However, we forged ahead and studied at least an hour every night, sometimes until we fell asleep.

In the midst of all of that, I had been auditioning as much as I could during my lunch breaks at work and on the weekends. I never landed another national spot, but I got a couple of regional commercials—they paid only scale, though, with no opportunity for royalties, so there wasn't another $50,000 payout.

Jermaine and I had spent so much time working to achieve our goals that we hardly ever found leisure time for ourselves. A full year had passed, and we had each completed three classes and were working on the fourth. We were so focused that we hadn't even discussed moving in together. With everything we had going on, we hadn't spent very much time together talking about our future as a couple.

In his usual, thoughtful fashion, Jermaine would surprise me and take me out to a nice restaurant every so often. Sometimes we'd even fit in a movie. One evening in particular, he invited me to an upscale restaurant that was a few notches above what we were accustomed to patronizing. He had asked me to dress up nicely, so I did. The restaurant he chose was spacious and was known for its great seafood and service.

"Wow!" I said when we took our seats. "So what's the occasion?"

"Us," he said. Then he took my hand from across the table.

"What about us?" I asked.

"Don't you think we deserve to be catered to every once in a while? Don't you think you deserve it?" he said.

"Yes, we do," I replied, "but I feel guilty."

"Why?"

"Because it seems that everybody in South Central LA is suffering except us. Because Rodney King was beaten a few days ago."

Rodney King was a twenty-five-year-old construction worker who had been severely beaten on March 3, 1991, by four Los Angeles police officers. The incident was a result of a high-speed chase in which King and some other passengers were spotted speeding in King's Hyundai down the San Fernando's Foothill Freeway, going more than a hundred miles an hour. When King, who was allegedly drunk, was stopped, he resisted arrest. Consequentially the officers, who weren't able to cuff him, knocked him to the ground. Three of the officers, Ted Briseno, Laurence Powell, and Timothy Wind, clubbed him and kicked him a total of fifty-six times in eighty-one seconds, while their sergeant, Stacey Koon, stood there and watched. Some of the blows King received were from a Taser gun, an electrical-shock device used by police to stun and subdue suspects.

Among his many injuries, King sustained a fractured skull and a fractured eye socket. The beating had been brutal and unnecessary, but it had also been videotaped. The graphic scene aired on national television within hours of the incident, which is when Jermaine and I found out about it. We sat and watched in disbelief that such extreme acts of racism could still exist in our society. Eventually the videotape was seen around the world, rousing international outrage.

"Which is exactly why we should be here in this bourgeois restaurant tonight, to show that Black people might be beat down unnecessarily and that we might be rightfully pissed off, but we're not out. We're showing that it's not over for us," Jermaine proclaimed.

We gave our orders and the waiter removed our menus. I looked over at Jermaine. He was so handsome, dressed in one of his best suits. He was wearing the tie I had given him for Christmas.

"You look stunning. I love when you wear dresses," he said to me.

I had on a dazzling red dress that had a low neckline. It was my favorite, but I seldom had the occasion to show it off.

"I'm wearing it specially for you," I flirted.

"And you'd better know I'm appreciating the view from here."

We toasted over our soft drinks.

"Let's toast to the only option being to complete what we began," he said.

We touched glasses. He reached over the table and kissed my lips.

"That was nice," I said.

"There's more where that came from," he replied.

The waiter returned with our order, and we held hands as we said a short prayer before eating. We often prayed together; we even went to church together. Once after church, Calvin approached me and asked me to forgive him for his actions back at the club. I told him I would. My relationship with God and with Jermaine's family continued to grow. Jermaine was a Christian man, and he—and I—wouldn't have had it any other way.

During dinner, we discussed the money I'd made from the toothpaste commercial.

"My major concern is how to spend it and help prevent it from being taxed to nothing," I said.

"Why don't you invest it?" Jermaine suggested.

"In what? Not stocks—my world would be shattered if I invested in the stock market and it suddenly crashed."

"Did you ever think about purchasing a house?" he suggested.

"It's not a bad idea," I said. "But what about D.C.? If I purchase a house, the odds of us moving to D.C. will disappear."

"You might be right, but you could also rent it out if and when we go to D.C."

"That's true, and it might be a good source of extra income," I agreed. "I always thought it would be nice to get a place in Inglewood."

"Yeah, Inglewood or Crenshaw."

"Either," I said. "Or maybe even Watts, if I had to."

"As long as you can get a good deal."

"Well, that would be the goal," I said. I took a deep breath. "So if I get a house, do you want to move in with me?"

"A few things would have to be right," he said.

"What does that mean?"

"How's your salmon?" he asked, skirting around the question.

"It's very good, thank you," I said. "So what do you mean? What has to be right?"

"Us."

"Aren't we right?" I asked.

"Not all the way."

"Is it because we haven't made love yet?"

"No, Lanita, that's not an issue. It never has been. I told you that before." He took a bite of his steak. "You'll understand eventually."

"Okay." I chose to drop the interrogation. We were having a nice time, and I didn't want to ruin it with too many questions.

We completed our dinner, and the waiter removed our plates. Then he returned with two champagne flutes and a huge piece of chocolate cake.

"The gentleman has a question that he would like to ask you," the waiter announced.

Just then, Jermaine fell to one knee next to my chair and placed my hand in his. "Lanita, we have been working toward getting our degrees together. And I know that it will happen for us. Now I want to work toward having it right with us," he said.

Jermaine squeezed my hand and kissed the back of it.

"Lanita Lightfoot, will you marry me?" he asked.

He pulled a ring out from I don't know where and slid it on my finger.

"Yes," I said, catching my breath. "Yes, I'll marry you, Jermaine Powers."

I stood, and so did he. We embraced and kissed while everyone in the restaurant cheered wildly.

"I wasn't expecting you to ask me to be Mrs. Powers—especially not tonight. You got me," I said.

"I hope I do," he replied.

.   .   .

We were married at the end of the summer, right after we finished our summer semester. The wedding took place in Miss Page's backyard, with Aretha and her fussing over every little detail. Aretha and I tried to contact my daddy, Paul, but we never got in touch with him. The service was lovely, nonetheless.

I stood nervous in the kitchen waiting for the music to cue my march down the aisle. Miss Page's husband, Donald, who was my escort, lingered close by. I stayed in one place fidgeting while he paced. Staring out of the sliding door window and over the deck, I caught a glimpse of all our friends and family all dressed up and sitting in the chairs on either side of the runner that lead to the gazebo.

Their new home located in Brentwood was beautiful, worlds away from Miss Page's humble home in Watts. Although I loved her old place, it was good to see the financial and social improvement a legitimate union between the two produced. And as always they graciously shared their wealth.

Miss Page used her connections to get a string quartet, which was set up on the side of the gazebo. They began playing while I watched Jermaine and Calvin take their places. I loved that man.

My music began—*Bridal March*. Donald jumped. "It's time," he said.

"Yes it is," I replied, beaming.

"Remember, today is your day. I will be by your side every step of the way. Take your time and everything will fall into place."

"Thank you, Donald, for everything," I said.

We embraced.

He gave me his arm and we proceeded toward the gazebo.

Jermaine followed intently with his eyes until I was directly in front of him.

"Who gives this woman to be united to this man?" the preacher asked.

"I do," Donald said proudly.

He handed me over to Jermaine and took his seat with Miss Page.

I always knew Miss Page was special to me, but in that moment I realized just how much Donald meant to me. Both were my family. They helped Aretha raise me. And even when I fell short, they remained constant. I thanked God for them as I took my husband's hand.

"I love you," I mouthed to Jermaine.

He winked, grinning from ear to ear.

The minister began speaking, and I was well on my way to becoming Mrs. Jermaine Powers.

After the ceremony, we continued the celebration. More people came over, and we partied all evening in Miss Page's backyard. Before we left the party, I pulled Miss Page aside.

"I never apologized to you about missing your wedding," I said to her. "I don't have a real excuse, except that I wasn't myself. There are a lot of things I did back then that I regret, but missing your wedding is the thing I miss the most."

She wrapped her arms around me. "We already forgave you, Donald and me. We're just glad you came back to us. Some people are not quite so fortunate."

"I love you, Miss Page, and I just want to thank you for everything you've done for me through the years."

"Every step of the way, it's been my pleasure," she responded.

•　　•　　•

Aretha stood near the door to see Jermaine and me off, standing there as proud as you please. "I believe you picked a good one," she said. Then she attempted to whisper to Jermaine, but I heard: "Thank you for rescuing my baby."

"Oh, Miss Aretha." Jermaine blushed.

She pulled him aside. "I knew what she was doing out there in Hollywood. She always tried to hide it from me, but I knew. You helped bring my baby back to me, and I just want to thank you for that."

"You're welcome, Miss Aretha."

"Now, y'all get on outta here." She kissed Jermaine's cheek, and then she kissed mine.

I looked at her. My mother had aged. So had I. She was still a pistol, but she was more controlled, less haphazard. I hugged her tight.

"I love you, Momma," I said. "You are a good mother."

She shooed me away with her hands. I saw the tears falling from her eyes.

I understood.

.   .   .

That evening, Jermaine and I spared no expense, spending the night at the Beverly Hills Hotel. It was our first night sharing a bed together. While I was ready to consummate our marriage, I was still nervous.

We played soft music and sipped on sparkling cider all night. Jermaine was the master at foreplay, which is exactly what I needed to be ready to give myself to him. He took his time, kissing and caressing every inch of my body.

"I want you to be inside me," I whispered.

Our hands locked.

He took his time, slowly and passionately pleasuring me. I wrapped my arms and legs around him and allowed him to take the lead. I gladly followed. Our bodies made love for the first time, but it was a familiar place, a comforting place, just more intense, the completion of the union Jermaine and I had made earlier that day, before the preacher.

I relished being there with my husband. We lay in bed all night, hugging and laughing and talking and dreaming, finally falling asleep in each other's arms.

.   .   .

The following morning we took a train down the coast to San Diego, where we honeymooned on Coronado Island. We spent four days and

three nights being near the water, hanging out in Coronado and downtown San Diego. We even went to the zoo. We took one day and walked
across the border to Mexico, where we shopped in the open market and
explored the city.

Each night before we went to sleep, Jermaine would hold me in his
arms and make love to me. "I love you with all my heart, Lanita Powers,"
he would say.

"I love you more," I'd reply.

"We are a special couple, you know? One that will beat the odds."

"Yes, because I'm lucky—and you're lucky to have me," I joked.

"Exactly," he replied.

. . .

We returned, refreshed and renewed, to Inglewood, where our newly
purchased home was located, a three-bedroom fixer-upper. It needed a
lot of work, but we loved it all the same. Jermaine constructed tables for
the entire place, including our kitchen table, dining room table, coffee
table, and end tables for the living room. He also created a unique array
of glass fixtures for the wall. We pulled together odds and ends we'd had
at our parents' homes and purchased a few pieces. We worked together to
build our new home and the best life we could.

Thirty

Deidra Michelle lifted Lanita's feet out of the water and rested them on a fluffy towel. She removed the tub of water, replacing it with paraffin. She dipped each of Lanita's feet in twice, then covered them with plastic bags, then cotton boots.

"When I remove the wax, your feet are going to feel extra soft."

"Wonderful," Lanita said.

"I hear purchasing a new home can be quite rewarding," Deidra said. "And quite a feat for a LA resident."

"It is. We've put a lot of money into fixing it up, turning it into a *home*."

"I have yet to begin the process of purchasing a home, but real estate in this city is so expensive, most of the people I know rent or buy condos," Deidra replied.

"The property value of our house has increased, so we are selling and looking for another house."

"What about children? Do you want any?" Deidra asked.

"Funny you should ask that question," Lanita said, winking.

. . .

By the spring of 1992, I had been dragging along. I was still working at the advertising agency and going to school, but I was beginning to slow down some because there had been a change in me. I had gained weight, was eating more and wanting to sleep more. I was eight months pregnant and couldn't wait until nature took its course and my baby was ready to be born. Any aspirations to move to D.C. were long forgotten, and I was okay with that. For me, home was wherever Jermaine and our soon-to-arrive baby were living, and that was Inglewood.

Although I had been sluggish, yet content in my space, every time I visited Aretha in Watts, turned on the television, or overheard conversations between Bill and Doug in the office, I was reminded of the aggravation and anger in the climate of Watts and South Central LA. It was a troublesome time that had begun to brew with the onset of the nineties. The country had stumbled into a deep economic recession, which was especially evident in South Central.

In recent years, heavy manufacturing companies, including Southwest Steel, Chrysler, Firestone, and Goodyear, had left the region, taking hundreds of thousands of jobs with them. It was a depressed time, when the lack of money, coupled with the rise of drug use, gang participation, and homelessness, sent a chill of uneasiness and destabilization through the very neighborhood I had called home for so many years. The mood had been intensified by the Rodney King beating, which had occurred just one year before. There was an unsettled anticipation as the jury and judges were finally selected for the trial. South Central and the rest of America, about 80 percent, were convinced that the officers were guilty and would be rightfully convicted by the trial's end.

Controversy surrounded the case, which continued to mount with apparent unfair logistics. LA Superior Court Justice Stanley Weisberg ordered the trial be held in Simi Valley, which was a predominately White community in Ventura County where only 2 percent of the population was Black. Furthermore, it was home to a large number of police officers and firefighters. Naturally, protests began to ensue.

The selected jury consisted of twelve members—ten White, one Hispanic, and one Filipino. Not one African American had been selected. Our faith in the system continued to slip as we eventually found out that of the jurors, who ranged in age from thirty-eight to sixty-five, three worked as security guards or patrol officers in the military, three others were members of the National Rifle Association, and one was the brother of a retired LA police sergeant. It was unfair, to say the least.

The trial went on for twenty-nine days. Each day Bill and Doug became increasingly vocal about their disregard for Rodney King. One morning I walked into the break room, where they were talking over coffee.

"He doesn't have a case. Those officers were just doing their job. Their families should be requited," Doug said.

"Yeah, they should be repaid for the unfair scrutiny that they and their loved ones are being faced with." Bill looked in my direction.

I shook my head and tried to ignore them while I poured myself a cup of decaf coffee. Then I walked away. After all, they were entitled to their own opinion. No matter how preposterous it was, they were entitled.

Concerned about our baby's future and the impact of the recession on so many of his friends' lives, Jermaine had taken on a second job as a security guard at an office building in Century City. In case the economy continued its downward spiral, he wanted to keep us from ever having our utilities turned off or from starving. He wanted to prepare for whatever the economy chose to dish out.

Because I didn't want to be home alone, I had begun to spend my evenings at Aretha's house. We'd watch television and talk, or I would study or read for pleasure. Aretha didn't move away from the television much when I visited. She was glued to the Rodney King trial. Any time she could find a program that mentioned the trial, she stopped whatever she was doing and tuned in.

"Why do you spend so much time obsessing over the trial?" I asked.

"It's not just the trial. It's the details," she said. "I'm waiting to hear something that will disprove what I already know."

"What's that?"

"That just as much as things change in the world—you know, like with surrogate mothers carrying babies for other women, people dying from AIDS, the prediction that every home will eventually have a computer, cash machines and CDs being invented, and the banning of leaded gas—things still stay the same. Unemployment among Blacks, Hispanics, and Asian men between the ages of eighteen and thirty-five is nearly fifty percent—fifty percent, Lanita. And the average household income in South Central is only twenty thousand dollars. That's a third less than the average for the whole of Los Angeles."

Aretha positioned herself on the sofa to get more comfortable.

"Things haven't changed for our people, Lanita, and believe me, I know. I've seen some things in my time, and if our brothers don't feel any relief soon, they're going to erupt."

"You think so?"

"I know so," she replied with calm wisdom. "Shhh, now sit back and listen to this. The doctor said that Rodney suffered a fractured skull that might leave him with permanent brain damage. Said that the damage to his right eye socket might cause his vision to be blurred. He might have partial facial paralysis. He has multiple burns from that Taser gun. That's just wrong."

It became a ritual. I would pull out my books and sit in the kitchen and study while Aretha closely followed the Rodney King verdict. The night of the verdict, I walked through the door, waddling in.

Aretha stared at me and laughed. "Whew-ee, girl, you sure are big. I believe that baby is coming sooner than you expect," she said.

"It would be nice, but we have several weeks to go," I said.

"How's Jermaine doing?" she asked.

"Momma, I love him so much. He's such a good man. Can you believe he takes his books over there with him to the office building and studies every free chance he gets and at least fifteen minutes a night before he goes to sleep? I don't know how he does it."

"A man can do whatever he wants to do, once he sets his mind to it."

"Jermaine's mind is definitely set." I walked into the kitchen. "Whatcha got to eat?"

"Some baked chicken and green beans," she said.

"Sounds good."

I went into the cabinets to find a plate for my dinner. Aretha came into the kitchen and sat at the table next to me.

"It's hard to believe that you're about to bring a new life into this world," she said.

"I know. I can hardly believe it myself."

"You're gonna make a good mother," she said.

"You think so?"

"Yep, a much better mother than I was," she acknowledged.

"You were a good mother," I protested. "You did the best with what you had to work with."

"I was okay, but I could have been better—I know that and accept it—

but look at you, you turned out just fine, anyway. Look at you, working a job, carrying a baby around in your belly, and still trying to get your degree."

"And I'm gonna get it too," I declared.

"Oh, I know you will, and Jermaine is gonna get his too," she said confidently. "See, I prayed for you a long time ago, back when I was too drunk to take care of you. I knew I was messed up, so I put you in God's hands and asked Him to look after you because I didn't think I was capable of doing it. And I know that He heard me."

"That's beautiful, Momma," I said.

"It is what it is," Aretha said.

"All this time I thought there were magical powers in the silver-dollar pendant that Daddy gave me. I felt that my luck was supposed to be better than anybody else's because I was Lucky Paul Lightfoot's daughter, who was born with a silver spoon handed to her on a silver platter by the Jewish community.

"Then when my luck turned sour, I didn't know how to pick myself up. It wasn't until I left that strip club that I realized that it was my choice and not fate that would allow me to be successful." I took a bite of the chicken. "This is good. Hard work and determination through adversity is what brings luck, not blowing out birthday candles or rubbing on a coin." I took a drink of my tea.

"I've had some fortunate things happen in my life, but I've come to find that true fortune comes from loving and being loved. That's what I have here with my family and friends."

"I know that's right." Aretha got up from the chair, kissed me on my cheek, and walked toward the television. "Now I'm gonna see what the outcome of this trial is gonna be." She sat in front of the television.

After I finished eating, I went in and joined her. King's lawyers appeared confident that the case was open-and-shut, that the videotape of the beating would speak for itself. They had presented only six witnesses. The defense attorneys, however, had been more aggressive in their strategy, using the videotape to try to prove that Rodney King had acted in a dangerous manner during the beating. They had presented forty-nine witnesses, almost all of whom were police officers and experts on law enforcement, who claimed that the accused officers had acted within LAPD guidelines. At the conclusion of the defense's delivery, the jury deliberated and returned with a verdict of not guilty, clearing the four officers of any wrongdoing.

"No way," I yelled at the television.

Aretha sat back in silence, becoming uncharacteristically subdued. A tear rolled down her eye.

"I can't believe it. This is bullshit," I yelled. Frustration and anger welled up inside me. I rushed to the phone and called Jermaine.

"Officer Powers, station three, how may I help you?" he said.

"Jermaine, this is Lanita," I said frantically.

"Hey, honey, is everything all right?" he asked.

"No, it's not all right. The officers got off scot-free."

"I know. I'm looking at it over here. It's messed up, isn't it?" I could hear the disappointment in his voice.

"Yes. What kind of society do we live in where cops can beat Black men to a pulp and then get off without so much as a tap on the back of their hands? What if we have a son? How am I going to sleep at night, knowing that if he makes one mistake, the cops can pound him senseless without reprimand?"

"Lanita, you've gotta calm down," he said. "How's Aretha? I know she's throwing a fit too."

"No, Momma's just sitting on the couch. I think she's in shock, Jermaine."

"Well, do the best you can. I'll be over to Aretha's in a couple of hours. Don't try to drive home tonight. People might decide they want to take the law into their own hands, and it might get dangerous, especially in Watts."

"Okay. I'll stay put. I love you," I said.

"I love you too," he replied. "Now you stay calm for Aretha and the baby."

"I will."

Aretha got up off the couch, went into the kitchen, and began to put the food that had been on the oven into the refrigerator. She began humming an old, upbeat disco tune. Her face and her demeanor were calm as you please as she sang, "Burn baby burn, disco inferno / Burn baby burn. Burn it."

She kept singing and cleaning. I sat back down on the couch and stared at the television in disbelief.

• • •

By the time Jermaine got off work and home to us, the country was in an uproar.

He rushed through the door. "We need to stay put tonight. There's mass chaos in the streets."

"We saw on the news," I said. "A mass of people were on the courthouse steps, yelling 'Guilty!' as the cops were led away."

"Yeah, but now they've broken into an all-out riot out here," he explained.

The news was too much for me to handle. Once I'd digested his words, my water broke.

"This can't be happening, not now," I said.

Jermaine was calm. "But it is. We need to close all the blinds and turn down some of the lights."

"Why? When the people choose to riot, they don't usually touch homes, just businesses," said Aretha, who was glued to the television, which was up way too loud. "It's just like the riot in 1965, when Lanita was born. You would think that nearly a quarter of a century later, there wouldn't be a need to revolt anymore."

"Y'all are not listening to me," I cried. "It's time! My baby is coming."

"Oh, honey, I'm so sorry I didn't know," Jermaine said, panicked. He looked over at Aretha. "What do we need to do?"

She stood and rushed over to me. "Lanita, are you sure?" she asked.

"Yes, Momma, my water has broken."

"Well, then I guess it *is* time," Aretha said. "We're not going to have time to get her to a hospital, so we're gonna have to do this here," she announced. "Jermaine, help me get her to the bed."

They got me into Aretha's bed.

"Have you ever done this before?" Jermaine questioned.

"Yes, I did give birth to your wife in a situation similar to this," she reminded him.

They monitored my contractions and prepared me for delivery. Through the hours of labor until the birth of my baby, I could hear the television playing in the next room. The newscaster was detailing the occurrences of the evening.

"When crowds gathered at the intersection of Florence and Normandie Streets in South Central Los Angeles today, April 29, 1992, a small group of about twenty-five officers tried to break up the crowd. Few arrests were made because the crowd overwhelmed them."

"Okay, Lanita, I'm going to need you to push," Aretha requested.

I pushed.

"Shouts were followed by a barrage of rocks and bottles, and finally the crowds started swarming the police, who had to withdraw and seek protection. The angry group, initially comprised of demonstrators expressing their opposition to the Rodney King verdict, turned into an uncontrolled mob of rioters."

"Push," Aretha instructed.

I pushed harder, attempting to keep the pace of my breathing steady between tries. Jermaine held my hand and rubbed it.

I looked over at him. He kissed me on the cheek and assured me. "Everything is going to be all right."

"The fires came, then the looting began. As the evening has progressed, the rage and violence has manifested itself by the rioters pulling passing motorists from their cars and beating them. It seems that the police are not making any attempts to contain the situation."

"I need you to push, Lanita," Aretha demanded.

Sweat was dripping down my face so Jermaine rushed to the bathroom and brought back wet towels for my forehead.

"Go and boil some water," Aretha said. "The blood is coming, and we want to keep her as clean as possible."

Jermaine came back with the water, and Aretha began to wipe me down.

"Push, Lanita, this time with all you have," she advised.

"Police Commander Robert Gil explained that unlike the Watts riots of 1965, which built and built, with the city going mad on the third day, this has been completely different. The city went wild in just an hour and a half."

"They'll probably never understand. Turn that shit off," Aretha yelled. "If they don't get it, how can they report it?"

Jermaine rushed to turn off the television and then came back to my side.

I felt his quiet strength and pushed with everything I had.

"I see the head—keep pushing," Aretha instructed.

I pushed and pushed until my baby entered this world. Aretha wiped it down and pinched its nose. It screamed at the top of its lungs.

"It's a girl!" Aretha announced.

"We have a girl," Jermaine said. He kissed my forehead.

"We have a girl," I said, with all the joy and pride I could muster.

Thirty-one

$\mathcal{A}$s Deidra Michelle finished Lanita's manicure and pedicure, Lanita had completed her servicing at the salon and was ready to go and get her degree.

"Thank you so much," Lanita said. "You did a fantastic job. Everybody did."

"Any time," Deidra responded. "You might want to sit here for at least five minutes and allow your nails to become completely dry." She began cleaning up her station. "So, Lanita, if you had your baby in 1992, she must be twelve by now."

"Yes, as a matter of fact, she had a birthday last month. We threw a big party. Took pictures, videotaped it. You know, the works."

"So what's her name?"

"Phoenix."

"Pretty."

"Unique," I gently corrected.

"Yes, unique." Deidra Michelle smiled. "Why Phoenix?"

"I named her after the fabulous mythological bird that rises from its own ashes to begin a new cycle of life. I have big dreams for her. I want her to have a more positive view on life, make better decisions than I did."

"I'm sure she's excited to see her mommy graduate."

"Yes, she's excited to see her mommy and daddy graduate on the same day. It took us a while. Things happened. After Phoenix was born, we both had to quit school again for a while. Working and taking care of Phoenix was all that I could handle for some time. Jermaine lost his part-time job as a security guard and picked up another one that didn't afford him the luxury of study time. Somehow we always managed to go back to school. Sometimes one of us took a class while the other sat out, but we made it happen. This has been our big dream. We've had to sacrifice a lot for this day, but it has been well worth it."

When Lanita's five minutes were up, she stood.

"So where do I pay?" she asked.

"At the receptionist's desk. I'll walk you up there," Deidra offered.

The two women walked up to the front desk and approached Natasha.

"Oh, Lanita, you look great," Natasha said.

Jimmy Choo must have heard Natasha mention Lanita's name because he came from around the corner and walked over to Lanita. He pulled her to the side and spoke in her ear. "What are you getting your degree in?" he asked.

Deidra Michelle whispered something to Natasha, who nodded.

"Education. I'm going to be a teacher. So is my husband," she replied. "I want to teach on the college level. He wants to teach high school. We expect to begin our careers this fall."

"Fabulous," Jimmy said, stepping back.

Lanita returned to the counter. "So what's the damage?" she asked.

Natasha gave her a folded piece of the salon's stationery.

Lanita took the paper and opened it, reading, "Congratulations on your graduation. Today's visit is on the house."

Lanita looked up at Natasha, and then around at Jimmy, Deidra Michelle, and Miss Lina, who had joined them.

"This is too much," Lanita said, feeling tears well up.

"No. It's not," Natasha said. "You should have expected it. Remember, you told me you were lucky."

"I am, but that's not the half of it. Luck is only a portion of all that I am." Lanita winked.

"I would have to agree," Natasha said, smiling.

"Now get out of here and go and make us all proud," Jimmy said.

"I will," Lanita replied from behind her smile.

After everyone hugged her and wished her and her family well, Lanita walked out of the salon with new supporters. She felt lighter and looked better. She was ready to graduate.

Epilogue

As Lanita pulled up to the designated parking lot on the USC campus, her heart raced with anticipation. She was finally going to put on her cap and gown and walk across the stage to accept her bachelor of arts degree in education. She and Jermaine were finally going to realize the dream they had been working toward for so many years.

She parked the car and grabbed her gown, purse, and tote bag, which contained her makeup, perfume, and other grooming items. Then she made her way over to the auditorium, where the ceremony would be held.

She dashed into a side bathroom and changed, situating her cap squarely on her head, making certain it was perfectly placed. Then she fussed over her hair and applied makeup to her face, which seemed softer. Before she left the bathroom to head to the check-in location, she gave herself one more glance. She straightened the silver-dollar pendant so that it lay perfectly around her neck and then blew a kiss at her reflection. She looked fresh, radiant. This was her day—their day—and she was going to delight in her victory.

Entering the check-in room, Lanita looked around and saw a sea of people, all dressed in black caps and gowns. She scanned the space, her eyes locking on Jermaine, who was standing by the door. In his cap and gown, he looked the same as everyone else, but there was something about seeing him dressed from head to toe in graduation attire that sent a warm sensation over Lanita's body.

He spotted her checking him out and smiled. "Honey, you made it," he said, dashing over and throwing his arms around her.

"You look so handsome," she said, proud of her husband.

He stepped back and looked at his wife, who was standing there waiting to be admired. "And you—you look fabulous," he said.

"That's what Jimmy Choo said." Lanita plumped her hair.

"Who?"

"Jimmy, the guy who did my hair. And guess what, honey, he didn't charge me! No one did. They did everything for free, as a gift for my graduation."

"I'm not surprised, Lanita, but it could only happen to you—or Phoenix. She's just as fortunate as you are. When my mother, Aretha, and I were walking across the parking lot with Phoenix earlier today, she stumbled on a five-dollar bill. Can you believe that?"

"Yeah, I used to find money all the time. Still do," Lanita said, laughing, thinking about the quarters she had found outside of the salon.

He shook his head in admiration.

"So Phoenix is in the auditorium with her grands, right?" she asked.

"You know she's with her grandmothers, being spoiled to death."

"Who else is here?" Lanita asked.

"I'm not gonna tell you," he replied with a sneaky smirk and kissed her on the cheek. "It's a surprise."

Lanita smiled. She had sent out several invitations, but wasn't sure who would show up. Based on her husband's enthusiasm, she assumed that those nearest and dearest to her were there.

"For now, you need to get checked in. Let's go over to the desk and sign in," he said, and then looked at his watch. "We'll be lining up in about five minutes."

The couple walked over to the check-in desk and Lanita signed herself in. Then they stood around with the rest of the graduates from the education department, waiting to be instructed to line up for the procession into the auditorium.

Once they received the word, everyone in the room moved about to form a line, based on the number they'd been given at check-in. Because Lanita and Jermaine shared the same last name, they were assigned to sit together throughout the ceremony.

As music of "Pomp and Circumstance" started, the group marched over to the auditorium and began to proceed inside. As they walked in, the graduates looked around the auditorium, seeing a large audience of people, all of whom were standing on their feet, watching.

Lanita tried to locate Phoenix and Aretha and her mother-in-law, but she couldn't find them. There were too many people. Once each graduate was in front of his or her seat, the dean, who was standing at the podium, asked everyone to be seated.

The ceremony began, and the dean said a few words to the graduating class of 2004. He spoke about the importance of education and teachers and the difference they could make in our society, one student at a time.

Jermaine held Lanita's hand, sporting a proud expression throughout the ceremony. He spotted their family and nudged Lanita, pointing. The two of them waved, and the group waved back, smiling from ear to ear.

The dean asked the graduates to stand row by row and began calling each graduate to the stage by name. When they got to the row where Jermaine and Lanita were seated, the couple stood, continuing to hold hands.

The dean said, "Jermaine Powers."

Jermaine took a deep breath and headed for the stage, while Lanita stood back and admired her husband as he walked across the stage. He shook the dean's hand and received his diploma.

When she heard her name, "Lanita Powers," Lanita's heart leaped. She sighed happily and headed toward the stage. It was a monumental moment, one she wouldn't soon forget. The walk she'd dreamed of for so long caused her to become choked up, but when she shook the hand of the dean of education, a feeling of relief and finality set in, and Lanita threw her hands in the air, waving as if she had just won a pageant. Then she blew kisses to her family, who was cheering her on. She stretched her moment out as long as she could.

Jermaine laughed as he watched his wife express her blessed happiness.

After the ceremony, Lanita and Jermaine met their family outside in front of the auditorium. When Phoenix saw them, she released her hold on her grandmothers' hands and ran to meet her parents.

"Mommy, Daddy!" she called. She jumped into Jermaine's arms and wrapped her arm around her mother's neck, squeezing both of them in her small arms. "Mommy, I found a five-dollar bill today."

"Is that so?" Lanita replied.

"Yes, we were walking across the parking lot and it was right there in my path. Daddy told me that I had to put it into my bank, but I want to spend it," she admitted.

"How about you do both? Put half into your account and spend the other half," Lanita said. "That is, if it's okay with your daddy."

"How does that sound, Daddy?" Phoenix asked.

"I can live with that," Jermaine replied.

Phoenix pulled her mother to the side and whispered in her ear. "Grandmomma told me that I was lucky, just like you and your daddy. Is that true?" she asked.

"As a matter of fact, it is," Lanita said.

"Grandmomma also said that you and I have just enough of King Midas's blood spilled into our veins to turn hard luck into gold, but not enough to keep it. Is that true?" she asked.

"That's your grandmother's truth, but I believe differently. I believe that God set aside a great many blessings for each of us, and that we must choose if we want those blessings to lead us to a life of abundant happiness and accomplishment. I eventually chose to do just that. I hope you'll do the same—only a lot sooner than I did."

"I'm sure I will, beginning with this five dollars. I'm going to save three dollars toward my college education and spend the other two for instant gratification. That way I can feel the blessing now and later."

The two shared a laugh.

"I love you, Phoenix."

"I love you too, Mommy," she replied.

Lanita looked up and saw she was encircled with all the special people in her life, Miss Page and Donald, Miss Powers, Calvin, Aretha, Stacia, and even Gloria, who had flown in from D.C. just for the occasion. They had surrounded Phoenix, Jermaine, and Lanita with hugs and kisses and congratulations.

The only person missing from the group was Paul Lightfoot, of whom Lanita had finally let go. She rubbed the silver dollar around her neck because Lanita knew that she would probably never see him again. But she took comfort in knowing that wherever he was, he was somewhere pressing his luck and riding it until the end.

"Lanita, we got everything set up at you and Jermaine's house. That's where we're all headed," Aretha said. Her voice trembled a bit, and she walked slower in her pace.

"Okay, Momma, that sounds good. So what's on the menu?" Lanita asked her.

"Just wait till we get to the house, and you'll see," Aretha assured her.

. . .

When the group arrived at Lanita and Jermaine's home, they gathered in the backyard. Lanita walked out of her kitchen and onto her patio, finding Jermaine and Calvin had fired up the grill. Donald was engaging them with conversation. Lanita gave her husband a fond kiss on the cheek and let him and the other men have their moment. She smiled when she noticed Aretha and Miss Powers laying out the spread they had prepared. Miss Page was passing out glasses of freshly squeezed lemonade. As Lanita walked toward her two friends, Gloria and Stacia, who were sitting under a tree getting along marvelously, she looked around to find Phoenix, who had curled up under a tree with a book.

Miss Page spotted Lanita observing her daughter and handed her a glass of lemonade. "The apple doesn't fall far from the tree, does it?" she said.

"No, I guess it doesn't," Lanita replied.

A huge smile grew on her face. She was the luckiest person she knew.

About the Author

TAJUANA "TJ" BUTLER is the founder of Lavelle Publishing and is also a writer and poet who speaks about women's issues and conducts poetry workshops. In addition to *Hand-me-down Heartache*, *Sorority Sisters*, and *The Night Before Thirty*, she is the author of a collection of poetry, *The Desires of a Woman*. She was born in Indianapolis and grew up in Kentucky, where she attended the University of Louisville.

About the Type

This book was set in Ehrhardt, a typeface based on the original design of Nicholas Kis, a seventeenth-century Hungarian type designer. Ehrhardt was first released in 1937 by the Monotype Corporation of London.